Illumination

Rowan Speedwell

RIPTIDE
PUBLISHING

Riptide Publishing
PO Box 6652
Hillsborough, NJ 08844
www.riptidepublishing.com

Illumination

Cover Art by L.C. Chase, lcchase.com/design.htm
Editor: Sarah Frantz
Layout: L.C. Chase, lcchase.com/design.htm

ISBN: 978-1-62649-051-2

First edition
September, 2013

Also available in ebook:
ISBN: 978-1-62649-052-9

Illumination

Rowan Speedwell

RIPTIDE PUBLISHING

For my scribal friends: Patty, Patrice, Shannon, Kerry, Terry, and Eva.
Thank you for all you have taught me.

Table of Contents

Chapter I

dam Craig worked his way through the crowd in the hotel suite, champagne bottle in one hand, cigarette in the other. Somewhere in this place was a balcony, he was sure; when they'd checked in earlier in the day he'd noticed it. And he was pretty sure this was the same hotel they'd checked into, since their manager had driven them back to the hotel and not that fucking drunk drummer Eddie.

He took a drag off the cigarette and elbowed his way past a skinny blonde who kept moving in front of him. The smoke was thick and the music way too loud and he was way too drunk and stoned. He needed that balcony, needed the fresh air—though "fresh" was probably a lot to ask for more than a dozen stories above Chicago's Loop. Okay, air that didn't taste of cigarettes and pot, but good healthy diesel fumes and smog. Yep, that's what he needed.

"Awesome gig, man!" someone shouted at him over the scream of metal rock blasting from the suite's high-end sound system. "You rocked 'em tonight!"

Adam waved the bottle at him and squirmed through the crowd. He nearly tripped over a pile of pillows where Eddie was cavorting half-naked with his girlfriend du jour and *her* girlfriend du jour, and holy shit, was that the lead from Unmet Potential? He'd thought those guys were in Slovakia on tour. No, he was pretty sure that's who that was; he'd had a bit of a crush on him until he met him and found out what a fucking dick he was. He stepped over someone's legs and worked his way along the wall to the sliding glass doors.

Fuck. The balcony was every bit as crowded as the room. Any minute now some asshole was going to get pushed over the railing and paint the sidewalk fourteen floors below. No point in going out there and guaranteeing it.

Someone grabbed his arm, and a Lady Gaga wannabe plastered herself to him. "Hey!" she shrieked. "Wanna fuck?"

"No!" he screamed back.

"Okay!" She wriggled away. A minute later, the crowd shifted and he saw her straddling Chuck the bassist's lap while Chuck fumbled with the buttons on his 501s. Not very discerning, Chuck—but then again, none of them were. It was kind of pathetic, he thought, and took a swig from the champagne bottle. Not one of the women here would turn down a fuck with one of the guys from either the band or the roadie staff, and he would be willing to bet a grand that none of the male hangers-on in the room would turn it down either—at least not from one of the guys in the band. The roadies would have a harder time of it. He snorted in drunken laughter. "Harder" time. Right. Himself—he was the lead singer and the public face of the band—*everyone* wanted to fuck him. Not that there was a soul here he actually wanted to fuck.

Suddenly the noise and the smoke and the letdown of this being the last concert on the tour, with only a few weeks in the studio to look forward to, all ganged up on him. "Fuck," he muttered, and this time worked his way across the room to his bedroom, seeking, if not quiet, then some measure of privacy.

There were three strangers fucking in his bed.

"Fuck!" he screamed, then threw the champagne bottle at them, spraying bubbly across the carpet and the bed and the three strangers. They got out of the way fast enough, but there was no way he was sleeping in that bed tonight. Instead, he ground out his cigarette on the marble table next to the door, and stormed out—out of the room, out of the suite, out of the hotel.

The wind from the lake was brisk and cooled the sweat on his neck. He reached behind and patted himself on the ass, checking to make sure his wallet was still in the back pocket of his leather pants, then hailed a cab. By the time one pulled up at the curb, the cool night air had brought a semblance of sobriety to his brain. He slid into the backseat, intending to tell the driver the name of a bar on Rush Street. Instead, he found himself telling the cabbie to drive to Milwaukee.

"Where on Milwaukee?" the cabbie asked.

"Milwaukee, Wisconsin," Adam said. "You know. In *Wayne's World*, when they went to Milwaukee to see Alice Cooper? I wanna go there."

"They don't make movies like that no more," the cabbie agreed, and put the car in gear. "Gonna cost you, though."

"You take plastic?" Adam handed him his AmEx card.

The cabbie ran it through and gave it back to him. "Cab's all yours, dude."

Adam lay back against the cracked vinyl seat and fell asleep.

He woke about half an hour later, according to the clock on the cab's dashboard, still sleepy, but less foggy. They'd left the city lights behind, and now only the occasional distant glint marking a residence broke the darkness outside. "How far did we get?" he asked the cabbie drowsily.

"Just past Gurnee."

"I used to love Six Flags Great America," Adam said. "We went there all the time."

"It was better back in the days when it was Marriott and really nice."

"You ever go there?"

"Sure. Take the kids every summer."

"I haven't been there in years. Is it open?"

"Not at this hour."

"Damn," Adam said wistfully.

They drove in silence another ten minutes or so, then Adam saw one of the ubiquitous brown highway signs that advertised local sights, with the legend "Indian Lake." "Indian Lake," he said aloud. "Indian Lake. Where have I heard of that before?"

"It was a hit back in the sixties. The Osmonds or the Cowsills or some group like that," the driver offered.

"No. No, I mean the lake. We just passed the sign."

"Oh, there used to be a resort up that way. About twenty miles off the highway."

"Go there," Adam commanded.

"Your dime." The cabbie took the exit.

"Dude," the cabbie said, "you sure you wanna do this?"

Adam shut the cab door and leaned back against it. The entrance to Indian Lake Resort was a narrow graveled road with a chain across it. A half-rusted sign read, "Indian Lake Resort. Closed for Season. Private access only," and another, "Private Property. KEEP OUT." Both the latter sign and the chain looked relatively new, and the gravel was well kept.

"I knew it," Adam said, more to himself than to the cab driver.

"Knew what?"

"My folks used to come here when I was a kid. Last time was probably when I was like eleven. Great place." It had been, with a terrifically clear lake to swim in, boats to mess around in, horses to ride, trails to hike, and rocks to climb. The perfect place, with the last visit the summer before the divorce, before his mother had taken him and his brother to California. He'd forgotten this place, and he hadn't realized how much he missed it.

"How long you gonna be?" the driver asked. "I only need to know cuz it'll be morning in about two hours, and I'm goin' off shift at eight."

Adam pulled his phone from his pocket and checked the signal. "You go on home. I don't know how much longer I'll be, but I got bars, so I'll just call for a ride when I'm ready to."

"Okay. Lemme give you a receipt. Keeps the credit card companies happy." The cab driver printed it out and handed it to him. "There ya go."

Adam gave him a hundred dollar tip. "If anybody asks, you ain't never seen me."

"Seen who?" said the cabbie. He grinned and put the cab in reverse.

Adam waved absently as he ducked under the chain and started up the road toward the lake.

He hadn't realized how dark it was until after the cab's taillights had vanished back down the road, but when they were gone, it was just him, the scrub trees along the side of the road, and starlight. The moon had set some time ago, he guessed, or maybe it wasn't up yet—he didn't know from moon schedules. But there was a glint of light close to the lake: either one of the private cottages that had flanked the old resort, or emergency lights around the resort itself. Either way, he headed in that direction, stumbling a few times from the drink, the pot, or the gravel surface.

It was probably a good twenty minutes before he came out of the trees near the lake, and he was fucking freezing. He was only wearing a leather vest over his leather pants, and neither of them did anything to keep him warm. *They make coats out of leather. Why, if it doesn't keep you warm? Maybe it's a different kind of leather . . .*

Up the slope of the hill he was standing on was one of the resort's cottages, the source of the light. He'd come off the gravel road at the foot of the short drive to the main building. The other cottages looked abandoned, dark and silent, and the main resort's windows were all boarded up, though what looked like construction equipment was parked around the front. He walked across the grass toward the lake, at the foot of the rise where the lighted cottage stood. A patio halfway up the slope was cut out as a terrace, with white iron furniture set around it and a closed sun umbrella propped against the table, but he walked past it, wanting to be near the lake.

The water lapped lazily at the pilings of the dock. Adam walked out and sat on the end of the dock tailor-fashion, his custom Docs scraping on the warped, peeling wood. The lights from the house stretched and flickered over the surface of the lake. A soft breeze stirred his hair and shirt and brought the smell of dark earth, new grass, and . . . dead fish. Yep. He was at a lake, all right. The smell brought back forgotten memories of good times; he could almost hear the laughter and shouts and splashing from those long-ago summer days. He chuckled softly to himself and settled in to enjoy the quiet.

After about twenty minutes, though, the edges of the warped wood started rubbing against his ankles and his ass, and he was beginning to get sleepy again, so he shifted back onto his feet and walked up the dock and the slope of hill to the little patio terrace. Someone must use it regularly; the cushion on the chaise was both new and dry. He sat there and looked out over the water, basking in the view. Maybe he should think about getting a place on a lake, or the ocean. Not Malibu—overpriced and overpopulated. Someplace quiet. He didn't even care if it was on the ocean. A lake, like this, would be just fine.

He fell asleep thinking about it, and dreamed of water.

Miles woke to the sound of a lunette scraping rhythmically over a cured goatskin. No, he thought a moment, calfskin—then the tenor changed again and he thought, no, definitely goatskin. "Grace!" he said sharply. Damn her. He'd been up late last night working on his most recent piece, and he'd really planned to sleep in.

"Love you!" caroled a woman's voice.

"God damn you, Grace!" He sat up, rubbed his eyes, and looked around his bedroom. There she was, sitting on the rocking chair. Well, on the back of the rocking chair. The African Grey Parrot opened her beak and echoed back in his voice, "God damn you, Grace," and then in his sister's, "Love you!" Then she went back to the sound of scraping, interspersed with muttering he recognized as his usual imprecations about uncooperative materials. Then his cell phone rang and he reached for it, only realizing after he saw no incoming call that it was Grace again.

"Damn you, Grace," he muttered. "I should've let Lisa take you when she moved out. But no, I've got to have some kind of company, she said; can't leave you all alone, she said. Ha!"

He raked his hands through his hair and looked at the clock. Seven fifteen. "I ought to have you stuffed," he said to Grace, who imitated his cell phone again in mocking response. "At the very least teach you to make coffee." Hmm. There was a thought. All he'd have to do was set up the coffeemaker the night before and teach her to turn it on in the mornings. That was assuming he'd remember to set it up the night before. Or he could just break down and buy a new coffeemaker, one that had a timer that actually worked.

Sorting through the pile of clothes at the foot of his bed, he pulled out a T-shirt that wasn't too smelly and a pair of paint-spattered jeans. Then he stumbled over the piles of books on the floor and into the bathroom.

Marginally more awake after a shower, he headed for the kitchen and coffee. The pot was dirty, of course, with yesterday's brew staining the glass of the carafe; he swore under his breath and filled it with water to soak while he put a new little white filter in the holder and filled it with fresh grounds. Then he rinsed out the pot and filled the coffeemaker and turned it on.

While it brewed, he dug into the refrigerator and found a not-too-badly-out-of-date package of rolls and popped it open, sticking them on a cookie sheet and into the oven, adding two minutes to the bake time to compensate for forgetting to preheat it. God, cooking was complicated.

There was a bowl on the counter full of the beaten egg whites from yesterday; he carefully slid the meringue out and into the garbage, and checked the clarity of the liquid left in the bowl. Ah, excellent—a good batch of glair, no white left to leave unwanted glossy patches in the paint. He took the clean bottle he'd prepared and poured the glair into it, adding precisely three drops of oil of clove to prevent the egg white from smelling as it aged. Still thinking about the glair, he went out onto the back porch to check the copper plate suspended over the bowl of ammonia. There was a solid buildup of verdigris on the plate; another day or so and he'd be able to scrape it and grind it. No hurry on that one, though; he had enough of the previous batch of verdigris to get him through this current project.

The coffeemaker stopped wheezing just about the time the oven timer dinged, and he took the rolls out of the oven and turned it off before pouring his coffee, automatically checking inside the mug first to make sure he hadn't been mixing paints in it. Most of the period pigments he used were innocuous, but there were a few that were pretty damn toxic, including the orpiment he'd worked with on his last project. Nasty stuff, orpiment, but no other period paint got that gorgeous shade of yellow.

He wandered into his workroom and set his coffee absentmindedly on the side desk, focused on the unfinished parchment on his worktable. The morning light picked up the gold leaf on the parchment, giving the piece the glow that medieval monks called "illumination." *Light*. He hadn't even begun adding color to it yet, but already the piece gleamed. He smiled contentedly to himself, pleased with the results of fifteen hours of gilding, fine gold leaf atop gesso made with slaked plaster using the period-accurate recipe in Cennini. Nothing gave gold that pure glow like the gesso in Cennini.

The calligraphy he'd be starting this morning was a poem the guy who'd commissioned the work had written—always an improvement over the morons who wanted him to put weeks of work into an illuminated manuscript with text copyrighted by someone else. He lost more commissions that way, but he would be damned if he was going to get into legal trouble because some asshole hadn't done his homework. Now he kept copies of the permissions with the photo documentation of the process. He preferred original text—even if, like this guy's, it was sappy and derivative. The best, of course, was text too old for copyright. Bible verses, medieval poetry, portions of epics—he'd done one with a fantastic portion of one of the Elder Eddas, in the original Norse or whatever, that had turned out to be one of his favorites, all intricate knotwork offset by runic letterforms. A twenty-four-color digital facsimile of it hung on his bedroom wall. The original had been commissioned by a huge Tolkien fan who had done his research. Those were the absolute best kinds of clients.

He hooked a bare foot around the rung of his stool and drew it over, settling down on it before adjusting the slant of his worktable. Without thinking about it, he reached over to the desk and closed his fingers around the ceramic beaker that held his quills (he'd cut and cured just enough for this project so he wouldn't have to stop and recut halfway through, as he'd too often done before). The beaker went into the cutout on the side of the custom-built worktable, and he drew out a goose quill, running his fingers over the feathers he'd left at the top. Unlike many calligraphers, he left most of the feathers on his quills, trimming off only as much as he needed for finger room; he liked the balance and weight they gave the pen, and the soft flick of the barbs against his wrist as he wrote. Odd term, barb—it sounded sharp and harsh, not silky like feathers, though he supposed that it came from the little hooklike parts that held them together. He smoothed his fingers over the feather, closing up the little splits, feeling the tiny clicks as the hooks caught. Then he put the feather back into the beaker and, with a faint sigh, drew out the stick of lead to begin lining the parchment. This was the boring part, but thanks to modern technology, he'd already done a computer layout of the text, and all he had to do now was pen the lines the text would float between. The placement marks for those were already on the parchment, laid out there when he'd done the original drawing.

His hand was steady as he drew the lines, using a T-square both for accuracy and to keep his hand off the parchment. Skin oils were a nightmare, sealing the surface of the calfskin and causing erratic absorption of the iron gall ink. Sometimes he wore a cotton glove to work, particularly in areas where precision called for a steady hand supported by the document, but cotton too often picked up ink and smeared it exactly where you didn't want it to go. Sometimes he'd rest his hand on a piece of paper or a scrap of vellum instead. Whatever kept his hand off the calfskin until the piece was inked.

Paints were more forgiving, but then the paints tended to float on the surface of the parchment, not etch themselves into it as the iron gall ink did. The painting was the easiest part of the project, even if it was the most toxic.

Lines drawn, Miles opened and stirred the contents of the ink bottle and set up the side tray with the stoneware bowl Lisa had made him in high school ceramics class. Pouring a little of the stirred ink into the bowl, he took out the quill he'd played with earlier and did a couple of test characters on a piece of scrap before starting the calligraphy. Then, with a faint sigh of pleasure, he set to work.

Chapter 2

ove you!"

Miles glanced up to see Grace perched on the top edge of his slant board, her claws shifting anxiously. "What's up, Grace?" he asked, and held out his hand for her to climb on.

"Love you!" she said again, bobbing her head. He frowned, then his brow cleared, and he looked out to see morning light bouncing off the lake. "Hell, I worked through the night again, didn't I?"

He got up and filled Grace's dish; she rubbed her head against his shoulder before stepping off his wrist and onto the perch where she ate. He watched her a moment, stretching. He'd remembered vaguely taking a break and noting that it was about four a.m.; he'd only intended to work a few more minutes, but he'd finished the calligraphy about midnight and started on his favorite part of an illuminated piece, the painting. And the few more minutes had somehow turned into—he glanced at the clock—two more hours. Oh, well. It wasn't like it was the first time he'd worked through nearly twenty-four hours straight. He poured himself a cup of cold coffee and stuck it in the microwave while he fixed a fresh pot, then took the cup outside and wandered barefoot in his paint-speckled jeans and T-shirt down to the patio.

He was halfway there when he realized that someone was asleep on *his* chaise.

"Son of a bitch!" he snarled, and stormed the rest of the way to the patio, his bare feet slapping as he lunged onto the cold flagstones, intending to wake the vagrant and kick him off *his* property—if not into *his* lake. But as he got a good look at the sleeping man, he froze, startled.

Not an ordinary vagrant—he'd had to chase off one or two in the past, and they generally didn't wear painted-on leather pants that looked expensive and butter-soft. The calf-high lace-up boots the guy wore probably cost as much as one of Miles's pricey creations. The stranger's leather vest laced up the front, and the black leather vambraces that covered his forearms were decorated with silver. Long brown hair, threaded with copper and gold that sparked in the morning sunlight, tumbled over his shoulders and face. An Aragorn wannabe, Miles thought, then amended, a *rich* Aragorn wannabe.

Then the wayward morning breeze lifted a lock of the silky hair off the stranger's face, and Miles's breath caught. The guy was fucking *gorgeous*. Fine, sharp features, an elegant nose beneath dark brows, and a mouth that looked cynical and sensual at the same time. Miles found himself caught up in a fantasy involving that mouth and vaguely wondered what color the guy's eyes were—and then he shook himself out of it. Was he *crazy*? This guy was *trespassing*. "Who the hell are you?" he roared instead, almost more angry with himself than he was with the trespasser.

The guy shot up into a sitting position and stared at Miles wide-eyed. "Jesus *Christ*!"

"The hair's right, but nothing else," Miles said caustically. "Now who are you really?"

The eyes that stared at him, still wide with shock, were gold. Not brown, not hazel, not even amber, but gold. Gold like the 23K stuff he used for gilding. Gold as Cennini. "Where am I?"

"*My* chaise," Miles snapped. "My patio, my lake. You're fucking trespassing, dude, and you need to get your ass gone."

The guy dropped his head into his hands. "Fuck. Don't yell. For the love of God, please don't yell. My fucking head is going to fall off and roll down the hill and end up in ten feet of water and I'll drown by remote control."

Miles stifled an involuntary laugh. The guy, hot as he was, was pathetic, and Miles couldn't help feeling just a little bit sorry for him. "How the hell did you get here anyway?" he asked at a more normal volume.

"Walked—I think. I—there was a cab, and the lake. Indian Lake."

"This is Indian Lake. It's private property, though. Why did you come here?"

"Used to come here when I was a kid." The guy lifted his head, and his gaze focused on the mug Miles still held, forgotten, in his hand. "Is that *coffee*?"

Miles took a sip. "Yep, tastes like it, sorta."

The guy groaned. "I'll give you a thousand dollars for a cup of coffee."

"Name first."

"Adam . . . Karoshewski. That's with a 'w,' not an 'f.'"

Had there been a bit of hesitation before the last name? "What?"

"It's spelled with a 'w' but it's pronounced like an 'f.' People are always messing it up." The guy rubbed his forehead. "Sorry. Babbling. Not awake yet."

Miles shrugged. "Well, Adam Karoshewski with a 'w,' you can have a cup of coffee while you wait for a cab. My hospitality will stretch that far. Are you hungover?"

"That would be an understatement, but yes." Adam threw his legs over the side of the chaise and stood up, holding a hand out for balance. "Okay. Vertical. Good start." He looked longingly at the mug in Miles's hand.

Miles shook his head, but handed him the mug. Adam took a drink. "God, this tastes like shit," he mumbled, but took another drink anyway.

"It's two days old," Miles said.

"Nectar of the fucking gods," Adam replied, and drained the mug. "Okay. I think I can walk now."

"Science-fiction convention around here somewhere?" Miles asked as they started up the hill toward the cottage.

Adam frowned. "What?"

"Your outfit. You look like you're auditioning for Aragorn in *The Lord of the Rings*. Figured you were with one of the cons; there are usually one or two running somewhere within a couple hundred miles. C2E2, Windycon, DucKon . . ."

"I have no fucking idea what you're talking about," Adam said blankly.

Miles opened the screen door and ushered him into the kitchen. He normally wouldn't let a stranger indoors, but there was nowhere on that skintight outfit that Adam Karoshewski-with-a-"w" could possibly be hiding a weapon. Even his wallet and cell phone were clearly outlined in the back pockets of those painted-on pants. And he was skinny, that tall, long-legged androgynous skinny, like a character in the yaoi manga Miles loved. Miles probably outweighed him by forty pounds.

Despite the androgynous look and the long hair, Adam didn't look girly. Maybe it was the firmly muscled chest underneath the tooled vest; maybe it was the lean muscle in his bare arms. It wasn't until Adam leaned up against the counter in the kitchen waiting for Miles to pour him coffee that Miles realized that he'd also subconsciously noticed the very nice package the guy was sporting in front. No. Nothing girly about that. Miles flushed and bent to look in the refrigerator for milk to hide his embarrassment.

The guy apparently didn't notice. "Black's okay, dude." He rubbed his eyes.

"So, if you aren't dressed for a con, why *are* you dressed like that?" Miles asked, and found another mug. He refilled Adam's and filled his own, then gestured for his unexpected guest to sit down. He turned around one of the two chairs that didn't have books piled on them and sat in it backwards.

Adam dropped into the other empty chair and sipped his coffee, rubbing his head again. Miles took the hint and went to dig around in the cabinet where he kept his meds, finding the familiar green bottle of Excedrin and tossing it across the table to Adam.

"You are a saint," Adam said fervently, and fumbled the bottle open. He took three and washed them down with the coffee. "Saint . . . ?"

"Miles," Miles said. "Miles Caldwell. Spelled the way it sounds, Adam Karoshewski with a 'w.' And you were going to tell me why you're dressed like an elf."

"A Ranger. Aragorn was a Ranger, not an elf. A human." Adam took a drink. "I may not know geekspeak, but I know my movies. And besides, I'm not in *costume*. I mean, except that I wore it on stage last night and haven't changed. I'm a musician."

Miles regarded him thoughtfully. "Of course you are. Metal, right?"

"We like to think of ourselves as being on a higher plane than an ordinary metal band," Adam said. "But yeah, essentially. A little harder than pop, a little softer than death metal. I call it light metal. Get it? As opposed to heavy metal?" His expression was anxious. "You listen to a lot of rock?"

"Nope. Opera. Classical. Nothing later than Beethoven."

"No *shit*? Not even the Stones? Beatles? The Who?"

"When I was a kid, sure—everyone did, right? Not since I've grown up. So. You any good?"

"We do all right." It appeared that Miles's disinterest in his guest's field of expertise was a good thing, because Adam seemed to relax. He even offered Miles a faint smile.

Miles liked the smile. He might not be interested in Adam's music, but his body reacted with interest to Adam's smile. He kept his voice neutral, though, as he asked, "So how the hell did you end up on my terrace? I don't recall any concerts being held around here last night."

"Not here. Chicago."

Miles nodded. Probably in one of the clubs on Rush Street or something—it had been years since he'd gone clubbing in the city and he had no idea where bands played nowadays. "Helluva long ride from Chicago."

"I think I fell asleep in the cab," Adam admitted. He ran long, graceful fingers through his hair. Miles admired the way his neck arched as he did. "I remember something about Milwaukee."

"What about Milwaukee?"

"I wanted to go there for some reason."

Miles made a face. "*Milwaukee?* You a Brewers fan or something?"

"No. I think it was something about Alice Cooper."

"Who's she?"

The look on the stranger's face was priceless. Miles snorted out a laugh. "Sorry. Couldn't resist." He went back to the coffeemaker; the carafe was empty so he made a fresh pot. "Sorry I don't have anything much to eat; there's some rolls on the counter, but they've been sitting out since yesterday so I wouldn't risk it."

Adam glanced at the rock-hard biscuits and said politely, "No, thanks. It's nice enough that you offered the coffee, considering I am a trespasser and all."

"Well, you did offer me a grand for a cup." Miles chuckled in spite of himself. "Don't worry, I won't hold you to it."

"I'm good for it." Adam pulled his phone out of his pocket and glanced at the display. "Crap. I got a voice mail." He pressed the buttons and held the phone to his ear, then away from his ear. Miles heard someone yelling and a lot of background noise; Adam listened a moment, sighed and disconnected, then pressed another couple of buttons and held the phone up, rocking the chair back onto its rear legs. "Bill? Yeah, it's me. I'm fine. What's up?"

Miles watched the coffee drip into the carafe and pretended not to listen.

A few moments of quiet on his end, then Adam went on, "Don't give me that crap. I told you I was fine . . . I'm from fucking Chicago, dickhead, of course I know where I'm going . . ." He frowned. "What the hell happened to Eddie? Swell. What a fucking asshole. Good thing the fucking tour's done; he can spend the next six months in fucking rehab. Is the girl okay? . . . Christ. Nothing like pissing away all the good press we got with the tour. I swear to God . . . What? No, I'm not shacked up with a groupie. Christ, like we ain't got enough of that bullshit to deal with. Hell, no, I didn't sleep in my own bed— there were three total strangers banging each other in it when I went in there last night. Jesus, Bill, can't you keep *some* control over who you let into the hotel room? You're just lucky nobody fell off the balcony . . . Yeah, yeah, I've heard it before. That's what we pay you for. Look, book me another room at the hotel, okay, and move my stuff down there. I'm gonna stay a couple more days but I don't need a fucking suite." He listened a few more moments, rolled his eyes, then said, "I don't know. Yeah, that's fine; beats having to find a cab." He put his hand over the phone. "You don't mind if I wait for a car to come up from downtown, do you? Shouldn't be more than an hour. Bill's gone all mother hen on me."

"No problem," Miles said, fascinated with the half of the conversation he could hear.

Adam returned to the phone. "No, send the limo. Indian Lake Resort . . ." Again, he took the phone from his ear and looked at Miles. "Address?"

Miles gave it to him, and the phone went back up as Adam repeated it. "No, I don't need anything. I'm fine. I'm fine. Yeah. See you then." He put the phone on the table and shook his head.

"Well, that'll save you the cost of a cab," Miles said.

The other man looked at him blankly.

"Having a car come up?"

"Oh, yeah. Right. Shit, I haven't thought about the cost of a cab for years. I take 'em all the time." Adam stretched, cracked his neck, and eyed Miles hopefully. "More coffee?"

Damn, his head ached. He wished he could remember what the hell he'd ingested last night—gin, he thought, probably in martinis with the preshow dinner he couldn't remember; then champagne after the show; pot, of course, maybe some E . . . He'd done a line of coke before the show, but not more than that; any more and the value of the buzz vanished in a haze of confusion, and as front man for the band, he needed to be sharp. He wasn't stupid enough to confuse the dizzy energy of coke with the real adrenaline high he needed to perform. And then the pot afterward to tone him down. He didn't remember anything else in between. No wonder he'd ended up in Buttfuck, Illinois.

Just lucky he'd ended up in the hands of someone who, while understandably cranky, didn't want to shoot his ass.

Speaking of asses . . . He shot a quick, surreptitious glance as his unwilling host turned to pour himself another cup of coffee. (That made three by Adam's count just since his awakening, so no wonder the guy was cranky.) The paint-covered jeans were baggy, but what they were covering wasn't. Nice shoulders, too, stretching out the T-shirt appealingly. And the rest of him wasn't too bad, either; pretty blue eyes, sexy, tousled, light brown hair, and a day's worth of scruff on a handsome face. Adam's gaydar was usually pretty good, but he was getting confusing signals from this guy: plenty of don't-touch vibes, but those blue eyes kept holding his a bit too long before glancing away. Adam sighed. Closeted, he'd bet money. *Severely* closeted. Just his luck. He looked like he'd give a guy a good fucking and what with the rock-star image thing going on, Adam hadn't been fucked in years. He'd done plenty of giving, with girls and even a few guys, but the front man for a metal band like his couldn't get caught taking it in the ass. And he fucking missed that. He didn't dare it with any of his pickups—and these days, weren't they all pickups?—and risk the publicity.

This guy didn't even know who Adam *was*.

A cell phone trilled in the next room. Miles just stood drinking his coffee. Adam said, "Aren't you going to get that?"

"Nope." Miles fished his phone from his front jeans pocket and held it up to show Adam the screen. No new calls. The phone trilled again.

Miles turned toward the door into the rest of the house and yelled, "Goddamn it, Grace!"

"Love you!" a woman's voice sang from the other room.

Adam's heart sank. Great. The first hot guy he'd met who didn't want to plaster his picture all over Facebook, and here he was not only closeted but *married*. Or shacked up, anyway.

Fuck. The day was just getting better. He couldn't fucking wait to see what happened next. The goddamn hotel would probably burn down with his guitars in it. He didn't care so much about the Rickenbacker 620/12, but the Fender acoustic had been a gift from his grandmother.

There was a strange whirring sound, and something *flew* into the kitchen in a flurry of gray feathers. Miles held out his arm casually and a big bird landed on it. A parrot or something, but not bright-colored like the ones Adam had seen before: this one was gray and white, with a wicked-looking beak and funky red feathers on its tail. It walked up Miles's arm and Adam winced as the sharp talons dug into his flesh. They didn't break the skin, though, and Miles didn't seem to notice. Instead, he reached into a bowl on the counter and put a peanut between his lips, then turned toward the parrot.

Gently, the bird reached out its wickedly sharp beak and took the peanut, ate it, then said, "Kiss, kiss," and Miles again turned his head so that the parrot could touch its beak to his lips. Then he said, "Say 'Thank you,' Gracie."

"Thank you, Gracie!" the parrot echoed.

Miles laughed and reached over with his other hand. Grace, as apparently that was her name, stepped from his shoulder onto his fist, and he carried her over to a wooden stand in the corner. "She's a Congo African Grey Parrot," he said to Adam's unasked question. "Smartest bird in the world."

"She's huge," Adam said. "Beautiful."

Miles grinned, the smile lighting up his fairly ordinary face. "Isn't she? She technically belongs to both me and my sister, but Lisa works all kinds of shitty hours, and CAGs need a lot of attention." He petted the bird gently. "Grace has a vocabulary of over four hundred words and phrases and can actually carry on a conversation. She's probably as smart as a chimp. Who's a smart girl, then?" This was addressed to the bird.

"Not you," she replied.

Adam laughed. "She's really cool."

"That she is. As long as I keep her away from my workspace when I'm not around. I use a lot of toxic chemicals and CAGs are notoriously curious. When I'm painting with anything poisonous, she goes in her cage."

"Dumb cage," Grace opined. Then, "Stinky. Stinky pot!"

"Stin . . . oh, crap." Miles went back out onto the porch. Adam got up to see what he was doing.

There was a largish basin on the porch that looked like hammered or galvanized steel or something. A platter was hung a few inches above it from a complicated hook setup anchored in the overhang of the porch roof. Miles crouched beside it and lifted the platter. It must have been copper, because the bottom was coated with green like the copper guttering on Adam's mother's house. When Miles raised the dish, Adam caught a whiff of what smelled like piss.

He said so, and was astonished when Miles nodded. "Yeah. Best thing for making period verdigris. It's mostly ammonia, but regular ammonia doesn't have the right chemical structure."

"You use actual piss to make—what's 'period verdigris'?"

"Paint. Green paint. For illuminated manuscripts."

It was English, but Adam didn't understand a word. "What the hell is that?"

Miles straightened the platter again and looked up. "You don't know what an illuminated manuscript is?"

"I know what illumination means and I know what a manuscript is, but not together. You make it sound like it's something specific. Is it like an illustrated manuscript?"

"It is to illustrated manuscripts what Notre Dame is to your local church," Miles said. "And I don't mean the football team." He stood up and put his hands on his hips. "Ready for a history lesson?"

Adam groaned. "Do I have a choice? I hated history."

"Think of it as art, then." Miles frowned at Adam a long moment, but Adam didn't think he was angry. It was more of an assessing frown. "The thing is," Miles said, "I don't know you from—you should pardon the expression—Adam, and I'm not sure I should let you see what I've got here. I live alone except for Grace, there are no neighbors for miles, and while I keep a gun in the house, I've never had to use it and hope I never do. What I have here is valuable, and for all I know you're likely to crack me over the head and take off with my artwork."

Adam stared back at him a long time. *Fuck, there goes my chance of hot sex with someone who doesn't know who I am.* But he was curious. "Shit." He took out his phone again. This time he pulled up the internet browser and linked up to the band's website. Then he handed the phone to Miles.

Miles took it and carried it back into the kitchen, looking at the phone's screen. Adam followed. "What am I looking at?"

"Click on the 'band photos' link," Adam said. His headache, which had vanished with Grace's arrival, was back in full force, and he swiveled his head to stretch his neck muscles.

Miles obeyed and frowned down at the screen. "It says Adam Craig under your picture," he said, then, "'Black Varen'?"

"Yeah. That's my stage name, Adam Craig. Black Varen's the band."

"I've *heard* of Black Varen." Miles's voice was aggrieved. "They're huge." His head shot up, and he stared at Adam accusingly. "Black Varen played the United Center last night."

"Yep." Adam leaned back against the counter and regarded him dispassionately. "I thought you didn't listen to any music later than Beethoven."

"I've never heard anything *by* you," Miles shot back. "I've just heard *of* you. Hell, I don't live under a fucking *rock*."

"No, more's the pity," Adam said. "So it won't come as any surprise when I say I don't need to steal anything of yours because I could probably buy all of it and not even notice the cost?"

Miles stared at him with narrowed eyes, then shook his head. "Okay, I guess you probably aren't going to mug me in my own house," he said grudgingly. "Come on."

"Another happy fan," Adam muttered. Jesus, this guy was cranky. And unimpressed. Which, now that he thought about it, was actually kind of refreshing. He followed Miles out of the kitchen and around a dogleg corner into what had probably originally been the cottage's living room, but was now sort of a workshop and library. Floor-to-ceiling shelves were crammed with books on one wall and wooden boxes on another. A third wall was mostly window overlooking the lake. Half of the room—the half with the wall of boxes—was scrupulously neat, with everything set in place around a tilt-top table. The other half, with the books, was cluttered and disorganized, sporting a battered couch covered with more books and sheets of newspaper; even more books were piled on the floor. A dusty CD changer sat in the corner.

Miles walked into the center of the room and pointed at the back wall. "*That's* illuminated manuscripts."

"Holy. Fucking. Shit."

The wall was covered with framed calligraphy pieces. Adam had played around with lettering in high school art classes, but nothing even remotely like these. The calligraphy was a bunch of different styles that he supposed were historical, and they were beautiful, but the painting that decorated the pieces was *amazing*. What looked like real gold was interspersed with designs and foliage and flowers painted in deep, bright colors, layered and detailed. He put his nose up close to the glass covering one of them to look at the tiny brushstrokes showing the minuscule hairs and veins of a leaf no more than a half an inch long. "Christ on a crutch," he breathed. "*You* did these?"

"Yeah. They're samples. That one you're looking at is a reproduction of a fourteenth century Book of Hours—that's kind of like a prayer book rich people carried around with them in the Middle Ages and Renaissance."

"Whole *books* of these?"

"Yep."

"Jesus."

"Yep."

Adam stood back and craned his neck to see the ones toward the ceiling. Those didn't have as much gold—one didn't have any at all—but they were even more intricate in the spiraling designs he recognized as Celtic. Others had amazingly realistic flowers and bugs painted so that they looked three-dimensional. One was entirely in shades of gray. The ones that had calligraphy all had the same text, which started out "Lorem ipsum . . ." The "L" was ornately decorated on some, with pictures inside the letter of flowers or people or animals. "So this is like, what, your catalog?"

Miles laughed. "Yeah, in a way. I do have a catalog, both physical and online—I have a professional facsimile photographer take pictures of finished pieces."

The paintings dazed Adam, already only semi-functional from the hangover. He turned and said weakly, "I need one of these."

"You look like you need to sit down." Miles sounded concerned. "Here." He cleared off a portion of the couch and led Adam over to it.

Adam sank onto the cushions. Miles knelt at his feet and took one arm, unbuckling the leather vambrace and pulling it off, then following suit with the other. "You okay?" he asked as he set the leather cuffs on the seat next to Adam and rubbed Adam's wrists gently, almost automatically, his concerned eyes on Adam's face.

Blinking, Adam said, "Yeah. I'm still kind of . . ." and he wiggled his hand. "Too much shit last night. And your art—fuck."

"Do you see why they called it 'illumination'?" Miles asked eagerly. "The way they seem to glow?"

"Hell, yeah." Adam looked down at Miles's face. It was glowing, too. Beautiful. "Fuck," Adam said, and bent his head to kiss Miles.

Chapter 3

iles held perfectly still as Adam's mouth brushed over his, tasting, then settling in for a serious kiss. When Adam's tongue flicked against his lower lip, he let him in, greeting him tentatively with his own tongue. God, it had been forever since he'd been kissed, and he didn't remember ever being kissed with such tender skill. Adam's lips were gentle, soft, and not too dry; he tasted of coffee, dark and bitter and hot. Miles felt a groan rattle his throat and heard Adam's answering moan. Adam's hands cupped his face and held it still for his gentle exploration.

He did nothing more, just kissed Miles for what seemed like forever, then finally drew back and released his grasp on Miles's head with seeming reluctance. "Sorry," he said in a rough voice. "I didn't mean to do that—it just sort of happened."

"It's okay." Miles licked his lips, drawing his tongue slowly over the upper as if tasting the remnants of the kiss.

Adam groaned again, closing his eyes. "Don't do that."

"Do what?"

"You're not in denial at all, are you?"

"No. I never said I was. Why? What did you kiss me for then, if you thought I wouldn't want it?"

Shaking his head, Adam said, "You really don't have a clue, do you? About how different you are?"

Different. Miles rocked back on his heels and stood up. "Yeah, whatever. Look, if you wanna fuck, we don't have to go through any of the mock-courtship preliminaries. You're hot, I'm easy, and I've got supplies. Just not in here, okay? I gotta work in here."

His guest slumped back against the couch. "Jesus, dude. It was just a fucking kiss. And I'm hungover." Rubbing his eyes with the heels of his hands, he added, "So while it was a really great kiss and you are really very hot . . ."

"Fuck." Miles's gut wrenched. He'd fucked up again. He should've known better than to attempt anything like trying to communicate outside business relationships.

Adam looked up, frowning. "What's the matter?"

"Nothing. I'm stupid, is all. Just ignore me. I'm not really good at reading people, and I make stupid mistakes. I apologize. Look, you want more coffee?"

Adam rested his arms on his knees and studied Miles thoughtfully. "You know, I *am* usually pretty good at reading people, but you're giving me whiplash."

The smile he got was thin and humorless. "Sorry. Coffee?"

"No, thanks." What had Adam said wrong? He was confused and tired. And he had to pee. "I'm caffeined out. I could use a couple minutes in the john."

"Sure. Second door on the right." Miles didn't move as he got up, just watched him out the door.

The bathroom was small but as scrupulously clean as the half of the living room with the worktable in it. When Adam had finished, he washed his hands and stared at the grubby face looking back at him in the mirror. God, it was a wonder Miles hadn't run screaming; he needed a shave, and the bags under his eyes had bags of their own. At least he'd taken off the makeup he'd worn on stage before they'd headed back to the hotel; he would have looked really horrendous with that shit smeared all over his face. He cocked his head and wondered idly if Miles would like the trashy rentboy look, then kicked himself. Miles gave the impression of white bread, all the way.

Though Adam had caught him giving the tight leather pants a lingering look . . . He visualized Miles in leather of his own, and the tight pants got a little tighter. Fuck. He needed to calm down before he went back out there. He recalled Bill's words about Eddie and the underaged chick, and that worked. Drying his hands, he went back out in search of Miles.

He checked the living room, but it was empty; then he saw that one of the windows was actually a French door leading out onto a deck overlooking the lake, and Miles was out there leaning his elbows on the back of a wrought iron lawn chair, watching some geese or something landing on the water. He went into the room and checked out the books on the wall behind the couch. He wasn't much of a reader; it was too hard to concentrate with the noise and confusion of life on the road, but he often thought that it would be nice to just take some time off and forget music for something else for a change. Something quiet and solitary. Miles had the life: art and solitude and books and the lake. He envied that.

Most of the books were science fiction, which he didn't know much about, though he'd heard that the name of the band came from some sci-fi book the previous lead Ray had been reading. Eddie had wanted to call the band Black Death, but that was Eddie. Ray had apparently been a pretty intellectual guy—not that his brains had stopped him from ODing on heroin. He was in some institution or nursing home or something now with cauliflower between his ears. Adam had joined the band five years ago, and Eddie, Chuck, and Neil all ragged him about not paying his dues. But he always shot back that they hadn't hit the big time until they'd had him fronting. Fact was, the chemistry was right, and Adam was a big believer in chemistry.

He ran his finger over a section of paperbacks and froze. There under his fingertip was a book called *The Varen Gambit*. It was labeled science fiction and had to be where Ray had gotten the band's name. He pulled it out and flipped through the pages.

Huh. The main character's name seemed to be Miles. That was a weird coincidence.

"You like Bellaston?"

He glanced up at Miles, who'd come back into the room and was leaning on the doorframe. "What?"

Miles nodded at the book. "Ingrid Bellaston. She wrote the Vargarian books."

"I've never read them," Adam admitted. "I think that's where the band got the name, though. The previous lead guitarist used to read a lot, I guess. BMT, you know?"

"BMT?"

"Before My Time. You know. It's one of those shortened words you use, like LOL."

"Why would I use words like that?"

"When you text, you know? Because you have to say stuff in less than 140 characters?" Adam stared at Miles blankly. *What the hell?*

"I don't text. Or tweet, or Facebook, or whatever. Nobody to text to. My sister calls or emails me." Miles shrugged. "Don't know anybody else. Bellaston's good. Saved my life a time or two. Her hero's named Miles. He's sort of a hero of mine, too." He crossed the room and took the book from Adam's hand. "This is one of my favorites. But they're all awesome."

"What do you mean you don't know anybody else? How can you not know anybody else?"

"I know the FedEx guy. And the UPS guy. And my doctor." Miles shrugged again. "And there's a guy Lisa hired to tend the grounds, though I only talked to him once. And the facsimile photographer. That's pretty much it. One or two old college friends I keep in touch with. Haven't left here in—oh, nearly ten years."

"What the fuck? *Why?*"

Again the shrug. "No reason to. Can get anything I want delivered. And Lisa does everything else. When's your car coming?"

Still stunned by what Miles had said, Adam had to take a moment to regroup and process the change of topic. "Bill said it'd be an hour, so it's probably more like a half hour by this point."

"No time to fuck, then," Miles said. "You like manga?"

"Dude," Adam said, "you're givin' me whiplash again."

Those blue eyes flicked his way, and the soft, sexy mouth gave him a twisted smile. "Gotta keep you on your toes."

"I think I woke up in *The Twilight Zone.*"

"Could be worse," Miles said, "you could have woken up in *The Twilight Saga.*"

"Oh, *Christ. That* he knows about," and Miles laughed.

God, Adam was so fucking *cute.* It had been all Miles could do not to throw him on the floor and fuck his brains out after that kiss, but Miles's stupid little reaction to Adam's comment about being different had pretty much cancelled any possibility of sex. He wasn't used to anyone thinking of him as desirable; it smacked of the insincere compliments he'd gotten when he'd been younger. He'd believed them then, not realizing that it didn't matter who he was or what he looked like: guys generally just wanted a hole to stick their dick in, whether it was a mouth, a cunt, or an ass. The couple of years between the accident and his coming to live here had been a series of one-night stands: the casual, endless search for the handy hole. He was done with that crap.

Adam had said he was hot. Yeah. Right. The correct word was "here."

That was why it was so confusing when Adam had backed off after Miles's acquiescence to sex. Hadn't that been what Adam wanted? He'd kissed Miles, not the other way around. But when Miles had offered sex, Adam had shut him down. Even after Miles had made the lame joke about not having enough time to fuck, he'd only joked right back. No interest there, as far as Miles could tell. But he never *could* tell—that was the problem. His radar or gaydar or whatever it was that people used to read other people had been fucked up for years and didn't give him a clue.

Just like everything else.

He shot another look at Adam, who'd turned back to the bookcase and was studying his shelf of yaoi manga. He looked tired and had admitted to being hungover. Maybe that was what it was. Maybe he didn't want to fuck Miles because he was still recovering from last night. That would make sense. Miles felt a little better.

"This what you're talking about? I've seen manga, but having to read the books backwards gave me a headache."

"You haven't seen manga like this," Miles said wickedly, and handed him *Cat x Dog*.

"Whoa." Adam looked at a page. "This puts the 'graphic' in 'graphic novel.'" He flipped to the back cover and read the blurb. "I've never heard of 'yah oy' manga. Are they all like this?"

"Ya-o-ee," Miles corrected. "And they vary. Some are really explicit, some not so much. The art's really beautiful, though. The stories—well, they tend to be sort of repetitive, but most of them have a sense of humor about them that I like." He shrugged. "Keeps me entertained, I guess."

"So," Adam said, not looking up from where he was paging through the book, "if you never leave here, and only ever see the UPS guy or the mailman or whatever, what do you need the supplies for? You fucking the mailman?"

Miles blinked. "What?"

Now Adam looked up. "The supplies, dude. You said you had supplies. You also said you never leave here."

Fuck. Miles bit his lip. "There's a guy, comes here sometimes . . ."

"Oh, dude. You should have said you had a boyfriend," Adam said. "I don't poach."

"He's not a boyfriend." Miles waved a hand helplessly. "He's just . . . he's just a guy. It's just . . ." He trailed off, feeling his face heat. "It's just sometimes when . . . It's not anything."

The golden eyes watching him widened. "He's a *rentboy*?"

"Jesus! That is so none of your fucking business!"

"Dude. Miles." Adam's voice was gentle. "I know, it ain't. But why the fuck are you settling for a rental fuck when you could have anybody?"

"He's discreet," Miles said weakly. Discreet, yes; but he didn't call Bobby unless he was really desperate for another person's hands. And Bobby didn't mind Miles fucking his ass the way Miles absolutely needed to do sometimes. He'd read enough books to know that he had it good, that the usual routine for a single gay guy was haunting the kind of bars you got diseases from. "He's not a rentboy or anything gross like that." Bobby was clean; he was in a committed relationship with Doug, who didn't mind if his boyfriend serviced his old college buddy who was too fucked-up to do the usual things gay guys did to get laid. Doug was the one who'd set up the arrangement years ago, when they'd finally gotten back in touch. He'd come with Bobby the first time and watched, and Miles thought he'd gotten off on it, but it had been too weird for Miles, and when he'd called a couple of months later, Doug had been cool with Bobby coming alone. Miles liked Bobby, he did; liked Doug, too, for that matter, but Doug had been his friend in college, and it was just too weird to think of fucking Doug. Plus Doug might have been okay with Bobby playing around, but Bobby was definitely not on board with Doug doing the same. Miles didn't understand their dynamic, but then, Miles pretty much didn't understand anybody's dynamic.

Like Adam's. What was with the guy? Was he interested or not? He seemed interested, but then he turned away. Like now: he was putting *Cat x Dog* back on the shelf and taking out the first volume of *The Crimson Spell.* "Hey," he said absently, "I like the costumes in this one. Maybe I should change the band's look. I'm pretty bored with the standard metal shit—this is more like French Revolution stuff. Kind of cool. There was this rock band, way back in the sixties, like around the time the Beatles came out. Paul Revere and the Raiders?" At Miles's blank look, he went on, "They wore like Revolutionary War shit. One of the first groups that had really long hair—not like Beatles bowl cuts, but hair long enough to put in a ponytail."

"You really are interested in the costuming stuff, aren't you?" Miles asked. It seemed a safe enough topic of conversation.

"Too many years in musical theater," Adam said offhandedly. "Drives the other guys crazy—they're traditional metalheads. But theatrical stuff sells. The tour we just finished was sort of an homage to old-school rock. That's why the leather and shit."

"Musical theater? Don't tell me—*Rent? Sweeney Todd?*"

Adam laughed and met his eyes again. God, the gold was gorgeous. Miles had always had a thing for gold. "Worse than that, babe. *Cabaret.* I played the Master of Ceremonies for four straight years in a touring company. I was *so* done with that by the time it was over. Fronting for a rock band was like a breath of fresh air."

"The MC is the best role in the movie," Miles protested. "Joel Grey was awesome."

"I wasn't." Adam chuckled. "And it's not the best role. The best role is Sally Bowles. I *so* wanted to play Sally Bowles."

Miles was laughing now, too. "Oh, seriously!"

"Seriously, dude!" Adam put the book back on the shelf and turned to face Miles. In a low, sexy voice, one that was female without being effeminate, he purred the lyrics about Sally's friend that made up the title song.

Miles listened with a growing sense of delight as Adam sang about poor Elsie, who'd died of drinks and drugs, but had a great time up to then. He had the role pitch-perfect, the gestures timed and elegant; clearly Sally Bowles but somehow not Liza Minnelli, who Miles thought would have been the pattern for the character. When Adam got the chorus, he flung his head and hands back and strutted, dancer-like, around the small space in front of the bookcase, which had suddenly become a backdrop for his performance.

And then he came to the climax of the song: "When I go . . ." and the note was so sweet and pure and perfect, and he held it longer than he should have been able to, and then his voice dropped into a growl that was just as perfect: "I'm goin' like Elsie . . ."

And then back into the chorus again, this time with grand, effulgent gestures and dance steps that had Miles laughing and clapping in delight. Adam flung his arms back, his head back, and held the last note again, until he ran out of breath and doubled over, laughing. Miles kept applauding.

"Jesus, that's harder work than a whole show with the band," Adam said finally. He threw himself onto the couch.

"You were great!" Miles said. "If I were a stage director, I'd cast you as Sally in a heartbeat."

"Well, if they ever do a gay version of *Cabaret*, I'll be sure to audition."

"Why did you quit?"

Adam shrugged. "Politics."

Miles frowned. "I would have thought theater was the one safe place for gay guys."

"Oh, it wasn't the gay thing." Adam shrugged. "Though I'd appreciate it if you kept that under your hat—my stage persona is primarily straight with only the occasional foray into the Dark Side, if you know what I mean, and the guys would be pissed if they knew it's actually the opposite. We've got a really strong male fan base and we decided, Bill and me, I mean, that I needed to play up the straight persona."

"So you fuck women?"

"Occasionally. If I have to." Adam shrugged. "The guys just think I'm more of a private person. Which I am."

"Yeah, I can see that," Miles snorted. "A regular shrinking violet. So what was the politics about, if not your sexual orientation?"

"Well, let me tell you something about theater. It doesn't matter if you're gay, straight, male, female—all actors are screaming queens. Emphasis on the screaming. My God, I never saw such hysterics about the stupidest things. Borrowed makeup. Stolen earrings. Lighting. Lines. Timing. We once had the two actors who played Fräulein Schneider and Herr Schultz not speaking to each other for weeks because one of them accused the other of stepping on their lines."

Max frowned again. "I don't remember those characters."

"Broadway version," Adam said with a sigh, "not the movie version. Movie version is way different. Different story, different songs, different characters. Though Liza pretty much owns Sally now." He stretched his feet out and studied his booted toes. "I do like the movie version, but except for a couple of things, it's not at all the same." He looked over at Miles. "In the play, the male lead isn't gay, and there's no Max."

"Too bad. One of the best lines in the movie is when Sally tells Brian she slept with Max, and he says, 'So did I.'"

"Yeah," Adam laughed. "I saw it on HBO when I was a kid, and when he said that line, I went, 'of course,' and it was then that I realized I was gay. 'Cause I so would have slept with Max too. I don't remember the actor's name; I just remember he was hot."

"Helmut Griem. So was Michael York, the guy who played Brian," Miles said. "I'da so fucked him when he was younger."

"Did you ever see that old sixties movie *Tom Jones*?"

"God!" Miles said. "Young Albert Finney? *Totally* fuckable."

"Yeah. Too bad they got old. Should be a law about that. So. Not into music but you like old movies."

Miles blinked. "Well, yeah. What's not to like? Music is complicated. Movies are just movies, you know?"

"Visual."

"Right. In case you hadn't figured it out, I'm very visually-oriented."

"Figured it out," Adam said. His eyes were locked on Miles's, and Miles swallowed, hard, at the molten heat of those gold eyes. Whoa. Maybe he *hadn't* read Adam wrong after all.

Adam's phone rang and he answered it, his eyes still on Miles. After a moment, though, he looked away. "What the hell happened?"

he asked whoever was on the line. Then he sighed and glanced back at Miles. "The limo had a flat. They're waiting for the motor club but it might be two hours." To the phone, he said, "You can't send another car?" Then, "Jesus Christ, Bill, I'm not a fucking kid. You don't have to escort me home, you know . . . Then it's your own damn fault you're stuck on the fucking expressway in the middle of a Sunday morning when the garages are all closed. No, don't give me that crap; I was perfectly willing to call a cab and get my own precious wittle self back to the hotel."

Miles said, "It's not a problem to wait. I've got nowhere to go."

Adam glanced up at him and gave him a quick smile. Miles's heart warmed. God, he was stupid. In a couple of hours, the guy'd be gone and he'd never see him again except maybe on TV or the internet. Just because he was the only halfway decent-looking guy (except for Bobby) he'd seen in the flesh—and why did *that* thought send chills through him?—in years, and he was right here, and he'd *kissed* Miles, and he wouldn't have done that unless he was interested . . . Would he? *Was* he interested? Miles couldn't tell. Why would he be? It wasn't like Miles was anything close to appealing. Hell, he couldn't even *talk* to the guy.

Miles's face heated, and he turned away to tidy his already compulsively tidy workspace. This wasn't good. He was hot for someone who couldn't possibly be interested, someone he had to be reading wrong—why the *hell* couldn't he judge people?—and now he had to put up with him and his smoky-gold eyes for a couple more hours. Not good. Over his shoulder, he said, "Have them call you when they get off the highway and I'll drive you up to the entrance to meet them."

"Thanks." Adam repeated the instructions to Bill. "Okay? Fine. Yeah, thanks." He put the phone back in his pocket. "Thanks," he said to Miles.

"No problem," Miles replied. Then he added, trying to hide the anxiety in his voice, "I do really need to get some stuff done, though, including laundry, inasmuch as I don't have anything that doesn't smell like two-day-old clothes . . ."

"Oh, hey, that's fine." Adam gave him his quicksilver smile. "Would you mind if I took a walk around the resort now that my head's not going to fall off? It's been—God, twenty years? How the hell did that happen? Anyway, I want to see if there's anything else I remember. Do what you gotta—I'll be okay."

"Okay." Miles let him out the kitchen door, throwing the deadbolt behind him. Then he raced back to his bedroom in a panic, scooped up the piles of dirty clothes, and stuffed them into the washer, adding detergent, and turning the washer on. Then he jumped into the shower (cold, because the washer was using all the warm water), and did a quick scrub-down and shave.

He found some clean sweats and a T-shirt on the floor of his closet and pulled them on, threw the wet clothes in the dryer and set it on low so the stuff wouldn't all shrink, then went to the kitchen to figure out what to feed his guest for breakfast. It had been years since he'd had a guest for breakfast other than Lisa, and he had no idea what Adam liked or didn't. So he played it safe and made pancakes. The expiration date on the pancake mix box was only a couple of days ago, and he used water instead of milk since he was pretty sure the milk was bad, but he had a couple of eggs that didn't look too funky, so pancakes it was. He made microwave bacon, too.

Adam wasn't back by the time he was finished, so he turned the oven on low and stuck the plate of pancakes and bacon in it to keep warm. Then he fed Grace, washed and reset the coffeemaker, and sat for a few minutes, breathing hard. *Okay*, he thought, *I can deal with him now.* He told himself he just wasn't used to people being around. It could have been anyone. It just happened to be this guy. He wasn't freaking just because he liked the guy. Or because he wanted him. He'd be the same if it were anyone: some old lady, some fat redneck, a lost kid . . . He'd be nervous just because he wasn't used to people being around.

Taking a last deep breath, he opened the door and went outside, down the well-traveled path to the lake. He didn't see Adam anywhere, though he turned around and looked up toward the resort building and other cottages. Had he gone off down the trails to the woods?

Then something fluttered in the corner of his eye, and he looked back at the dock. Frowning, he walked toward it. Just as he reached the dock, he realized that there was a pile of clothing anchored by a pair of knee-high black Docs.

Clothing. Oh, holy fucking shit.

With a splash, Adam surfaced a few feet away from the dock, in waist-high water. "Hey!" he called, grinning. "Done with your projects already? I thought a bath sounded good and the water's not too cold."

Miles stared at him blankly. Adam's grin faded. "Um . . . What's wrong? Is there something wrong with the water? Or am I not supposed to swim? What, is it a nuclear dump site, or an environmentally sensitive—?"

"No, that's okay." His voice cracked. "It's fine. It's just . . ." *You're naked*, he thought, then said aloud, "If it's not too cold." He stared; he couldn't help but stare. Without the distraction of Adam's vest and vambraces, and with the drops of water sparkling in the sunlight, he realized what a gorgeous build the guy had. He should have known that jumping around on stage the way rock stars did—didn't they?— would keep Adam fit. He was lean, but not skinny; he had defined abs and strong shoulders and arms, and not a lot of body hair, just enough to be interesting. Miles licked his lips involuntarily, watching a stream of water from Adam's hair trail down his chest to where his hips vanished beneath the surface of the water. And thought about licking it off.

Oh, God, he thought, *now what?*

Adam watched his host lick his lips as if he were looking at something delicious and felt heat rise, along with his cock, despite the chill of the water. Christ, did Miles have a *clue* how hot that was? He'd had guys ogle him before, plenty, but for some reason this sort-of-cranky hermit was just pushing all of his buttons. He slid back down into the water so that his erection didn't show. Jesus.

He managed to grin and say, "Come on in then, the water's fine," as if it were nothing.

Miles stared at him a moment, then in a rush peeled out of the sweats and T-shirt and ran along the dock, diving in a low, flat arc that cut cleanly into the still surface of the lake.

And Adam was catapulted back nearly twenty years to his last summer here.

He'd been goofing around in the shallows with his brother and their friends. Some of the older kids had swum out to the big floating platform anchored fifty or sixty feet out in the deeper water, and he and his friends were daring each other to swim out there as well. And then there were footsteps on the dock, running footsteps, and he saw Mike, the teenager who was the lifeguard and Adam's secret crush all summer, executing an absolutely perfect, beautiful dive off the end of the dock. A moment later he'd been swimming back to the beach, towing a little girl who'd gotten away from her mother. No big rescue; the little girl hadn't been in trouble, but she'd clearly swum out too far for her mom's peace of mind, and the mother had been all over Mike, burbling in gratitude. Adam's young heart had swelled with pride over "his" Mike.

That dive . . . He'd seen it far too often that summer to forget it, had watched it, *memorized* it. "*Mike?*" he said as Miles surfaced.

Miles froze, treading water and staring at Adam as if he'd grown a third eye.

"It *is* you, isn't it? But everybody called you Mike, not Miles. Was 'Mike' a nickname?"

"I took Miles from the Vargarian books." Miles looked away from Adam, dragging his hand through the water as if trying to catch something invisible floating there. When he spoke again, his face was expressionless. "I told you they saved my life. The hero's named Miles—he's got pretty much everything going against him, he's physically damaged and is up against all kinds of shit, but he figures it all out. He's smart. I wanted to be like him." Miles shrugged. "It's just a thing. No big."

"You used to be the lifeguard here. I remember now."

"My parents owned this resort," Miles said woodenly. He swam past Adam and climbed up the overgrown beach to where he'd dropped his clothes.

Adam followed and caught his arm. "No, wait."

Miles turned and their eyes met. At first Adam saw anger in Miles's face, and was that fear? But then his expression changed; his eyes widened and went dark and hungry, and Adam realized they were both standing there stark naked. And both of them were hard.

"Fuck," Adam breathed.

Miles took a breath, then whispered, "Okay," and buried his hand in Adam's hair, dragging him closer and covering Adam's mouth with his own.

He'd brushed his teeth. That was all Adam could think before Miles's mouth and tongue swept him under, like one of those big waves from an earthquake, tsunami, yeah, that was the word, oh who fucking cared what the word was because Miles's hand was digging into his wet hair and Miles's other arm was clamped around his waist, holding him hard against his own wet body, and their tongues were playing tag and it was even hotter than their earlier kiss and Miles was *naked* and so was he and if he wasn't going to get fucked this time he was just going to sit down and cry like a little baby.

Miles dragged his mouth away from Adam's and rasped, "I hope to God you have a rubber in your wallet."

Adam's bones melted, and he stammered, "Yeah, think so, God, *hope* so," and he was diving for the pile of clothing two endless feet away from him. He fumbled through it, tossing aside the leather vest, finding the pants and digging through the pockets for his wallet. Hands slid around his chest as Miles knelt behind him, stroking, tugging the darker hair around his nipples, and he moaned, throwing his head back against Miles's shoulder, his fingers tight on the wallet.

"Is there?" Miles whispered in his ear, and the warmth of Miles's breath on his cheek sent heat ricocheting around his brain. He managed to get the wallet open and found the little packet.

Then, still on his knees, he squirmed around to face Miles and kissed him again, pressing the condom into Miles's hand and drawing back long enough to gasp, "Oh, God, *please* fuck me," before diving back into the kiss. He ran his hands over Miles's chest and down to curl around his sweet, thick cock, feeling the silk and steel of it, hot and damp and so hard. He put a hand on Miles's chest and pushed him back onto the grass, and slid down between Miles's legs, desperate to taste him. He didn't mess with preliminaries, just took him in his mouth and slid down the shaft until Miles filled his throat and his nose was buried in the brown curls.

"Christ!" Miles shouted, and dropped the condom.

Adam slid off him and grabbed the condom, opening it and unrolling it onto Miles's cock with hands that trembled. "How do you want this?" he stammered, his hands smoothing the latex, then moving lower. "On my knees, what?"

Miles just stared at him, his eyes wild and uncomprehending. Then he looked down at Adam's hands cupping his balls, shuddered, and surged up off the grass, tackling Adam and pinning him down on the ground. "I can't do this easy," he growled, "nothing fancy, nothing like what you're probably used to ..."

"I'm not used to nothing," Adam cried, "just fuck me, for God's sake."

"There's no lube!"

Adam half sat up, grabbed Miles's ears, and snarled, "I. Don't. Care. Fuck me. Use spit. Just do it. *Now.*" He hiked his legs up over Miles's shoulders, locking his ankles over his back. "Now!"

And Miles, still growling, shifted his weight. The pressure, almost too painful for him to take, even with the spit and the water and the lubrication on the condom, pushed against his involuntary resistance, and then Miles was there, in him, and the head of his cock scraped right over the magic spot. Adam cried out, and Miles froze. "No," Adam said dazedly, "it's good. Good. God, *move ...*"

Miles moved, hard and fast, rocking into him, damp skin against damp skin, eyes locked on Adam's face. His hands moved to clamp around Adam's wrists, holding him pinned to the ground. There was a sound, a low moan like the wind, and Adam thought vaguely that it was the water, and then he realized it was him. Miles was staring at him as if he held the answers to all the universe, and somehow that struck him as funny, that this smart, *clever* man, so much smarter and so much better read than he himself, would be looking at him that way, and then he remembered a science-fiction book he *had* read, and with a stupid, insane grin, cried "Forty-two!" And shot, coming hard without anything touching his cock at all, just from the fucking and the sheer goddamn relief of having a dick up his ass at last after so long. And it was Miles's, Miles the guy who didn't know him from the original Adam, but wanted him anyway.

Shouting wordlessly, Miles bucked hard, his back arching and his head thrown back. He thrust a couple more times, then collapsed onto Adam's chest. He released Adam's wrists long enough to let Adam's legs slide off his shoulders and to the ground, then slipped his fingers between Adam's so that their hands were linked.

They lay still and silent a long moment, then Miles raised his head and said blankly, "Forty-two?"

"The Answer," Adam murmured. God, he felt good. The sun was warm, the grass was soft, his ass was full, and Miles was heavy. Solid. He felt anchored. His ass hurt, but it was a good hurt, a great hurt, like he'd had a really good workout, or a really good performance, all achy and positive. Endorphins or something.

Miles rested his forehead on Adam's shoulder, then turned his face to nuzzle at Adam's neck. Adam tilted his head accommodatingly. "I should ask if it was good for you," Miles murmured, "but given that evidently you acquired the answer to life, the universe, and everything, it must have been—excuse the word—cosmic."

"Mmm," Adam said. Miles's hair smelled of lake water—green and slightly musty and faintly, very faintly, of fish. It was a great smell. The ground was warm underneath him, Miles heavy and warm on top of him and inside him, and Adam thought he could just maybe lie here forever.

But Miles was moving, shifting back and sitting up, careful with the condom as he drew himself out of Adam's reluctant body. "You got come all over your chest," he said, not looking at Adam.

"You do too. Looks good on you."

Miles looked up then, flashing him a quick grin before settling his face back into its sober lines. Adam loved that, the little quick flashes of humor; he couldn't help but grin back up at Miles from where he lay.

Miles dropped the tied-off condom with a squelch next to where he'd left his sweats, and stepped back into the shallow water to wash himself off. Sighing—he was really very comfortable where he was— Adam joined him. They stood staring out across the water for a while, and then Miles said, "You ever get out to the island when you were here before?"

"No, my parents wouldn't let us. It was for the older kids." Adam shot him a sideways look. "You must have been out there plenty. Did you live here year round?"

"Most of the time, then. We had a house in Forest Park, on the west side, but we only lived there during the school year, and spent almost all our weekends up here, all winter." Miles fell silent, still gazing at the shoreline of the island a quarter mile out into the lake. "After they died, I didn't come here for two years."

"What happened?"

"Car crash." Miles didn't elaborate, and Adam didn't want to ask. Instead, he said, "So what's with the construction equipment?"

"Lisa wants to reopen the resort. I don't. We compromised on renovating the lodge since it needed it anyway and then debating whether or not we want to do the bed-and-breakfast thing, just for the summer." He glanced at Adam, his mouth quirking in one of those grins again. "Needless to say, this sort of thing would no longer be an option, in that case."

"In that case," Adam quipped, "I vote no."

"I'll take it under advisement," Miles said gravely. "I was thinking more about the noise bothering me when I'm trying to work. Lisa's thinking about the fact that I've become even more antisocial in the last couple of years."

"You seem pretty social to me," Adam said. He walked over the grass-infested sand to the pile of his clothes and dug in his vest pocket for his cigarettes and lighter. Sitting carefully on the edge of the dock, he lit one and took a deep drag, letting the smoke out slowly. God, the first smoke of the day always tasted so good. Too bad the rest of them didn't so much, anymore.

"You don't taste like a smoker," Miles said. He wasn't looking at Adam, but staring down into the water around his knees. "Kissing a smoker is like eating an ashtray. Or so I've heard."

"I don't smoke a lot," Adam admitted. "And frankly, if I do, it's just as often weed. Someone's always passing a joint around. I just like having something to do with my hands. Particularly when I'm drinking—or after sex."

"So the key to you not smoking is keeping your hands busy?"

"Why? You got something in mind?"

"If I did? Would you not smoke then?"

"I would take it under advisement," Adam said in the same grave tone Miles had used. "I take it you don't indulge."

Miles snorted. "I deal with enough poisons on a daily basis. I don't need to add nicotine to the mix. Besides, I'd probably forget I lit one and set the place on fire. I'm not the most organized person in the world."

Adam considered this, smoking thoughtfully. It was true that the part of the cottage he'd seen was mostly pretty messy—not dirty, just messy, with clean dishes piled in the drainer and on the counter, books and papers strewn over half the table, and more books and what had looked like mail piled on most of the horizontal surfaces in the living room. And then there was the bucket of piss on the porch. The only space that was immaculate was the area where Miles worked. "You're organized for what you need to be organized for," he pointed out. "Who gives a shit about anything else?"

"Can I give you my sister's phone number, please?" Miles said.

"Babe, she has never seen the mess that is the hotel suite of Black Varen." Adam sighed. "I'll show your sister one of these days and she will never criticize you again. It's a special little slice of hell." He took a long drag off the cigarette and stubbed it out on the damp wood of the dock.

Miles said, "More like 'Black Hole'?"

Adam laughed. "You said it."

"Can't you afford your own room?" Miles sloshed through the shallow water and hiked himself up onto the dock next to Adam, the muscles in his strong arms flexing. Adam wondered if he worked out; he didn't have the build of a sedentary man, like he'd have thought an artist would. "I mean, I'd think the expense account would stretch that far. *Do* you have an expense account? Does the record company pay for it? How does that all work?"

"Record company pays for it, but for security reasons they want us all in one place when we're on tour. Bill almost had a stroke this morning when he found out I'd gone walkabout." He leaned against Miles's shoulder. "You think you were suspicious when you found me? Bill was all paranoid about who I was with, like you were some kind of freakazoid stalker or something."

"Who's to say I'm not?" Miles said dryly.

"Are you?"

"No."

"Then I'm not worried. Besides, you said you never left this place, so it'd be kind of hard to stalk me."

"There is that. Hey, you hungry?"

"Starving. But you don't have to feed me. I can wait 'til the car gets here."

"I already made pancakes. I'm relatively sure they're not poisonous. I try not to go near the kitchen with any of the really dangerous stuff."

"God, I haven't had pancakes for breakfast in forever. Hell, I haven't had breakfast in forever. I tend to focus on lunch as the first meal of the day, if not supper." Adam scrambled up and picked up his clothes, eyeing his leather pants doubtfully. Miles laughed.

"I've got some drawstring sweats you can borrow until you're ready to deal with the painted-on shit. I don't know how you wear those."

"Some days, man," Adam said ruefully, "neither do I."

ou're not at all what I thought a rocker would be like," Miles said over the pancakes.

Adam picked up a slice of microwave bacon and inspected it. "This is really weird bacon," he observed, then Miles's words seemed to sink in, and he winced. "Dude. You sound so seventies saying shit like that. 'Rockers.' Crap. That sounds like some K-tel record your mother mighta had."

"What do you call yourselves then?" Miles forked in a mouthful of food.

Adam shrugged. "Musicians. The band. Self-defined by the instrument—the bassist, the lead, keyboards, drums. And what did you think we would be like?"

"Arrogant. Stuck-up. Wild. Or semicomatose."

A snort was the response to the last. "There are those of us whose natural state is that, that's for damn sure. But most of us are just guys, you know. Working for a living. Trying to have fun while we're doing it."

"What kind of fun?"

"Depends." Adam ate quietly a moment, then said, "Sometimes the 'fun' gets to be too much, you know? And having people around who pretend that they want to give you the world when they're really out to get it from you—that gets old. Your perspective gets screwy. Like Eddie, for instance. Dude's thirty-four years old. Been in the band fifteen years. Never grew up; still thinks he's twenty. Last night he was making out with this chick who showed up at the after-party. Bill sees 'em, gets the vibe that there's something weird about the chick. Pulls her aside and checks ID. It's fake as they come. Gets the girl's real name from one of the girls she came with. Turns out she's fucking *fourteen*. Bill calls hotel security and gets them to call her parents. Fortunately nothing more than some necking went on. But Eddie's such a loser he spends the rest of the night bitching at Bill that he took his girl away. Fourteen. What kind of loser his age wants to fuck a fourteen-year-old girl?"

"You ever make out with an underage girl?" Miles asked.

Adam laughed. "Hell, no. But I came into this late—I was twenty-five and already had a sort-of career behind me. Was a little older than the other guys, even if I'm younger in years. Didn't stop me from falling into the stupid zone for five years."

"When did you stop being stupid?"

Adam glanced at him. "I'll let you know when it happens."

Miles met his eyes and suddenly felt as tired as Adam looked. "Today was stupid?" he asked quietly.

"Hell, no." Adam's voice was surprised. "Today was nice. A break. I needed it." He rested his elbow on the table and his chin in his hand. "Coulda been boring, with someone else. But it wasn't. I like you, Miles. Or Mike, or whoever you are."

"It says 'Michael' on my birth certificate," Miles admitted. He glanced at the dregs of the pancakes on his plate and pushed them around with his fork. "But I'm Miles."

"I like Miles. It's different. You're different."

"Yeah," Miles said bitterly. "I'm real different. You done?"

"Yeah. What did I say? It wasn't an insult."

"That's okay." Miles rose and took the plates to scrape into the garbage. He washed them off and put them in the dish drainer with the rest of the dishes. "I know I'm different. Kind of messed up."

"Hey." Adam followed him and took his arm. "You ain't messed up. You're okay. You're different, but not *not* normal . . ."

Miles barked a short, humorless laugh. "Oh, yeah, right. Haven't been off my own property in ten years except once when I got hurt and my regular doctor was on vacation. Fuck. Never mind." He finished loading the dishwasher and turned it on.

"Why?"

"Why never mind?"

"Why don't you leave here? I mean, hell, it's a sweet place and all, but you don't strike me as the hermit type." Adam leaned against the counter and grinned. "You're perfectly hospitable to me, and then some."

"Long, boring story." He reached over and took hold of the waistband of the sweats Adam was wearing, tugging him closer. "I can think of better things to do." He ran his hand over Adam's chest, feeling the crisp spring of the sparse hair, the hard nub of his nipples, the sleek, strong muscles in his belly. "God, you're pretty."

Sighing, Adam wound his arms around Miles's neck and nuzzled his jaw. "You're not so bad yourself. Wish I could take you home with me." He drew back, his arms still linked behind Miles. "Why *can't* I? I know it's been years, but hell . . . It'd be fun. I'm booked at the Hyatt a couple more days; the rest of the guys are leaving tonight, so it'll just be you and me. We could do a little partying, just the two of us . . ." He trailed off as Miles went rigid in his arms.

Reaching up, Miles unhooked Adam's arms from around his neck and stepped away. He rubbed his own arms, as if suddenly chilled at Adam's words. "Thanks, but no thanks. You might want to take a shower before your manager gets here. I need . . ." He made a vague gesture toward the living room.

"What? You need to go paint or something?"

Miles just nodded and vanished through the doorway.

Adam stared, nonplused, a moment, then sighed and followed.

His host was sitting on a stool, hunched over the slanted desk, not working, not anything, just sitting there with his attention on the empty desktop. His hands cupped his elbows as if he were cold. "Hey," Adam said softly from the doorway, "whatever I said, I'm sorry. Are you okay?"

"Fine." Miles angled his face toward Adam, damp brown hair falling over his eyes. "Sorry. Told you I was weird."

"Seem more scared than weird," Adam said.

Miles swiveled around on the stool and rubbed his hands on the thighs of his sweats. "Look, thanks for the invitation, but it just wouldn't work out, okay? I can't. I got issues. Not your problem."

"Okay." Adam shrugged, disappointed. "It's just that, well, I *like* you, dude. Not just the sex, which was fabulous, by the way, but you. You're interesting. You probably don't realize just how rare that is."

Miles snorted. "And you must surround yourself with brain-dead losers if you think I'm interesting."

"Well, there's that, too."

Miles laughed at that, and a warm glow bloomed in the pit of Adam's belly. "Okay," he said reluctantly, "I really do need a shower. Care to join me?"

"No, thanks." Miles shook his head. "I mean, it would be nice, but I can't, okay?"

Another *can't*. Adam said, "Okay," and went to take his shower.

When he came out, Miles went in, ducking his head in embarrassment as they passed in the hall. Adam rubbed his hair with the towel and went looking for his clothes. He thought they'd dumped them in the living room, but they weren't there, so he went to the kitchen. As he ducked down the dogleg corridor he heard Grace caroling, "Miles, darling!" and smiled to himself.

Then he walked into the kitchen, still rubbing his head, and nearly ran into a woman coming out. They froze, staring at each other, and then she let out a bloodcurdling scream.

"Holy fuck!" Adam yelled, and jerked down the towel he held to hide his nakedness. "I thought you were the fucking bird!"

"Who are you?" she panted, and grabbed the pancake pan from the drainer, brandishing it like a sword.

Miles came skidding around the corner, shirtless but thankfully still wearing his sweats, and said, "Lise, sorry, shit, I wasn't expecting you! It's okay. This is Adam. Adam—my sister Lisa."

"Shit." Adam adjusted the towel and pushed his wet hair out of his eyes. He held out a damp hand, dropped it in embarrassment, then when she held out her hand, he put it out again, eyeing the skillet nervously.

She glanced at it, then giggled and set it on the counter. "Sorry," she said, and shook his hand firmly. "Not expecting to see a naked man in here—Miles always wears clothes even if he's by himself."

"My clothes are around here somewhere. If I could just . . ." He eased past her and scooped up the bundle from the chair. "Here they are. I'm gonna . . . if you'll just excuse . . ." and retreated back to the bathroom to dress.

Lisa looked after him, then back to Miles. "Spill."

He sighed and ran his hand through his hair. "Would you believe I found him?"

"Found him where?"

"Asleep on my patio. This morning. I guess he was drunk and wandered down here from the gate. He used to vacation here when he was a kid."

"Huh," Lisa said skeptically, but moved in to give him a kiss. In his ear, she whispered, "Be careful."

"It's fine. It's nothing. He's got a ride coming to pick him up; I'll take him up to the gate, and then it's done." He shrugged. "No big."

"You gotta be more careful, Miles. You live out here all alone—what if he's a front man for a criminal gang? They might be looking for a good hideout, and here you are, all alone, and this place is miles from anywhere . . ."

"He's not a front man for a criminal gang, unless you consider metal rock criminal." Miles sighed. "He's Adam Craig, from Black Varen. They're a—"

"I know what they are." Lisa stared at him, her eyes narrowed. "You're asking me to believe that Adam Craig of Black Varen just wandered out of nowhere onto the resort and you, you picked him up like a stray puppy or something?"

Miles flushed. "Well, he had to call for a ride, so I gave him coffee. And breakfast, and we kind of talked, and then we had a swim, and everything's *fine*, Lise, I don't need to explain everything . . ."

"Oh, shit. You screwed him, didn't you?"

Miles could feel the grin spreading on his face. "I sure did."

"God, did you at least use a condom? God only knows who he's been with, and . . . wait a minute. Since when is Adam Craig gay? Nobody's ever said anything about—"

"And if you don't mind," Adam said from behind Miles, "I would appreciate it if you wouldn't, either. My manager knows, but the other guys in the group don't. It would be kind of a public relations fiasco if it came out."

Miles turned to see him carrying his vest and boots. He smiled at Miles. "Hey, can I get a grocery bag or something to put the rest of my crap in? Getting the pants on was hard enough; I don't want to mess with the arm things or the vest."

"Sure." Miles went to the cabinet where he stashed the extra plastic bags. He handed one to Adam, who stuffed his gear in it before sitting down to put on his boots.

Lisa said, "So you're *the* Adam Craig?"

"Yep. And you're *the* Lisa Caldwell."

There was a piercing scream from the cage in the corner that mimicked the one Lisa had uttered on seeing Adam. Miles groaned. "Oh, good grief. I spend hours trying to teach her a phrase or two and she picks up on a fucking scream. That's gonna make me crazy. *Er.* Crazier."

"You're not crazy," Adam and Lisa chorused. They looked at each other, then grinned.

"Shut up," Miles grumbled.

Lisa got up and poured them all coffee, checking the mugs just as Miles had taught her. "So. Adam. What brings you around this neck of the woods?"

"I told you—he used to come here when he was a kid," Miles said, then thought *Oh, shit*, when she turned hopeful eyes on him. He shook his head minutely; she looked disappointed for a second, then the cheerful expression returned.

Adam was watching them, frowning faintly, but Lisa said, "I don't remember a Craig family from back then. I used to do the bookings . . ."

"Karoshewski. Craig's my stage name."

She thought a minute, then her brow cleared. "Right! Two boys, mother blonde, father dark. You were the younger one."

"Wow." Adam laughed. "What a memory! That's gotta be twenty years ago."

She tapped her skull. "Mind like a steel trap."

"That's one of us," Miles said.

Ignoring him, she focused on Adam. "You seem pretty normal for a musician."

"Well, I've only been with the band for five years. Maybe I haven't had time to develop yet."

"He used to be in musical theater," Miles supplied.

"I love musical theater," Lisa said. "Broadway?"

Adam made a face. "I wish. No, just a California-based touring company. We played mostly midrange venues in the Northwest—California, Oregon, Washington. Good experience. Then someone was at one of the performances who knew that Varen was looking for a new lead singer because their current lead was ... um ... incapacitated, and introduced me to them. I also compose, and play guitar, so that helped." He shrugged. "They're not a bad bunch of guys—kind of hedonistic and self-indulgent, which I guess is understandable. Talented, though."

"I've heard," Lisa said dryly. "You can't turn on the radio without hearing you guys somewhere." She glanced at Miles. "Unless, of course, you never move the dial off NPR."

"Hey," Adam said, "I listen to NPR. Okay, most of the time I don't have a clue what they're talking about, but I listen to it. Sometimes. At least I don't have to worry about picking up a musical hook that ends up in a song and then we get sued for copyright infringement. And I've gotten some ideas from it. Like 'Boy Meets Girl'? That was from one of their StoryCorps pieces. People's history is so interesting."

Yeah, Miles thought dryly. Real interesting. He avoided Lisa's eyes, knowing the expression in them all too well. Instead, he asked, "What brings you out today, Lise?"

"It's Sunday."

He blinked. "It is? Already?"

"Well, that explains your utter surprise," she replied with a quick glance at Adam.

Adam grinned at her. "I'd say he wasn't the only one who was surprised."

"Nope," she agreed. "Although I do have to say ... it was kind of um, nice to be greeted by a naked Adam Craig."

"Hey," he said, "I had a towel on."

"Your *head*," she shot back.

Miles laughed. Despite the usual undercurrents of stress between him and his sister, he was enjoying himself. Had been all morning, except for a few sensitive moments—and he really did need to let some of that stuff go . . .

Lisa was saying, "So someone's coming to pick you up? I guess that means you're not sticking around for Sunday dinner."

"I wish, if only for the reason that I'm curious as to how you'll find edible food in this house."

"There isn't any," Lisa said. "But there is up at the lodge. Miles and I always have Sunday dinner at the lodge. It's closed, but the kitchen is still kitted out and everything works, and I keep the freezer stocked. Fresh food's in a cooler in my car. So it's sort of like going out to dinner, which . . ." She hesitated, and Miles nodded for her to go on. ". . . isn't really an option."

Adam looked at Miles. "So why don't you go up to the lodge to get food instead of eating expired stuff?"

Miles shrugged. "Too much trouble. I'm too busy."

"Which is why I make him eat Sunday dinner with me. Then I know he at least has leftovers to reheat the rest of the week." She made a face at Miles, and he made kissy-faces back at her.

Adam laughed. "You guys are cute," he said. "Like, I don't know . . . meerkats or something."

"Great," Miles said, "we remind him of rodents."

"Could be worse," Lisa mused. "Could be capybaras. Or chupacabras."

"Or chimichangas," Miles added.

There was the sound of a phone ringing, and they, as one, looked in Grace's direction, then all realized at the same time that it wasn't Miles's ringtone. "Shit," Adam said, and dug his phone out of his pocket. "Bill. Okay. See you in a few." He looked up at Miles, his expression dismayed. "They just turned off I-94."

"Oh," Miles said. "Okay. I'll drive you up to the gate. Lise, I'll meet you at the lodge in about fifteen minutes?"

"Sure." She turned to Adam, holding out her hand. "It was nice meeting you again, Adam Karoshewski."

"You too. Next time we're in Chicago, I'll reserve tickets for you."
He glanced at Miles. "No chance of your coming, though, right?"

Miles shook his head grimly.

"That's okay. It's cool. Oh, and I need your email address or
website or something—I'm serious about wanting you to do a calligy-
thing for me."

"MilesCaldwellDesigns dot com," Miles said. "Lisa manages the
website, but it's got an email link that comes to me."

"You a web designer?" Adam asked. "We're sorta looking for a
new one."

"Sorry, no." She smiled. "I'm a lawyer. A friend of Miles's did the
design; I just manage it."

Miles listened to them talk, bemused and envious of the level of
comfort between them after only talking a few minutes, then turned
to find his keys.

They walked out to the Jeep in silence, Adam swinging the plastic
bag from his hand, Miles watching him out of the corner of his eye.
He was always in motion, Miles thought, seeing him looking around
at the cracked surface of the parking lot, the construction equipment
at the far end of the lot, the back of the lodge—or front, depending
on whether you were arriving by car or by boat. On the back side, the
car side, a set of double doors was padlocked shut, the chains along
with the abandoned-looking lot giving the lodge a feeling of lonely
emptiness. Miles hated this side of the resort; it only reminded him
of everything he'd lost. The front, by the lake, was easier to deal with;
the lake was something he saw every day, unchanging, reliable. But the
Jeep was too heavy to park on the grass near his cottage. He pressed
the button to unlock the doors and climbed in.

"What year is this?" Adam asked as he followed suit, patting the
passenger side doorframe in illustration.

"I don't know. I got it two, maybe three years ago. I don't keep
track of stuff like that. That's Lisa's job."

"Lisa buy this for you? It's a pretty sweet ride."

"No," Miles said curtly, then relented. "Well, she made the arrangements, had the salesman bring it out here so I could sign the papers and everything. But I paid for it."

"Researched it online, huh?"

"Something wrong with that?"

Adam spread his hands. "Hey, Miles, it's just conversation. I'm not attacking you. There's no need to get defensive."

"Sorry. I . . . sorry." He turned the key in the ignition and put it in gear. "I bet you think it's stupid for someone who doesn't go anywhere to have a car."

"Nope. I figure you probably drive around the property, and if that Miata's Lisa's, then I bet she borrows this whenever she has to haul stuff, right?"

Miles snorted in agreement.

"And you'd need it if you ever had an emergency or something."

This time the snort was decidedly negative. "I don't drive off-site. I don't *go* off-site."

"Yeah, I got that."

"I did, once."

Adam just looked at him. He flushed hotly, not sure why he'd brought that up. He supposed Adam was expecting an explanation.

Finally, he said, "I cut myself on a piece of metal. It wouldn't stop bleeding. Lisa came out to bring me to the hospital. We got about two feet from the gate and I freaked out. I jumped out of the car and ran back to the gate, and just curled up there, kind of catatonic. She had to call an ambulance, and they sedated me. Then they patched me up and gave me a tetanus shot, and then drove me back to the resort. Didn't even try to get me to the hospital. I guess I was pretty scary."

"Oh," Adam said. It didn't sound judgmental; Miles glanced over at him and saw him looking thoughtful.

"What?" he demanded.

Adam blinked. "What what?"

"What are you thinking?"

"Nothing, really. Just that it explains why you kind of shut down when I was talking about you coming into the city for a day or two."

Miles felt the cold rush of fear down his spine. "I can't do that," he said hoarsely.

"I get that. It's okay. We all have our hang-ups." The voice was calm, the expression mild. Miles wasn't sure if it was understanding or indifference—but that wasn't unusual. He never could tell. He hunched his shoulders and kept driving.

The road ended some yards from the gate; not quite ended, but the stretch between here and the gate wasn't kept up: the gravel was uneven, with patches of vegetation sprouting among the stones. He stopped the car at the end of the pavement and put it in park, then sat staring straight ahead, both hands clenched on the wheel.

"Can I ask something?" Adam said quietly.

Miles shrugged, not looking at him. It hurt too much to look at him.

"I really liked being here. Being with you. I know you can't leave, but I could stay in town for a couple more days. We aren't going back into the studio for a couple of weeks. I could rent a car, maybe come back?"

Sweat beaded on Miles's neck and ran down under his T-shirt. Adam here. Maybe overnight. Maybe sleeping with him, his arms around him, those long, lean legs wrapped around him again, Miles losing himself in those warm, wet kisses. He saw it, Adam straddling him, his dark hair hanging like a curtain, shutting out the world, the soft, sensual smile on his beautiful face all he could see in the dimness.

And he saw other possibilities—impatience with his ineptitude, scorn for his lack of anything resembling skill in social intercourse, boredom with his limited interests. No. Better to leave it like this, with the memory of those kisses and those sleek limbs twined around his body. He opened his mouth to explain, to excuse, but all that came out was a strangled "No."

He didn't look at Adam, just sat there, his face burning and his voice silent. After a moment, Adam said, still in that quiet voice, "Okay," and he got out of the car, closing the door carefully.

Stupid, Miles thought savagely to himself. *Stupid, stupid, stupid.* He sat there a moment, then glanced up to see Adam looking in the passenger side window. Adam held up a hand in farewell, smiled regretfully, then turned away.

Miles didn't even remember lunging from the car, but he was suddenly outside, on his feet. He slammed the door and was around the car in a few steps, catching Adam's arm and dragging him back, turning him so his back was against the side of the car. He put his hand on Adam's face and leaned forward, his mouth finding Adam's.

Adam made a faint sound and opened for him, one hand pressing against Miles's waist, the other burying itself in his hair. Miles groaned and pressed into Adam, trying to put everything he felt into the kiss, everything he couldn't say, everything he couldn't *do*. Adam seemed to understand; he was soft and supple under Miles's hands, but didn't push, didn't demand anything, just took what Miles needed to give.

Finally Miles dragged himself back and stared into Adam's bemused golden eyes. "I can't," he rasped helplessly. "I *can't*."

Adam stroked his cheek gently. "It's okay. I get it. It's okay."

Letting go of a heavy sigh, Miles dropped his head to Adam's shoulder and just stood there, his hands on Adam's waist. Adam hugged him gently, and said "It's okay" again, then, "But you don't mind if I email you, right? 'Cause I really do want that picture."

Miles barked a humorless laugh. "Sure. I can handle email."

"Then it's all good." Adam hugged him again, then eased from Miles's grip. Miles, feeling as if he'd had a layer of skin ripped off, turned and leaned against the Jeep.

Tires crunched on gravel, and a white stretch limo rolled around the corner and came to a stop outside the gate. Adam bent and picked up the plastic bag he'd dropped sometime during the last few minutes, and put his other hand out for Miles to shake. "There's my ride," he said cheerfully, as if they were relative strangers. Miles shook his hand, and shook his head at his own thoughts. Of course Adam was a stranger. Miles might know that body, but he knew very little else about Adam Craig Karoshewski-with-a-"w."

"Good trip," he said stiffly.

An older man had gotten out of the limo, and now he waved at them. "That's Bill," Adam said. "Mother Hen. I'll be in touch, Miles."

"Good," Miles said. "Bye."

"Bye."

He stood and watched as Adam walked the rest of the way to the gate, stepped over the hanging chain, and got into the limo, Bill following. Then the limo backed into the wide space everyone had always used as a turnaround, before driving back down the blacktop and vanishing around the corner.

He stood there a long time.

Chapter 5

o," Bill said, after they'd driven back to the expressway and were heading south toward the city, "you're unusually quiet. Still have a hangover?"

Adam considered the question. "No. I did when I woke up, but Miles—that's the guy who owns the place—gave me coffee and breakfast, and I went for a swim in the lake."

"How the hell did you end up out there anyway?"

Sighing, Adam shrugged. "I was stoned and decided to go to Milwaukee. Don't ask me why. Anyway, I saw the sign for the resort—my family used to go there when I was a kid—and at the time it seemed like a good idea. It's closed, but Miles was pretty nice. He's an artist."

"Oh." Bill fell silent. They drove for another fifteen miles or so, then Bill said, "There isn't anything I need to know about that's gonna come and bite me in the ass, is there?"

"You mean did I fuck him?" Adam asked wearily. "Yeah. We fucked. No big. Guy's a hermit—it's not like he's gonna turn into some crazed stalker. Anyway, it was a one-time deal. I'll probably never see him again. Done. Donerino."

"Adam, baby, you know this shit worries me," Bill said. "There's the publicity, which if it gets out, will be brutal—"

"It won't get out."

"And then there's the health issues—"

"Jesus, Bill, listen to yourself! Eddie's more likely to pick up an STD from one of his jailbait girlfriends than I am from the one guy I fucked who's a hermit to boot. Plus the fact that with all the shit going around before, during, and after the concerts, one of us is gonna end up like Ray, brain-dead from an overdose. Or real dead. Fuck." Adam slouched sullenly back against the leather seat. "Do you have a *clue* when the last time I got fucked was? Three years. Three fucking years, Bill. *You* try going without sex for three fucking years."

"You don't go without sex," Bill pointed out. "You've slept with a couple of different women—"

"Four times. Four women over the course of five years. And just because I *can* fuck women doesn't mean I *want* to. Christ. I can't believe I'm having this conversation. In fact, I'm not. Conversation over."

"I just worry about you, kid. Neil's pretty much a loss, Chuck and Eddie just want to get laid, but you—you've got potential. It ain't a coincidence that the group took off when you joined up—you're the one with the charisma, you're the one with the talent. They don't care about the band—they only care about what they get with it. Without you they'd be nothing. So you're the one who's the most vulnerable. Anything happens to you, the group is over." He regarded Adam with beagle-y sad eyes. "I wanted to talk to you about maybe thinking about putting out a solo album, just testing the waters, you know? I think that might be a good thing—build a solo rep so when the group implodes—'cause they all do—you'll be ready to move on."

"Not all groups implode," Adam said, his eyes closed. "The Stones have been around forever, and The Who."

Bill waved his hand dismissively. "They're different. You can't tell me that Varen's in that class. You—you're in that class."

"You—you're hedging your bets," Adam said without opening his eyes.

Bill laughed. "Busted. But still. I know which star to hitch my wagon to. I'm not stupid."

"No. Neither am I. The fact is, Bill, you know that as long as people think I'm occasionally bisexual, like Jim Morrison, they're okay with it. If it came out that I'm really just plain gay, that won't work so well. Stupid distinction, but there it is. So, yeah, I'll keep the girls happy—maybe one a year—if you shut up about the guys. You know I'm not stupid."

"No. But you get stoned, or buzzed, or whatever, and you end up in the ass-end of nowhere on your way to fucking Milwaukee. Doesn't give me a lot of confidence in your judgment."

"Conceded. I promise not to run away to Milwaukee again. Now. What's the deal on the hotel?"

"I got you a suite on the sixth floor of the east tower under the name Craig Karoshewski, as usual. Use the appropriate credit card when buying anything outside the hotel. Otherwise bill it to your room. The label'll pick it up through Wednesday; after that you're on your own. I had your stuff moved there already. The rest of the boys and I have a red-eye flight back to L.A. tonight, so we'll be out of your hair. You need to be back in L.A. in two weeks at the latest; that's when you go back into the studio."

"Thanks."

"What are your plans?"

"Right now? Change into comfortable clothes, go shopping, then a nice quiet dinner."

"Shopping for what?"

"One of those e-readers. There are some books I want to read."

"What kind of books?"

"Science fiction."

"Since when do you read science fiction?" Bill thought a moment. "Since when do you read books at all?"

"Since this afternoon. Did you know the name of the band came from a science-fiction book?"

"Yeah, I'd heard that."

"Well, those are the books I'm going to read. Someone recommended them. It'll be a quiet couple of days. Maybe I'll walk down to the lake and read all day tomorrow, out in the sunshine."

"Just keep a low profile," Bill said.

"Always," Adam sighed.

"Do you want to talk about it?" Lisa asked quietly over dessert.

Miles poked at his cherry cobbler with his fork. "Talk about what?"

"What you're upset about?"

"I'm not upset."

She didn't answer, and he looked up to see her watching him, a worried look on her face. "I'm not," he said. "Not really. It's just . . ."

When he didn't go on, she said, "Today was different. Your routine was upset, even if you weren't."

"Yeah."

"He seemed like a really nice guy. Do you think you'll see him again?"

"No."

"Did you ask him?"

"No." Miles sighed. "He asked. I said no."

"Oh, Miles," Lisa said.

"This," Miles said savagely, "is why I don't talk. I don't know what to do or say or anything right. Or do anything right. Oh, fuck, whatever, I can't even *talk* right."

"You seemed to be getting along fine with Adam. He seemed to get you."

"I don't know why. I don't know why he'd even want to come back. And if he did, I'd only screw it up worse. So I said no. End of story."

"Do you *want* to see him again?"

He ate a piece of cobbler. It was his favorite, but it tasted like ashes. "It doesn't matter. I won't."

His cell phone blurped. He took it out of his pocket and looked at it. "Speak of the devil," he said with a humorless smile at Lisa, "he sent me a text. Probably about the thing he wants me to illuminate. Yep. That's it."

That wasn't what the text said, but he didn't tell her that. It was just a brief message: *if u chg ur mind let me kno.* God, he wanted to, but it was better this way.

"All right," Lisa said doubtfully.

Later that evening, he logged into his email. Adam had sent a follow-up to his earlier text, attaching a PDF of some sheet music. The email was considerably longer.

From: aceydeucey@premierrecordings.com
To: miles@milescaldwelldesigns.com

Miles: just to let you know I'm cool with whatever design you want for the picture thing. Anything you do will be beautiful. Like you. I just started those books—I'm reading them in order so I won't get to the Miles ones for a bit, but I'm liking the first one. I'm serious about if you ever change your mind. I'll be at the Hyatt on Wacker until Wednesday if you do. Love, Adam

Chapter 6

To: miles@milescaldwelldesigns.com
From: aceydeucey@premierrecordings.com

Miles: just got the sketch. Wow. It's gonna be gorgeous. Can't wait to see the real thing. I like how you made it look like music from some old book or something.

Walked down to the lake today and am just sitting and watching the sailboats. Do you sail? I seem to remember sailboats on your lake there and thinking I'd like to try to crew someday. You'd think living in L.A. with the ocean so close I would have eventually gotten around to it, but I never have yet. I'd probably be better off trying it on a lake instead of the ocean. But not Michigan—that lake looks as big as an ocean from here.

It's funny—I haven't written any songs in about six months—that's part of the reason we're taking a break from touring, so we can go into the studio and work on some stuff. The thing I sent you yesterday was just my first recorded song, but I haven't written in a while. Then last night I came up with one and it kind of just flowed out. And I woke up this morning with another one.

I think you were good for me.

Finished the first book and started on the second. I
am completely in love with Miles's old man Aaron.
Too bad he's imaginary.

I wish you'd change your mind. Love, Adam

To: aceydeucey@premierrecordings.com
From: miles@milescaldwelldesigns.com

Adam: glad you like the sketch.

Miles stared at the curt message. There was so much more he
wanted to say, but couldn't. So much banging at the back of his teeth:
I *have* changed my mind, I love Aaron too, I want to hear your songs,
you were good for me too, yes, I sail, yes, I'll teach you, yes, please
come back, please let me love you, please love me.

He hit send.

"Hey, dude!" Doug's voice came from behind him, but at the
door, so he couldn't see what Miles was doing.

Miles closed out the email program and turned around. "Hey,
Doug."

"Cruising internet porn?" his friend asked, pushing aside a pile of
books on the couch and dropping down, stretching his legs out.

"No. Just confirming a new commission. What are you doing
here?"

Fortunately, Doug knew him well enough not to take offense at
his unintentional rudeness. "Rob had a thing going on in Gurnee—
some medical software seminar or something—so I dropped him off
and swung by here to hang out for a while. Hot day, you got the lake,
so." He tilted his head back to look at Miles. "You busy? I can swim on
my own, if you are."

"No. I have some painting to do, but I haven't started yet today."

"Mikey, it's two in the afternoon. You're usually elbow-deep in
that crap by this time."

Miles shrugged. Doug, as usual, didn't press it; it was one of the reasons why he liked Doug and had managed to stay friends with him so long—Doug never pressed, never harassed, never put Miles on the spot or made him uncomfortable or misinterpreted his frequent faux pas. Doug and Bobby had been the first two of his friends from college to come see him in the hospital after he'd come out of the coma, and the only two who were still around. Even after Miles had retreated here and shut everyone else out, Doug and Bobby still kept after him. They, along with Lisa, were the only ones with keys to the gate chain and to Miles's cottage, and were on his medical records as emergency contacts, even though they weren't officially related. "Give me a minute and I'll meet you out by the dock."

"Bring towels," Doug instructed, then shifted back off the couch and went out the French doors, pulling his T-shirt over his head.

"Sunblock."

Miles reached up and fumbled for the tube lying in the grass, then tossed it idly over at Doug without raising his head. Doug, equally nonchalant, reached up and caught it.

It was something they did without thinking, having done it a couple dozen times a summer over the last ten years. It was part of the routine when Doug came by: drop the clothes and towel and sunscreen in a pile on the grass, swim, then crawl out to lie in the sun for a while to dry off. Miles himself swam every day, unless deep in a project, clear up until the shorter days in late October failed to warm the water up enough to bear. And he was back in the water by mid-April, cold or not. During the winter he shoveled the parking lot for exercise, or cross-country-skied, and on clear days when there wasn't any snow on the ground, he'd run a couple miles on the hiking trails that meandered along the lake. When he remembered. So he always had a good tan, but he supposed he should put some sunscreen on if they were going to be lying around here for any length of time.

Doug, of course, having a job downtown, had less opportunity for sunbathing, so sunblock for him was a necessity. Even with his naturally dark Italian skin, he still burned.

Adam was fairer-skinned than one would expect with his dark hair and an L.A. residence, Miles mused. He looked as though he spent a lot of time indoors rehearsing or recording or whatever it was rock bands did when they weren't touring. He had to work out sometime though; he was in pretty good shape for someone with such a slim build. Miles groaned faintly as he thought of those long, slender-but-strong legs, the smooth, sleek torso, the lean-muscled arms wrapped around him.

"Dude," Doug said in amusement, "I hope it ain't me got you excited like that. Cuz, you know I love you, but Rob's kind of possessive."

"Shit." Miles grabbed the closest piece of fabric he could reach to throw over his erection. It was a towel. Could have been worse; could have been Doug's shirt. "Sorry. Just thinking of . . . something."

"Someone, I'd say," Doug snorted. "Okay, give. Who's got your knickers in a twist? Some porn star?"

"Nobody."

Doug was silent, and finally Miles turned his head to see him sitting up, his arms around his knees and a skeptical expression on his face. "Spill," he said when he saw Miles looking at him. "You know you will sooner or later."

"It's nothing, really."

"Uh-huh."

"No. Really."

"Uh-huh."

"God, you're worse than Lisa."

"Lisa's all right, for a chick."

"Yeah," Miles admitted. Had he been thinking earlier that Doug wasn't a harasser?

"So?"

"Just a guy. Got lost and ended up sleeping on my patio."

"And this random guy was hot enough to give you a boner?" Doug cocked his head. "Dude. Tell me more."

"Nothin' to tell. He hung around awhile, then his ride got here, and he left."

"Did you fuck him?"

Miles didn't answer. Doug crowed, "Dude! You so did, didn't you?"

Miles sighed.

"So, *was* he hot? Or were you just desperate?"

"He was hot. And a nice guy, too." Miles sat up, echoing Doug's posture, but put his forehead on his knees.

"So what's got you bummed?"

"What if," Miles said painfully, "you met someone, a guy, and you liked him, and he was hot. And he asked you if he could see you again?"

"Oh, shit fuck, Mikey," Doug groaned. "You said no, didn't you."

Miles didn't answer.

"Did you at least get his cell phone number?"

"No."

"Shit."

"He sent me a text message though. I don't know how to answer it."

"Shit, Mike, you just type a response and hit send."

Miles shrugged. "It was yesterday. He probably doesn't even remember."

Doug shook his head and gazed at him pityingly. "Dude, you aren't that forgettable."

"He says that," Miles said abruptly. "'Dude.' He says that like you do. Made me feel kind of comfortable, you know?"

"Why didn't you let the guy come back? Did he freak you out or something?"

"No." Miles put his head back down on his knees. "He was . . . he was great. I liked him a lot."

"Mike, baby, you know I love you, don't you? But I'm tryin' to understand . . ."

"I don't make sense." Miles got to his feet and started picking up his clothes and towels. "I know that. I just don't. That's why."

"You told him no because you don't make sense? That doesn't make sense."

"No. You get it. You get me. He's . . . he's *new*. He's different. He's the Visconti Hours. I'm the Book of Kells."

"Christ, Mike, I don't speak fucking Manuscript! Explain!"

"Come in. I'll *show* you." He stomped up toward the house. Doug gathered up his own stuff and followed.

In Miles's workroom, he went straight for his bookcase of facsimiles and pulled down one slip-cased volume, then a second. The first one he opened up to page in the middle. "This is the Book of Kells—what's called a 'carpet' page, because there's no real text, just decoration, in this case an abbreviation, the Chi Rho."

"Do I care what a Chi Rho is?"

"No. Shut up. The point is—well, look at that. It's all twisty and complicated, and you can't really see a pattern or a theme. It's just knotwork for knotwork's sake."

"But still beautiful, and really cool, Mikey."

Miles waved his hand dismissively. "That's not the point. The complexity of the design was perceived by the ancient monks who drew it as a way to describe the glory of God as a reflection of the complexity of life. That and there really wasn't much else to do in an Irish monastery in the eighth or ninth century. The point is that it's twisty and complicated and doesn't really make rational sense. Anyway." He drew the other, smaller book from its slipcover and opened it. "Now look at this. Visconti Hours—Renaissance Italian. Look at the bright colors, the beautiful artwork, the florals, the animals and birds and how fucking gorgeous this thing is? It's complex, but understandable. Relatable. The colors, the *gold*—God, Dougie, this is fucking amazingly beautiful. You can see this, understand this, appreciate this. *This*—this is Adam."

"It blows my mind," Doug said, "that you get positively fluent when you start talking art. You don't hesitate, you don't say the wrong thing, you don't get all nervous and anxious."

"But when I'm not talking art, I *do*. *That's* the point, Dougie." Miles shut the books and put them back on the shelves. "I get all, all *stupid*, and my brain stops working."

"You ain't stupid, Mike. Yeah, sometimes your tongue gets hung up, but hell, that happens to everyone."

Miles just shook his head.

Doug slung his arm around Miles and squeezed gently. "You're a dork, you know."

Miles nodded.

"Come on, let's have a beer, and you can tell me about this Adam dude. Cuz you know you want to."

"I can't, really," Miles said, but put on his jeans as Doug did the same, then followed his friend out to the kitchen. Doug hunted around in his refrigerator and found a couple of bottles of PBR he'd left there the last time he was here, and popped the tops.

Miles sat at the kitchen table and stared blankly at the bottle of beer. He rarely drank; he was barely comprehensible at the best of times, and alcohol seemed to tongue-tie him even worse. So he just took a sip of the brew and let the buzzy sharp taste linger in his mouth a moment before sighing and saying, "There really isn't an awful lot to tell. He got drunk, or stoned, or both, was going by in a cab and recognized the name of the resort from when he was a kid, and had the cab driver drop him off. He fell asleep on my chaise and I found him in the morning." He remembered how quickly his fury on finding a trespasser had abated when he'd seen just what the trespasser looked like. "I was mad."

"And?" Doug asked when he didn't continue.

"And nothing. He was hungover, I gave him some coffee, we went swimming, we fucked, I fed him pancakes. He left." Miles took a bigger drink. "He asked if he could come back while he was still in town. I said no."

"Why?" This time the inquiry was quiet, concerned.

Shrugging, Miles took another gulp of beer.

"Was it because it was a good fuck and he just wanted another?" Doug asked. "Or some other reason?"

Miles shrugged.

"*Sacacorchos*," Doug said.

"What?"

"When we were in college Spanish classes, that's what our professor used to say when she was trying to get answers out of us. It means 'corkscrew.'"

Miles didn't get it, and apparently his confused expression made that clear. Doug laughed. "It means I can't get answers out of you without a corkscrew."

"Sorry," Miles said unrepentantly.

Grace flew down off the top of the cabinets and landed on Miles's shoulder. "Love you!" she told Miles.

Miles started laughing. Grace got indignant and flew to her perch, settling with her back to them. Seeing Doug's nonplused expression, he explained, "Lisa came by for Sunday dinner—I'd forgotten about it as usual. She called out, but I had just turned on the shower and didn't hear. Adam had just taken one and walked into the kitchen starkers, just as she came in. He heard her call, but thought it was Grace. You should have heard her scream. *That* I heard. I don't know who was more upset, her or Adam."

"Mikey," Doug said solemnly, "you should see your face when you talk about him. Please. Call him or text him or something. Don't walk away from this. Even if it doesn't work out, don't you owe it to yourself to see if it does? And don't give me any of that Book of Kells and the Viagra Hours—"

"Visconti Hours," Miles corrected.

"—because none of that crap means anything. Don't you want to see if maybe this could turn into something?"

"No, because it *can't*," Miles replied. "He's got to go back to L.A. eventually."

"So? That's eventually. Hell, even if he's here a few days, it'd be worth it. Come on, Mikey. This is the first guy besides Rob you've fucked in how many years? And you still want him. That's gotta mean something."

"Yeah. Means I'm stupid." Miles polished off the rest of his beer.

"Mike." Doug's voice was quiet and serious.

"Okay! Okay. I'll do it." Miles's hands were shaking as he took out his cell phone and pulled up Adam's text. "What do I do?"

"Just click 'reply' and then type your response."

Fumbling with the tiny keys, Miles laboriously typed *Come*, then added *Please*, and pressed the Send button. He held the phone tightly in both hands.

A moment later the screen flashed. *Srsly?*

Yes, Miles typed, and sent.

Again the flash of the screen. *Thk Gd. 2 hrs.*

"Well?" Doug asked.

"He's coming. He says two hours." Miles took a breath.

"This time of the afternoon? Better figure three, on account of rush hour and all. Particularly if he doesn't already have a rental—you said he took a cab out here before?"

"Yeah. His manager picked him up in a limo, but the rest of them all went back last night, he said."

"Did you say 'manager'?"

"Yeah." He glanced up into Doug's curious eyes. "He's a musician. In a band."

"Good. Maybe he can get you to listen to something more recent than Frank Sinatra."

"I don't listen to Frank Sinatra, you hoser."

"You should. He's good. You know what I mean."

Miles shrugged. "I don't get pop music, you know that. That was one of the things I liked about Adam. He's into musical theater. Used to be in a touring company of *Cabaret* as the Master of Ceremonies."

"Holy. Fuck. Shit," Doug said. "Adam is *Adam Craig*?"

"How did you know?"

"Dude, you may not be into pop music, but I am. And everyone who knows Black Varen knows that Adam Craig did theater before he joined up. The *Cabaret* thing. Jesus, Mary, and Joseph. And Black Varen was in town this weekend. You fucked Adam Craig. Rob is gonna shit bricks."

"Do not tell anyone," Miles demanded frantically. "Jesus, Dougie, do not tell anyone! I don't want to fuck things up for him."

"Shit, he's closeted or something, ain't he? Makes sense—I never heard he was gay." Doug nodded. "I gotta tell Rob. But he won't tell anyone, you know that."

"No, I know. Okay. Rob. But nobody else, okay? I don't want it getting out and messing up his career or anything. And it could."

"Yeah, I know. Okay, just Rob." But Doug was shaking his head and grinning like a fool. "That's crazy, you know. You never leave this place and still manage to meet the hottest piece of ass on the planet. Aside from yours truly, of course."

"Shit." Miles put his head down on the table. "Shit. What if some reporter or something follows him or something? Maybe I shouldn't have sent that text. Damn it, Doug, why did you let me send that text?

Maybe I can tell him to forget it . . ." He was reaching for the cell phone he'd set down on the table, but Doug beat him to it.

Holding it out of reach, he said, "No. Fucking. Way. You are not telling him no again. This is awesome, Mikey. A night to remember. Jesus. Rob will *shit bricks*. I kinda feel honored, you know? I fuck the guy who fucks the guy who fucks Adam Fucking Craig."

"You," Miles grabbed the phone from Doug's hand, but put it back in his jeans pocket, "are insane."

"Maybe, but I'm hanging out here until it's too late for you to call and tell him forget it without feeling horribly guilty about wasting his time. Which you know you will, because if there's one thing you know how to do, it's guilt."

"What about Bobby? Don't you have to pick him up?"

"Nice try. He's tied up until six. So I've got a whole two hours to hang here and annoy you."

"Fucker." Miles sighed.

"And if I might make a suggestion? Clean your room while you're waiting? That place is a pigsty. When was the last time you changed your sheets?"

"Fuck you," Miles said, but went to his room to follow Doug's instructions.

Chapter 7

he concierge had arranged for a rental, and Adam took the risk of checking out while he waited for the car, but even working as efficiently as possible, he was still nearly an hour late by the time he turned off I-94 onto the frontage road. Following the instructions on the rental's GPS, he wound down a couple of country roads he didn't remember from his previous visit, and was just about to panic when he saw a faded sign that said "Indian Lake Resort" pointing down another road. The GPS, a fruity British voice, told him to turn left, and he did, and a few minutes later paused at the gate.

He'd expected he'd have to call Miles to come and unlock the chain, but the links were lying on the ground. A piece of paper fluttered on one wooden post; Adam dropped the driver's side window and reached out to pluck it from the nail it had been stuck on.

"Dude," the note read, "lock the chain when you're in. Doug."

Doug? Who the hell was Doug?

He drove over the chain and parked the car, getting out and walking back to re-hook the chain and snap the padlock closed before climbing back into the car and heading down the gravel road toward the lodge.

Miles was waiting when he got to the parking lot: pacing, his hands shoved into his pockets. He turned when Adam pulled into the lot and parked, but didn't approach, just stood there. When Adam got out, he saw that Miles's hands weren't in his pockets anymore; they were at his sides, clenched tightly. His stomach sank. "Hey, Miles."

"What do you want?" Miles asked. His voice sounded funny: tight and strained.

Adam looked at him, at the white knuckles, the expressionless face, and thought, *This is bad.* But it seemed familiar. Then he had it. His nephew Ryan sometimes stood in that same pose, wearing the same expression. When he was afraid, or nervous, or faced with something new. Okay, Ryan was *eleven*, but still . . .

He pulled off the ball cap he was wearing and tossed it back through the open car window onto the seat, then said, "What do I want? First, I want you to take me to bed, then maybe later a moonlight skinny-dip in the lake, then I want to sleep in your arms all night. And then in the morning, I want breakfast—pancakes made with questionable eggs, and weird bacon."

Miles blinked. The fists unknotted. Then he was in motion, lunging across the space that separated them, driving Adam back up against the side of the car, and kissing him the way he had yesterday, fierce and hot and throwing his whole body, his whole self into it. Adam reveled in the heat and passion of it, running his hands up and down the taut, muscular back. When Miles's mouth slid from his, kissing his jaw and down his throat, he said, "I am so fucking glad you changed your mind . . ."

Miles growled low, then suddenly his shoulder was in Adam's gut, and Adam was flying off his feet, Miles's arm around his knees and his ass in Adam's direct line of sight. "Miles!" he yelped. "What the fuck?"

Saying nothing, Miles charged down the path to the cottage, slamming through the screen door and down the hall to the bedroom Adam had glimpsed on his previous visit. The room had been cleaned, but that was all he noticed before he was flying again, this time landing on the bed. Miles landed beside him, taking up the kiss again.

Adam sighed happily and wrapped his arms around Miles's neck. "That was hot," he said against Miles's mouth.

Miles growled again and drew back, sliding off the end of the bed and pulling off Adam's Vans and purple socks before climbing back onto the bed and starting work on the buttons of Adam's baggy jeans. "Not you," Miles said. "These. Not you."

"No," Adam gasped as the last button came undone and Miles yanked off the jeans, tossing them onto the floor. "Camouflage— Ack!" This as Miles's mouth came down on Adam's cock inside the black silk bikini briefs. He tongued Adam through the silk, and Adam's brain went away for a while.

Then Miles looked up at him with a grin. "These . . . are you."

Adam just grinned back. He reached for the hem of his T-shirt, but Miles stopped him, one hand on Adam's. "No. Mine," and he pulled the shirt up over Adam's head and twisted it, tangling Adam's arms in the fabric.

"Miles, dude," Adam gasped. Jesus, could it *get* any hotter?

It could. The twist of knit fabric pulled on his arms, and then they were immobilized somehow, caught on something, so he lay helpless, naked except for the skimpy black briefs that were, at this moment, sort of pointless. His lover sat back on his heels beside him and looked at him. Then he reached down and gently, carefully, removed the black-framed glasses Adam wore and set them on the nightstand. "Miles," Adam moaned, totally turned on by the contrast of strength and gentleness. "Miles . . ."

"Shhh." Miles slid back down his body, dipping beneath the elastic of the waistband to pull off the briefs and cup Adam's balls in his long, clever fingers. Then his mouth took Adam and Adam lost all sense of reason, just reveling in the sensations of Miles's mouth and tongue and hands, helpless to resist and why the hell would he want to anyway? It felt *fanfuckingtastic*.

This was what he had wanted to do with Miles yesterday, down by the water, but he'd been too hungry for Miles to fuck him then, and Miles had been just as desperate. It seemed now that Miles wasn't quite as desperate, despite the kiss in the parking lot. It seemed that Miles was at the opposite end of desperate, content to tease and lick and suck and *torment* Adam. "Miles!" he shouted. "God, Miles!"

Miles raised his head, and Adam almost wept at the hunger in Miles's eyes. "Go ahead," he whispered, and bent his head to take him in his mouth again.

Adam bucked and came.

An eternity later, he opened dazed eyes to see Miles looking down at him, an amused look on his face. "Jesus Christ," Adam croaked, "give a guy a little warning, will ya?"

The amusement fled. "Warning about what?"

"The fact that your mouth is a registered weapon of mass destruction."

Miles laughed and lay down beside Adam. "That was nice," he said.

"That is an understatement." Adam came up on his elbows. Apparently when he'd been zoned after his climax, Miles had released whatever it was he'd caught Adam's shirt on. "But you didn't get off."

"We have time, if you're planning on eating questionable pancakes tomorrow. Besides." He sighed. "I never get to suck dick anymore, and I really love it."

"That guy, you know," Adam probed. "He doesn't . . .?"

"Nope. Did it a few times, but he doesn't like me to. It's too intimate."

"Dude, if you fuck him, how much more intimate can you get?"

Miles rolled onto his side and regarded him thoughtfully. "Plenty," he said. "Plain vanilla sex isn't really intimate, you know. Kissing is intimate. Holding hands is intimate. Eating weird bacon together is intimate. Fucking? Not so much."

"I guess," Adam said. He grinned. "Can I return the favor?"

"Nope." Miles leaned over and reached in the nightstand, then dropped a condom and lube on Adam's belly. "Gonna do this right this time. Nice and slow. Real slow."

"Oh, fuck," Adam said faintly.

"That's the idea."

He didn't say anything more, but reached out and ran his fingers gently over Adam's cheekbone, trailing them around his ear as if the curve of cartilage were something rare and precious. His attention was all on his hand, not on Adam; his eyes gone smoky blue and deep in thought, the way they did when he was thinking about his art. Adam felt like art, felt like Miles's attention was on him the way a curator's might be on a sculpture he was deciding to acquire. When Miles's fingers stroked down the nape of his neck, Adam shuddered, and Miles smiled slowly. "Ticklish?" he murmured.

"No, it's just . . ."

Miles's fingers stroked his nape again, and Adam felt his eyes roll back into his head. "Oh," Miles said, still in that low, smoky voice, "it's like that, is it?" He cupped the back of Adam's head and drew him forward into a kiss that tasted of Adam and Miles together. A moan rumbled in Adam's throat. He was dizzy—how could he be so aroused again so quickly after such an intense climax?—but Miles's tongue was so sweet and his hand in Adam's hair was like an embrace itself . . .

Miles drew back and his smile was gone, replaced with an expression so intent, so focused, that Adam shuddered again. Miles bent his head and kissed Adam's throat, drawing the skin up into his teeth and biting gently. Adam gasped.

"Turn over," Miles rasped. He grabbed the condoms and lube from Adam's belly, and set them aside. His hand on Adam's hip, he drew him over, then that delicate, assessing touch slid over his ass and down the back of his thighs. "You're so beautiful," Miles murmured. "I wish I could paint you."

"I don't know," Adam got out, "my skin's kind of sensitive to chemicals."

Miles chuckled, and Adam felt the breath of it on the back of his neck just before the touch of warm lips and warmer tongue. Miles did the same thing, tugging up the skin to nip at it gently before releasing it and moving down an inch to do it again. And again, all the way down his spine, giving Adam's back the same meticulous attention he did to everything. Despite the rising tide of his arousal, Adam was boneless, floating, anchored to earth only by Miles's touch.

When Miles's mouth touched the base of Adam's spine, Adam felt his hands nudging his thighs apart. Obediently, Adam spread his legs so Miles could shift over to kneel between them. He felt Miles's hands again, parting his ass and licking down the crease. Miles's tongue flicked over Adam's hole, then moved further down to nuzzle his balls. "You shave," Miles whispered. Adam shivered at the feel of his breath on the damp skin.

"Yeah," Adam managed. "It's kind of a thing."

"Do you mind that I don't?"

"Oh, hell no." This time when Miles's attention settled on his cock, he whimpered, and again when Miles mouthed him, taking one side, then the other, into warm wetness. "Miles . . ."

Miles chuckled, then pushed his legs farther apart to lick again at Adam's anus. Adam closed his eyes, buried his face in the clean, fabric-softener-scented pillowcase, and gave himself over to the pleasure.

He didn't notice when Miles opened the lube, but felt the slick—cool, not cold, which meant Miles must have warmed it a little in his hands before touching him, a little Miles thing that made Adam only appreciate him more. Miles applied the lube as if he were mixing his precious paints, steadily, with sure hands, his fingers firm but gentle. When he slid a pair of them inside Adam, he moved carefully, and stroked over the bump of Adam's gland. Adam jerked a little.

"Too rough?" Miles asked, a faint note of worry in his voice.

"No. Good." So good. The last time he'd been fucked by someone else who'd bothered to finger him open first, the guy had gone for Adam's prostate like it was the button on one of those animal testing things that the rat had to press for a food treat. At the time Adam had been so hot it was okay, but he'd felt a little bruised afterward. He hadn't been sure if that was his imagination, but it was enough that he hadn't bothered to try to find the guy again.

But Miles had the right touch, not too soft, not too rough, with the same bump and pressure as a nice thick dick gliding over the spot.

Speaking of which—Adam heard the rustle of the condom packaging, then Miles dropped a kiss on the top of one buttock, and pressed himself inside. Adam tensed against the slight burn, then relaxed and welcomed Miles in.

Miles put his hands on Adam's hips and drew him up onto his knees. Adam came easily, letting himself be manipulated like a rag doll. He folded his arms and rested his cheek on them, rocking back, arching into the movement, not thinking, just feeling an odd sort of restless peace, if there ever was such a thing. Hmm. Might make a good title for a song . . .

Thoughts fled as Miles's cock slid just exactly right, and Miles leaned forward, one arm propping himself up, the other curving beneath Adam to take him in hand. His body lay along Adam's, not on him, but above him, his weight on his arm and just his skin against Adam's. With every slide-bump, a little fluid leaked from Adam's cock, and Miles put it to good use, working Adam's erection with the same sure, steady hand.

Adam was making noises he'd never heard before and hadn't realized himself capable of: soft breathy gasps, squeaks, groans, whimpers. He was constrained, shackled by Miles at his back and Miles's hand in front, just as much as he had been by the tangled T-shirt earlier, and against all logic it made him feel like he had been freed. He floated, safe in Miles's hands, and when he felt like he was going to come, it was as if he'd broken the tether of earth.

"Oh, no," Miles murmured against the skin of his shoulder, and tightened his grasp on the base of Adam's cock to hold back a climax Adam would have thought inevitable. "Wait for me, love . . ."

Always, Adam thought, and even though what little mind he had left was boggling at the thought of falling so hard, so fast for a guy he just met, his heart and soul was right on board with the idea. *Forever*.

Miles's movements sped up, but the slap and squelch of sex was only background music. Adam drew his head back and turned his face to Miles's, catching his lips in a kiss just as Miles thrust home hard— once, twice, and on that one Adam came, his hips jerking forward and back, caught between Miles in him and Miles on him and Miles around him, hard and strong and loving.

Adam lay on the grass in the moonlight, watching Miles. He was like an otter, or a seal, so at home in the water, his sleek dark head breaking the surface and sending the moonlit shards of lake scattering. He flipped upside down, standing on his hands, his legs straight upright, his head and torso invisible beneath the surface. When he came up, laughing, Adam called, "Dude, that looks so weird. Like a pair of disembodied legs. Creepy!"

"Come on back in," Miles responded, wiping his hair from his eyes. "You were the one who wanted a moonlight swim."

"You wore me out."

"Bullshit. You just got lazy."

Adam laughed. "Busted. Okay." He rolled onto his feet and took a run down the battered dock, cannonballing into the water and sending up a tsunami. He was still underwater when something grabbed him around the waist and hauled him back up. Miles grinned at him, stole a quick kiss, then threw him out further into the lake. "Too small to keep!" Miles called at him when he came up for air.

"Weasel!" Adam shot back, and sent a spray of water at Miles.

Miles went down again, and a moment later pulled Adam's feet out from under him. The minute Miles had vanished, though, Adam had wisely taken a big breath, so when he got dunked, he stayed under, reaching for Miles and pulling him down as well.

They both came up together, face to face, laughing. Miles reached out and dragged Adam into his arms—not kissing him, just holding him, his breath warm and ragged in Adam's ear.

"This is nice," Adam said softly, his arms folding themselves around Miles.

Tree frogs and crickets and the soft wash of waves against the shore were the only sounds as they stood there in breast-high water, their bodies warm against each other in the coolness of the lake. Adam breathed in the scent of Miles wet, running his hands down the long line of Miles's back, over his solid muscular rump, and back up again. Miles held him, motionless, wordless, just strong and solid and *there*. Adam sighed happily and rested his head on Miles's shoulder.

"There used to be a float." Miles's voice rumbled at last against Adam's ear. "Out in the lake."

"Yeah, I remember. The big kids used to commandeer it every summer. Got to the point that my friends and I would swim out at the crack of dawn, before anyone else was up, before the big kids would throw us off. But it was cool, being out there before anyone else, lying on the float and staring up at the sky, all of us just hanging out and talking about what we were going to do when we grew up."

"Did you want to be a rock star then?"

"Didn't everyone?" Adam laughed and nuzzled Miles's neck. "It was more socially acceptable than saying I wanted to be an opera star."

"Seriously?"

"Seriously. I was a weird kid. What happened to the float?"

"Rotted out. We got rid of it a couple of years ago. Not much point in replacing it."

"Too bad."

"I sail," Miles said.

Adam blinked and drew back. "What?"

"I sail. You asked in your email if I sailed. I do. But the boat's in storage. Has been for years."

"Maybe sometime you could teach me."

Miles didn't answer. Adam's heart sank. Oh, boy. He'd fucked up, assuming Miles was interested in carrying on after their little interlude. Shit. "Sorry," he said wryly, drawing back out of Miles's arms and giving him a grin. "Didn't mean to get all clingy. Doesn't mean I'm like, expecting things or anything."

"I don't understand." Miles stepped away from Adam, turning toward shore. "I'm sorry."

"Wait, what?"

"Look, I'm kind of bad at communicating, if you haven't figured it out so far. I don't know what you want."

"I told you earlier."

Miles waved a hand. "Yeah, I got it. It's cool. But what about after breakfast?"

"What?"

"Breakfast. Are you hanging around after breakfast? You only went as far as the questionable eggs and weird bacon."

Adam's heart was thumping against his breastbone. "I kind of thought maybe? I mean, I don't have a set schedule—I don't have to be back in L.A. for a couple of weeks. If it's a problem—you got other plans—no big. I can book a flight and if I can't get anything right away, I'll find someplace else to stay 'til then. Lots of hotels in Gurnee."

Miles turned to stare at him. "You checked out of your hotel?"

"Well, yeah. Like I said, though, no big."

"You want to stay here a couple of weeks? The whole time?"

"Well, that was the game plan. But like I said, no—"

"Shut up," Miles said. He sloshed back toward Adam, and caught his face in both hands. "You want to stay," he said again. "For two *weeks*."

"Um, yeah? 'Cause I just said so?"

The smile that bloomed on Miles's face took Adam's breath away. He'd seen Miles's quicksilver grins, but nothing like this. He looked like a kid who had just gotten everything he'd asked Santa for. "Okay," he said simply, and kissed Adam. Not a messy, lustful kiss, but a soft, affectionate kiss. Then he let Adam go.

Adam gazed at him a moment, then fell backward into the water in a mock swoon. As he came back up, he heard Miles laughing.

Chapter 8

ewsies? You've got a copy of *Newsies*?" Adam said from the floor in front of Miles's DVD collection.

"I've got a copy of just about every musical ever made," Miles said. "Including the god-awful Woody Allen ones."

"They weren't that awful. Okay, they were marginal, but not *that* awful. Do you have . . . oh, yeah. *Love's Labour's Lost*, the Kenneth Branagh Musical Years. Now *that* was awful."

"Alicia Silverstone does Shakespeare. And sings."

Adam shuddered. "That is just so wrong. Oh, you've got the original *Fame*. I love that movie. It was one of Mom's favorites when I was growing up. The finale always makes me cry."

"Me too."

"Then that's it." Adam sat up and looked around. "Where's your setup?"

"Bedroom."

"Oh, man. We get to watch this in bed?"

"Well, you could stand, but yeah, that's the general idea."

Adam got up off the floor and leaned over Miles where he was sprawled on the couch. "Best. Vacation. Ever."

Miles set up the movie, then crawled into bed beside Adam. Adam expected him to lean on the pillows propped against the headboard, as he was, but instead he rested his head on Adam's chest. Adam gazed down at the dark hair, surprised. It had been a long time since anyone had done that; most of the guys Adam had dated in his high school and college years were the kind he would have laid on, not the other way around. The big guys, the football players and surfers, he'd bottomed for happily, and when they'd lain like this, Adam had been the one curling into the large solid bodies. Now he moved his arm and settled it around Miles's shoulder; Miles sighed softly and relaxed into Adam's casual embrace.

They watched the first half of the movie in silence, except for the dance scene where Leroy stole the audition from his talentless girlfriend. Then Miles just sighed and said, "Hot," and Adam murmured, "Fuckin' A."

Then a little while later, Adam felt Miles's fingers exploring his belly, and slowly trailing down under the waistband of the sweats he had put on after their swim. Adam didn't say anything, but made a soft noise in his throat when Miles curled his hand around his cock and rubbed his thumb across the head. Miles looked up at Adam and smiled that sweet, slow smile again, then edged the sweats down Adam's thighs. "Roll over," he whispered, and Adam shuddered with anticipation.

The pillows smelled of Miles: lemony, grassy, and a faint hint of healthy sweat. Earthy scents. He wondered vaguely what he smelled like to Miles, and then Miles spread his cheeks and licked him, and his arms went weak, and he buried his face in the linens and lost himself in the smell and feeling of Miles in him. Taking Miles in. Breathing Miles in.

He supposed he was just too relaxed, because even with Miles's hand on his cock, Miles finished long before he was ready to, and he sighed faintly as Miles eased out of him. "Roll over," Miles said again, and Adam obeyed, leaning up to kiss Miles before Miles slid down Adam's body to take him in his mouth and coax him to his own climax. Miles stayed down there a few minutes more, nuzzling into Adam's groin like a puppy looking for a teat; Adam reached down and stroked his hair gently.

Finally, Miles crawled back up to lay on the pillows beside Adam. To his surprise, Miles's face was set, his mouth hard and unsmiling. "Hey," Adam said, "what's the matter?"

Miles didn't answer right away. Finally he said, "Sorry." His voice was stiff, his body more so.

"Sorry for *what*?" Adam demanded, coming up on one elbow to glare at him. "Jesus Christ, Miles, I thought I was gonna lose my mind, coming like that. What the hell are you sorry about?"

Miles blinked. "You didn't."

"Uh, you got a mouthful of come to say otherwise. Assuming you can, with a mouthful of come."

"No. I mean, before. When I . . . before."

"Dude." Adam shook his head. "It don't always happen that way, you know. I mean, sometimes, yeah, getting fucked will bring me off, but not always. And it's not a bad thing. I mean, being fucked is a beautiful thing by itself, but sometimes it doesn't go all the way and I need a little extra help. Most guys are like that. It's just a thing, you know."

"That's just it. I don't know."

"Does what's-his-name get off just from you fucking him? I mean, without any extra help?"

"That's different. He doesn't . . . it's just different, that's all."

"Whoa. Miles." Adam sat up and looked at him seriously. "Are you telling me what's-his-name . . ."

"Bobby. Doug calls him Rob but he calls himself Bobby."

". . . Bobby doesn't get off? Ever?"

Miles stared at him, his eyes bleak. "He did once, when Doug was there. But he says he'd rather not, anyway. Since I just, you know, need him, not want him."

"What a fucking prick!"

Miles got up and picked up the sweats he'd thrown on the floor. "Sorry," he said again, his voice tight.

"What . . . Jesus, Miles, I didn't mean *you*! I meant that Bobby dude. You are like the farthest thing from a prick I've ever met."

His lover turned and looked at him, and Adam nearly wept from the naked hope in his eyes. "I am?"

"Oh Jesus, Miles." Adam shook his head, his eyes never leaving Miles. "You are so not a prick. Yeah, you can get cranky, and you're not *easy*, but you're not a prick. Or an asshole. Come here and let's finish watching this movie."

Miles dropped the sweats and crawled back onto the bed. Adam reached down and drew the sheets up around them, then Miles settled back in his original position, his head on Adam's chest. Adam put his arm around him, stroked his hair gently, and turned his attention back to the movie.

Adam's skin was warm and solid beneath Miles's cheek. He stretched out an arm and laid it around Adam's waist, relaxing for the first time in what seemed like forever, warm and comfortable and safe. How did Adam do it? He seemed to be able to look past Miles's weirdness and insecurities and awkwardness to see *Miles*, himself, what he was—whatever he was—inside.

And Adam seemed to *like* Miles. Maybe it was because he knew Miles wasn't about to do anything to wreck his life; he couldn't very well when he was as close to a hermit as one could get in this day and age. Maybe it was because Miles didn't make any demands on him— didn't know who he was outside the resort (although Miles had done a lot of internet research in the last twenty-four hours) and more importantly didn't care who or what he was. Well, he did care. Adam was the first new person he'd ever had a connection with who really didn't know him from before the accident—knowing him when he was a kid didn't count, and he really hadn't *known* Michael Caldwell then, anyway—the first person who knew only Miles and not the old, forgotten Mike. Miles couldn't help but care about that. Besides, he really liked Adam, not only for the sex but because Adam didn't seem to care either—about the weirdness, the fumblings.

Miles ran his fingertips lightly across Adam's ribs, feeling the bumps of bone beneath the casing of taut skin and muscle. Skin. He'd heard of something the shrinks called "skin hunger," the need for human beings to touch, to be touched. He rarely touched anyone these days: a brief guy-hug from Doug, a longer hug from Lisa, Bobby when he was fucking him, and that had last been, what, a good eight months ago . . . Touching Adam was different, was like sucking understanding through his fingertips, as if his fingers were knowledge vacuums. Every touch was an education. He stroked Adam's hip gently. The skin there was still soft though Adam had to be about thirty; still young and silky, but with lean strength beneath. He'd be wiry when he got older,

Miles thought, envisioning a whipcord-thin old man with gray hair and a shit-eating grin. He would have hair, too, probably; he didn't have the thick body hair that men doomed to male-pattern baldness all seemed to have.

He froze a moment. How did he know that? He knew so very few people, and none of them balding. A movie? A pop-up ad on some website? Had Doug or Bobby mentioned something about that? He was sure Lisa would have no reason to. But he couldn't remember.

Of course, that was the problem, wasn't it? If he could remember, he would know how his lovers from high school and college had reacted when they'd made love, if they came easily or if it took extra effort, if they kissed like Adam or if they didn't kiss at all. He and Bobby never kissed—that was Doug's territory.

He was grateful for Doug and Bobby's generosity, but it irked him so much to ask for it. Not that he ever did; Doug watched out for him, and either he or Bobby seemed to be able to tell when Miles needed Bobby. Miles tried not to need him more than once or twice a year; the rest of the time he got along with just his hand for company. He supposed that if he hadn't had Doug and Bobby, he would have gotten along okay, but knowing that he could have Bobby made it harder to do without.

"Miles? You asleep?"

"No," he said.

"'Kay. It's coming up on the finale. Just thought you'd want to be awake for that."

"Yeah. Thanks."

He turned his head and watched the movie: the scramble and confusion and subdued hysteria leading up to graduation. He wondered if he'd been like those kids—scared and excited and nervous, not sure what waited ahead, but eager to find out, even if it meant leaving someplace safe and familiar. He supposed he must have, but the idea seemed alien now.

But the finale was as glorious as ever: the slow buildup, the pure clear young voices, the rising tempo and tenor of the theme, until it burst into a wild thrill ride of a music video. You could see the electricity, Miles thought, you could see the enthusiasm and excitement and sheer joy in those young faces, those young bodies.

He felt a thousand years away from that. Had he ever been young?

He turned his head to Adam. His lover was grinning, tears in his eyes along with delight in the spectacle he was watching. He held his emotions so close to the surface, so honest, so open. Miles hadn't expected that from someone who lived so much in the public eye. Was it only in private that he left himself so exposed? Was it only with Miles? The thought terrified him, exhilarated him. He turned back to the movie, forcing himself to drop that line of thought and focus on the film. Adam's hand came up to stroke his head, and he relaxed under his touch.

And drifted off, not even noticing when the movie ended and Adam turned off the TV with the remote.

Chapter 9

iles was alone when he woke, and for a moment thought he'd maybe dreamed the whole thing, but then he heard footsteps in the hallway and Adam came into the bedroom, a pair of coffee mugs in his hands. "Hey," he said.

"Hey." Miles reached out for the mug Adam handed him.

"I checked for paint and stuff," Adam said with a grin, "so I'm relatively sure there's nothing poisonous in it."

"It smells different."

"Oh. Yeah. I like fancy-ass coffees, and brought some from home, but didn't spend enough time in the hotel to make it worth making some. So I thought I'd see if you liked it." Adam's face was a little anxious.

"Smells good," Miles reassured him. "What kind is it?"

"It's a fair-trade orgasmic bean from Costa Rica."

"'Orgasmic'? Or 'organic'?"

"Yes."

Miles snorted, but took a sip. It was good, far better than his usual supermarket coffee. "Sweet. Where do you get it?"

"I order it online," Adam said. "I can give you the website if you're interested. I mean, as much coffee as you drink, you should at least be drinking something good." He sat on the bed, his legs folded. He was back in the sweats he'd been wearing last night, but hadn't bothered with a T-shirt. "So what's on the agenda for today?"

"I dunno. Breakfast, I guess. Then . . . whatever."

"It's raining like a banshee, so it'll have to be something indoors. Unless you *want* to get electrocuted by swimming in the lake during a thunderstorm."

"Not my idea of a good time. If it weren't storming, we could go fishing—fish bite great when it's raining. But not in a storm."

"Okay. Grace is up, by the way. I'm surprised you didn't hear her scream."

"Did she scream?"

"Yep. I came into the kitchen and took the towel off her cage, figuring she might need some water or something, and she let fly. Sounded just like your sister."

"Gah." Miles blanched.

Adam laughed. "I'm kidding, dude. She just looked at me and clucked disapprovingly, so I let her out of the cage. I hope that's okay."

"Yeah. I think everything's cleaned up, so she won't get poisoned or anything."

"It is. I almost didn't recognize the place." Adam shot him another grin. "Guess having company is a great motivator to clean the house."

"I wouldn't know," Miles said. "You're the first company I've ever had. Except Lisa and Doug and Bobby, but they're used to it."

There was a fluttering noise and Grace sailed through the door, landing on the headboard. "Love you!" she caroled in Lisa's voice, then, to Miles's shock, "Hey, you're one hot cootchie papa," in Adam's. Miles nearly choked on the sip of coffee he'd just taken.

Adam laughed uproariously. "It worked!" he said when he could catch his breath.

"Brat," Miles said. "She is going to be saying that forever now!"

"Good! Then maybe you'll always remember me."

Miles's smile died, but he said politely, "I don't think I'll have a problem with that."

Adam reached over and put his hand on Miles's sheet-covered thigh. "Hey, dude. Did I say something wrong?"

Miles just stared at Adam's hand a long moment, then, as Adam flushed and started to draw it away, put his own hand over it. "It's okay," he said numbly. "It's just . . . something I can't explain, okay? But it's not anything you said. Well, it is, but you didn't know any better. And it's my fault, anyway." He looked up into Adam's puzzled, beautiful face, and tried for a smile. "And you haven't got the vaguest idea of what I'm talking about."

"Nope," Adam said quietly.

"I don't remember you from when we were kids, but I don't think I could ever forget you now. Not without forgetting my own name." There. That was his out, the one way he could promise what Adam asked for.

"Me either," Adam said, his voice raw, then added all in a rush, "Miles . . . Miles, can I come back sometime? Maybe the next time I get a break? We're booked in the studio through most of the fall, but I could maybe take some time off around Thanksgiving? Not actual Thanksgiving, because my mother would *kill* me if I blew off the holiday, but maybe around then, sometime?"

"You come back," Miles said, and now his voice was raw and shaking, "any fucking time you want. Anytime."

Adam carefully took Miles's cup from his hand and set them both on the nightstand. Then he flowed into Miles's arms. Miles met his lips with his own, letting Adam's weight carry him back down onto the mattress.

"I've never known anyone like you before," Adam said hoarsely. "You're like . . . I don't know, something out of a fairy tale. You're so fucking *giving*. Don't you ever take?"

"I don't know what you mean." To shut him up, Miles rolled them both over and took his mouth, hot, demanding, *fierce*. Adam whined deep in his throat, wriggling beneath him until the sheets were out of the way and he could wrap his legs around Miles's waist and rock against him.

And the phone rang.

"Shut up, Grace," they both chorused, but she said, "You're one hot cootchie papa," just as the phone rang again. "Don't answer it," Adam said urgently, and tried to drag Miles's head back down.

"Gotta." Miles reached for the phone. Adam fell back against the pillow, but he kept his legs locked around Miles. "Hello?" Miles reached around himself to try to unwrap Adam. Adam tightened his calves and crossed his ankles.

"Miles, dude," Doug said on the other end. "What you doing?"

Adam apparently heard him, because he whispered, "Tell him you're just about to get wildly fucked by a famous rock star."

Miles grinned at him. "I'm just about to get wildly fucked by the hottest famous rock star you ever fucking saw." Adam blew him a kiss.

"Dude, you are a god," Doug said. "He gonna be around awhile?"

"Yeah. Why?"

"'Cause Rob and I are coming over for dinner. We'll be there before seven and will bring food and drink. Rob so does not believe me when I tell him who's there, but he has sworn to God not to tell another living soul. And he's a doctor, he keeps those kinds of secrets." In the background, Miles heard Bobby say, "You're the one who doesn't believe him," and Doug shushed him. "But we gotta come over and meet him. It would be just wrong to let an opportunity like this go."

Miles said to Adam, "They want to meet you."

Adam shrugged. "Your call."

"He says they'll bring dinner."

"Hmm. Okay. As long as they're not total dickheads."

"I heard that," Doug said.

"Well, they are, but they're manageable," Miles told Adam.

"I heard that, too. Pizza okay?"

"Giordano's," Miles said.

Doug sighed. "You and your stuffed pizza."

"That sounds kinda dirty," Adam said.

"Tell your boy-toy rock star to quit eavesdropping," Doug said.

Adam took the phone from Miles's hand. "Sorry, dude," he said, "but the fucking is about to commence and Miles will no longer have a free hand to hold this phone, so hanging up now."

"Spoken to by the rock god Adam Craig. I may faint."

Laughing, Adam said, "Fuck off, dude. Just don't forget beer."

"Beer is on the list, rock star dude," Doug replied.

"Hanging up now." Adam did so, tossing the phone onto the pile of clothes on the floor. Then he turned to Miles. "Now."

"Now," Miles agreed.

By noon it had stopped storming, but the sky was still overcast and spitting rain. At least the power hadn't gone out. Although the resort was on the same grid as the surrounding forest preserve districts, it had its own generator for backup. The trouble was that the generator was on the other side of the lodge in one of the service buildings, which meant either braving the elements or freezing or boiling to death. Thunderstorms were bad enough. Sometimes the power went out during blizzards and Miles had to plow through knee-deep drifts to get to the building.

Adam had offered to clean up the breakfast dishes, since Miles had done the cooking. It was weird how natural he looked in Miles's kitchen, as if he'd always been there; he leaned on the sink in a T-shirt and sweats and washed the dishes, humming absently to himself. Miles stood in the doorway, staring at him; finally, Adam glanced up and said with a grin, "I promise I won't break anything."

Miles opened his mouth to protest that that wasn't what he'd been thinking, couldn't find the words, and was distracted by the happiness shining out of Adam's face. He didn't know what to think or how to react, so he just ducked his head and mumbled, "No," and went red-faced into his workroom, hearing Adam's chuckle behind him. Grace was sitting on the back of his writing slope, bobbing to some internal music of her own—maybe to Adam's humming; Miles couldn't hear it in here but it didn't mean she couldn't—and he sat down, staring blankly at her. She bobbed her head a few more times, then leaned forward, her head outstretched. "Kiss, kiss."

He obliged, then put up his hand. She carefully stepped onto his fist, and he set her on his shoulder. "What am I gonna do, Gracie?" he murmured. She rubbed her head against his cheek as he pulled one of his projects off the shelf beside him. It was damp out, and humidity was good for gilding, so he could probably get part of this piece gilded while Adam was washing dishes. Then he could figure out what they were going to do the rest of the afternoon. Maybe by then Adam would be ready to go back to bed . . . He shook himself. It probably wasn't good that he really, really wanted to have sex with Adam again. Did Doug and Bobby do nothing but fuck? No, they had a relationship, talked and stuff. Miles wasn't so good with talking, though Adam didn't seem to mind. Adam liked to talk. But Adam was leaving eventually, probably for good, for all he talked about Thanksgiving and that. Maybe fucking was all they had together. It had to be. There wasn't anything Miles could offer Adam except that, after all . . .

Absently, he took his gilding supplies out of their container and started to set up, the movements so automatic he didn't even notice. A few minutes later he was wrapped in his work, not even noticing when Adam came to the door, wiping his hands on a towel. Adam looked at him absorbed in his project, smiled faintly, then went back to the kitchen, where he sat at the kitchen table and opened his laptop.

Miles finished gilding the last of the projects he'd had pending for that stage and leaned back, stretching. A good afternoon's work, he thought, glancing at the clock on the shelf across the room. Grace was sleeping on the perch he had set up near the window, her head under her wing. The rain had started up again, giving the light from the windows a watery look, but that was okay. Rainy days were just part of a Midwest summer.

Then he heard the music and wondered vaguely if he'd left a CD playing in the bedroom. It was a song from the movie *Fame* he and Adam had watched last night . . .

Fuck. Adam.

He jumped up, steadying the slant board as he bumped it with his leg, then went into the kitchen. Adam was sitting in front of an open laptop, an acoustic guitar on his lap, absorbed in his playing. Miles stood in the doorway and listened to the plaintive ballad, about being reminded of his lover when he saw something they'd seen together, or a photograph of his lover's smile. Then Adam stopped and smiled up at Miles. "Did I disturb you? You were pretty into your work."

"I am so fucking sorry." Miles raked a hand through his hair. "I get caught up, and then I forget everything. I'm really sorry. I didn't mean to and I wasted so much time . . ."

"Hey, whoa," Adam said. "You weren't wasting time—we've got time. Besides, you were working. So was I. I got a couple of songs down, which is good, 'cause we're supposed to be going into the studio to work on the album and all we have is a couple pieces of crap Neil came up with. So now we have a couple pieces of crap that I came up with. Makes for variety."

"I bet they're not crap, though," Miles said.

"Nah. I'm pretty sure they're not. I made more coffee."

"The good stuff?"

"Well, yeah. Duh." But he said it with a grin, and Miles grinned back.

Adam set the guitar in its case and closed the latches, then closed the laptop. "When are your friends coming by?"

"Probably after work." Miles raked his hand through his hair again, watching Adam as he got up from the table and walked toward him. "That's usually around six, depending on if Bobby's on call or something. Doug works from home a lot—he's a website designer—but if he's working downtown in his office it'll be more like seven. If Bobby's on call, then they might be even later . . ."

"Miles?"

"Huh?"

"Shut up." Adam ran his hands up Miles's shirtfront, then twisted in the T-shirt fabric and pulled Miles close so he could kiss him. He didn't seem angry, Miles thought absently as he wrapped his hands around Adam's narrow waist and met Adam's tongue with his own. God, could Adam kiss. It had been so long since Miles had sucked face with anyone—in fact, Miles couldn't remember the last time he'd sucked face. But he had to have, right? He knew what to do—at least his body did, and that was good. As long as he didn't think too much about it.

Adam's hands were busy undoing the drawstring of his sweats; he caught them and said thickly, "Bedroom. Stuff. Lube." Something about Adam reduced him to monosyllables.

But Adam didn't seem to care; he practically dragged Miles down the hallway to the bedroom, pushing Miles onto the bed and climbing on top of him. Between kisses, Adam gasped, "Even if . . . they get here . . . at six . . . we have . . . a good . . . three . . . oh fuck, yes, right there, oh fuck. Fuck. Miles, love, baby, beautiful, suit up and get that cock where it belongs . . ."

Miles chuckled and worked Adam's dick. Adam closed his eyes, threw his head back, and keened.

Chapter 10

iles was still asleep when Adam got out of the shower: sprawled naked on his back, his long, muscled arms and legs spread out over the tangled sheets. The lines that bracketed Miles's mouth and the upside-down V that punctuated the space between his dark eyebrows were smoothed out, his face soft and open in sleep. He looked younger than, what, thirty-five? It was weird, thinking of Miles as thirty-five; at thirty-one, Adam sometimes felt so old, but he didn't, couldn't, think of Miles that way. Maybe it was the way Miles behaved: sometimes so smart, and other times so confused and innocent. Even when they fucked; sometimes Miles seemed to slow down in the middle, as if he were experimenting, testing, exploring, his touches tentative and sweet, only in the next moment turning domineering and demanding. Maybe it was that whole not-fucking-anyone-except-the-borrowed-boy-toy-for-ten-years thing. Whatever it was, Adam thanked God for it. He hadn't had an experience like that since he was a kid. It made him feel . . . something. Alive. Engaged. Involved. Something like that.

Adam toweled his hair dry, watching his lover, then stretched languorously, feeling the ache and burn and relishing it. He'd feel Miles for a week, at the very least.

He checked the clock: they'd slept for over an hour. No, closer to two. He supposed he should wake Miles up so he could have a shower before their guests arrived, but Miles looked wiped. He grinned smugly, enjoying the memory of his contribution to that state. He himself was full of energy, as if he'd had an injection of joy juice. His grin widened at the thought. Oh, yeah. Plenty of joy juice. Better than coke any day.

His jeans were on the chair where they'd thrown them sometime in the last twenty-four hours; since then he'd been in sweats or naked, but if they were having company, he figured he should at least make an effort to get dressed, so he dug around in his duffel for clean underwear and a fresh T-shirt. It was hard to put the jeans on, the fabric heavy and stiff after soft fleece. He pulled on his Vans, too, and ran a comb through his still-damp hair, then went to find something to drink.

He was sitting in the kitchen drinking a hard cider he'd found in the back of Miles's refrigerator when Grace, who'd been sitting quietly on her perch, started to bark. It was an amazing bark, deep and rough—a Doberman bark, or a Rottweiler. It sounded weird coming out of a bird. He started to say, "What the fuck?" when the back door opened and someone stepped inside. No, not just someone, but Someone. Adam blinked. Holy. Shit.

The guy was a good six-four, no, an *excellent* six-four, his blue T-shirt stretched tight across his muscular chest and jeans clinging to slim hips framing a substantial package. He wore his golden-blond hair short and sort of spiky; not in the fashionable-spiky style, but in the just-got-finished-playing-two-hours-of-basketball-because-I'm-that-macho kind of spiky. His eyes were sky-blue, his features drop-dead gorgeous, young-Brad-Pitt gorgeous. Adam could only stare at him, stunned.

Then he moved, stumbled, actually, forward into the kitchen, and a crabby voice said behind him, "Move, you big lummox!" and another body, this one shorter, darker, and less ripped, squirmed past him. The newcomer blinked at Adam and said, "Holy fucking shit— he wasn't kidding!"

"Told you," the blond said in a low, testosterone-infused rumble. Adam looked back at him and realized he was holding two thick pizza boxes, which he set on the table. The dark-haired guy followed suit with the two six-packs of bottled beer he carried. "Miles doesn't bullshit like that."

"I didn't think it was bullshit," the dark-haired guy retorted, "I thought he was hallucinating." He pushed past the Adonis, and held out a hand to Adam. "Doug Carter," he said, "and this is Rob Halloway."

"*You're* 'Bobby'?" Adam swallowed hard. Holy fucking shit, how the hell could he compete with this, this . . . Greek god? He gave his hand to Rob, and Rob's—Bobby's—swallowed his up, but the guy shook it gently.

"I am. And pleased to meet you. I'm pretty fond of your music."

"Rob likes teenybopper shit," Doug said. "But your stuff's okay." He moved around the kitchen with great familiarity, pulling out paper plates and napkins. "Where's Mike—Miles?"

"Sleeping," Adam said, then flushed.

Doug laughed. "Wore him out, huh? I tell you, Adam—I can call you Adam, right? You're not gonna be all pissy at me or anything, are you?"

"Of course he isn't," Rob rumbled. "Miles wouldn't put up with that shit."

"Right. Anyway. It's good to see him making contact with the real world, you know? He keeps cooped up here too much." Doug opened one of the boxes. "Rob, honey, go wake up Mike. Adam, you put this"—he handed him one of the six-packs—"into the fridge for later."

Adam obeyed automatically. Doug reminded him so much of his older brother that he found himself responding to him just as he did to Eric. Apparently Rob did, also, because he wordlessly left the kitchen.

As soon as he had, Doug turned to Adam. "So. What are you doing here with Mike?"

"I think that's kinda obvious," Adam said in surprise. "What's it to you?"

"Mike is my best friend, and he's been through a lot of shit over the years, and I've kinda taken it on myself to look out for him, because as you might have figured out, he's not so good at taking care of himself."

"That's bullshit," Adam said tightly. "He's smart. He's really smart. And he's talented and he's got his own business, and lives by himself just fine, so what the hell does he need you—or your *boyfriend*—for? He could have anybody he wants!"

"Yeah, he could. Except for the little issue of how he never leaves the lake. Have you figured that out yet?"

"Yeah, he told me." Adam sat down and rocked on the chair's back legs. "I don't get why, but that's his business. And frankly, if I were that big Frankenstein of yours, I'd dump your skinny ass and take on Miles instead."

To his surprise, Doug grinned. "Yeah, ya'd think, right? He's pretty, and Mike is pretty, and I'm just a tough little bastard from the South Side. But for some reason, Rob likes me. And he and Mike never did connect that way."

"From what Miles tells me, they manage to on occasion," Adam said darkly.

Doug hooted. "Oh, jealous?"

Adam thought about how Miles was with him, so open and loving and eager, and how he described his encounters with Bobby, and said, "No. Bobby doesn't treat him as well as he deserves, that's all."

The other man's eyes narrowed. "Mikey told you that?"

"No," Adam admitted. "He just said some things that made me think it. Like the fact that Bobby doesn't kiss him, and won't let Miles blow him, and stuff like that. Miles is so fucking giving that it pisses me off that someone has like, unlimited access to him, and doesn't ..."

"Doesn't what?"

"Doesn't love him," Adam muttered.

There was silence in the kitchen, and then Doug echoed, "Love him. You're saying you love him?"

"No, I mean ... well, no. But I just met him. You guys know him. How can your Bobby not love him?"

"Rob does love him," Doug said quietly, "and so do I. But we're together. We've been together since we were in high school. Rob gives him as much as he can, and I give him Rob. Because we do love him. And you," he went on, his tone unchanging, "have a helluva lot of nerve to come here and criticize what we do when you have no idea what's going on or what Mike is dealing with."

"No." Adam flushed. "I don't know what's going on. I only know that it hurts Miles."

"What hurts Miles?" Miles came into the kitchen in jeans and a T-shirt that read "Calligraphers Do It With A Flourish," and no shoes, as usual. Adam found himself staring at his naked feet, so solid and graceful, with their long, shapely toes. Then he blinked. *Toes?* He was losing it. "What?" he said stupidly.

"Adam here thinks that it hurts you to be with Rob." Doug popped the lid off a bottle of beer and handed it to Miles. "I think it's none of his business."

Miles blinked at Adam. "What?"

"Nothing. Never mind. Are we going to eat that pizza or stare at it?"

"Well," Rob rumbled from behind Miles, "that bottom one has enough crap on it that it's likely to start moving on its own any minute now."

Adam perked up. "Garbage pizza? You guys brought garbage pizza?"

"*Giordano's* garbage pizza," Doug said. He opened both boxes and started shoveling out the thick, gooey mess.

For a few minutes, they were too busy stuffing their faces with the melted cheese and various toppings to talk. Adam was amused to see that elegant, gorgeous Rob—Bobby? Rob?—was just as enthusiastic about the food as wiry little Doug was. Not that there wasn't anything to be enthusiastic about—it had been years since he'd had Chicago pizza, and even longer since he'd had Giordano's, with its thin upper and lower crusts and inch-thick layers of cheese and add-ons. It was just as good as he'd remembered, and he got through two pieces before slowing down.

"We are all going to die of coronaries," Rob said contentedly.

"Miles said you're a doctor," Adam said. "What kind of doctor?"

"Interventional radiology," Rob said absently, helping himself to another piece of pizza.

"What's that mean?"

"I use radiology—X-ray technology—to do things like minimally invasive exploration. Angiograms, arteriograms, some laser surgeries, angioplasties . . ." Rob paused, seeing Adam's blank face. "The balloon things when arteries get blocked. Which all of ours will be momentarily."

"So are you a surgeon?"

"I went through a surgical residency. But I'm not so big on the cutting-open stuff. I like the challenge of fixing up patients without messing them up more than they are already. Surgery is pretty traumatic in itself. Whenever we can, we go for less invasive procedures."

"Where do you work?"

"Northwestern Hospital, in Chicago."

"I've heard of that," Adam admitted.

Doug snorted. "Hear that, Rob? He's heard of one of the biggest hospitals in the country. Amazing."

"Shut up, Doug," Rob said.

Miles had been quiet while they'd gone through the first round of eating, but as they slowed down, he looked up at Adam with confused eyes and said, "It's really okay, you know."

"I know," Adam said softly. He shook his head and grinned. "Chuck says I'm kind of a den mother—always trying to take care of the boys. Sorry. I didn't mean to step on anyone's toes."

"Wait, what?" Doug said. "What are we talking about?"

"Rob." Adam took a bite of pizza.

Rob was looking puzzled, too. "Me?"

"How did you know what he was talking about?" Doug demanded.

Adam shrugged. "I don't know. I just did."

Doug's face wore a peculiar expression a moment, then he went back to eating. The conversation moved on.

They hung out awhile after dinner; the rain had stopped and they'd brought their beers down to the little patio where Miles had found Adam Sunday morning. The cushions were wet, but they just tossed them on the ground and sat on the wrought iron. Miles and Adam took the chairs and Rob lay back on the chaise, Doug sitting between his spread thighs and leaning back against Rob's broad chest.

"When does the construction crew come back?" Doug asked Miles.

"Next month, probably. The stuff for the septic tank renovations is on back order, and in the meantime they've got an indoor project that they don't need the earthmoving machines for. So they're just sitting there. It'll get noisy enough when they get back. And smelly." Miles cast a glance at Adam. "You timed your visit just right—you'll be gone by the time they start digging up the septic tanks. I think I'll go camping on the other side of the lake."

"And hope for a southerly breeze," Doug said.

Adam wished he could suggest that Miles come visit him while that was going on, but he didn't want to disturb the mellow, laid-back feeling that had settled over them. Instead, he reached over with one bare foot and nudged Miles's ankle. Miles glanced at him, giving him a shy smile from underneath his lashes, and turned his foot slightly to tease Adam's too.

Adam sighed and eased back in his chair, the wrought iron cool and hard against his back. The breeze smelled of evening, he was full from the pizza and relaxed from the beer. Doug and Rob had turned out to be okay, not assholes as he'd worried they would be, and he had a whole two weeks with Miles yet. Life was good.

"So Mikey says you used to come here when you were a kid?" Doug asked lazily. "I don't remember you."

"Well, I hope not," Adam said. "Being as how I was this scrawny, geeky little kid. You might remember my older brother though. Eric. He was maybe two years older than you guys?"

Doug shook his head. "I don't recall an Eric Craig."

"Not Craig. Karoshewski."

Doug sat up. "*Eric Karoshewski?* Jesus, dude! Eric Karoshewski is your older brother? Hot damn! Rob, you remember Eric Karoshewski, don't you?"

"Could hardly forget," Rob drawled. "I was pissed at you the whole summer we were fifteen. Eric this, and Eric that, and Eric, can I suck your dick?"

"I never sucked his dick."

"Only because he never even saw you, Dougie. You trailed after him like a lovesick puppy."

"Did not."

"Did."

Adam glanced at Miles, who was smiling faintly. Good—this stroll down memory lane wasn't upsetting him the way talk about the past sometimes seemed to. "I did a lot of that trailing after, myself," he offered. "I had a huge crush on Miles back then."

"I don't remember," Miles said quietly.

"You wouldn't, for the same reason. I was eleven," he said to Doug and Rob. "And you guys were older—and apparently Doug was in love with my brother." He chortled. "I can't wait to tell him."

"Don't you dare," Doug said, then added wistfully, "I don't suppose he's gay?"

Rob pinched him, and he yelped.

"Nope. Happily married for the past ten years with three kids."

"Probably just as well. So you live in L.A.?"

"Yeah. I have a condo in Santa Monica. Nothing fancy—I'm hardly ever there, anyway. Most of my family lives south of the city, so I'm there if I'm not touring or working."

"You like SoCal?" Doug asked.

"Yeah, it's great. Great weather, great parties, always something to do. Though it's been really sweet to just relax like this. Haven't had a real vacation in a long time."

There was a rumble of thunder, and all four men looked up at the sky. "Crap," Doug said. "So much for a nice evening."

"We should probably get going anyway," Rob said. "It's after eleven, and I have a carotid arteriogram at eight tomorrow."

"I love it when you talk medical," Doug said. Adam and Miles laughed.

"Besides," Rob went on, unruffled, "Adam was going to show me the music program he's got on his computer. It uses the microphone and actually hears the music and can translate it into notes."

"That's it," Doug said. "I may be the tech geek in the household, but once you get Rob going on voice recognition software, he's all squee. We'll be here all night."

"Five minutes," Rob assured him.

Miles and Doug exchanged skeptical glances. Then another rumble of thunder and a scattering of raindrops sent them all bolting for the house.

Standing in the kitchen doorway, Doug beside him leaning on the jamb, Miles watched as Adam showed Bobby the program on his laptop, his face alight with enthusiasm and delight as he picked out a tune on his guitar. Miles's chest hurt. "He's not coming back, is he?" he said in a low voice to Doug.

Doug didn't answer right away; then he sighed. "Probably not. That's how it goes, you know. He'll *mean* to come back, and for the first few days or weeks, you might keep in touch. But people don't,

Mikey. Life gets in the way. Like Paul and Nate and Nick—they didn't stop liking you or being your friends, they just sort of . . . forgot."

"He'll forget, too," Miles said.

"Probably. Oh, not on purpose, and not entirely. You're doing a piece for him, right? Then he'll always have a reminder. He won't forget you. You'll just sort of slide down his priority list." He hesitated, then went on, "It's not a slam against you, Mike, really. It's just that his usual real life is so waaay different from yours. You got nothing in common."

"You didn't forget."

"No," Doug said. "I'm your fucking best friend, Mikey. Always have been."

"I forgot *you*," Miles said bitterly. "*Twice*."

"It don't count. I remember you. And so does Rob. We've got a shared past, stuff in common. I *know* you, Mike." He glanced back at Adam. "He doesn't know you."

"Sometimes it feels like he does," Miles argued. "Sometimes he gets it."

"Yeah, and that's great," Doug replied. "Or would be great if he lived around here. If you guys had a shot at building a relationship. But a couple of weeks of fucking does not a relationship make. No matter how hot the fucking." He shot Miles a quick, rueful grin. "And I gotta apologize. When I told you to take the chance, to text him back and tell him to come . . . I didn't know who he was then. I didn't know you had hooked up with someone like him—someone with the kind of responsibilities that come with fame and all."

"You wouldn't have told me to ask him back if you had, would you?"

Doug was quiet a moment, then shook his head. "No, probably not. But don't regret it, Mikey. He's great. Enjoy him while you can. Remember him as a good thing. Just know you gotta deal with it ending."

"This sucks."

"Yeah." He reached out and rubbed Miles's shoulder. "But enjoy the rest of your time with him, Mikey. Build some good memories. And if nothing else," he grinned, "take pictures."

Chapter II

fter Doug and Rob had gone, Miles busied himself with cleaning up: rinsing out the beer bottles and putting them in the recycling bin, packing up the pizza boxes in the garbage, washing the forks and putting them away. Adam, who'd taken two seconds to shut down his laptop, watched him until he couldn't stand it anymore. "What's wrong, Miles?"

Miles jumped, as if he'd forgotten Adam was in the room. "Nothing," he said hastily. "Just, you know, cleaning up . . ."

"I don't know you very well," Adam said, "but I'd be willing to bet that under normal circumstances you'd leave all that shit for the morning and just go to bed."

Miles closed the drawer he had dumped the clean forks into and finally—finally!—turned to face Adam. He didn't say anything, just gazed at Adam with a numb expression. It shocked Adam, that look—not fearful, not sad, just . . . desolate.

"Miles," he said helplessly.

"It's not anything."

Adam didn't know what to say, so instead, he crossed the kitchen and stood in front of Miles, running his hand up his arm to his shoulder, curling his fingers around Miles's nape. "Leave the dishes," he said, "and let's go to bed."

Miles stared at him a moment, then with a sigh, all the tension bled out of him, and he put his head on Adam's shoulder.

"See," Adam murmured, "it's as simple as that."

His lover chuffed a snort, but when Adam drew back a little, Miles was smiling. "That's better," Adam said, and led Miles by the neck down the hall to the bedroom.

Once in the room, though, Miles took over, stripping Adam out of his jeans and T-shirt and tumbling him onto the bed. Adam laced his fingers through Miles's dark hair as Miles kissed his way down Adam's belly, relishing the heat and damp of Miles's mouth on his skin. Too soon he'd be going back to his regularly scheduled life, hiding what he was, pretending to be what he wasn't, all for what? Money, fame, the sake of the band, the people whose livelihoods were tied up with what he was pretending to be . . . He resolutely pushed the guilt and responsibility aside and focused on what was going on here, now; on what that beautiful mouth and those beautiful hands were doing to him.

That mouth was nuzzling tenderly at his groin, kissing the soft skin between his hip and cock, one hand curling around to tug gently on his balls. Adam groaned in delight as Miles's lips brushed the base of his cock and licked gently upward before closing around him. "God," Adam moaned, "your mouth . . ." Miles chuckled, then, amazingly, started to hum: a little off-key and gravely, but who could expect more when the mouth in question was full of cock? It felt fantastic, and sounded familiar . . . wait. He knew that song, the one from *Fame* he'd been playing earlier.

Then Miles slid two fingers into his ass and hit home, and all thoughts of songs went straight out of his head.

The weather stayed beautiful, hot but not too humid, a miracle for the upper Midwest. Miles grumbled some about needing the humidity for gilding, which Adam didn't follow. He knew gilding was the gold leaf that Miles put on the pictures he painted, and that it was a big project in really small doses, involving a velvet pad and a tiny brush and Miles blowing into a feather that had all its feathery parts taken off and the gunk inside the shaft pulled out. Adam didn't even know there *was* gunk in the shaft until Miles showed him. But there was a lot of stuff Adam didn't know until Miles showed him. Like how the green stuff that grew on the copper Miles had hanging over the bucket of pee turned out to be a really pretty green paint, and that the parchment Miles painted on was made out of honest-to-God animal skin, like leather, only scraped thin with this curved metal thing Miles called a lunette but that looked like something a crazed butcher serial killer would chop people up with.

It wasn't just about Miles's art, either.

Miles ran just about every day, and Adam ran with him. It was a bitch, keeping up—he'd thought he was in pretty good shape, what with all the energy he spent on stage, and he'd only just come off the tour, so he didn't think he'd gone to pot that quickly. But when he'd staggered to a halt, wheezing and sweating, after only about a mile, Miles had turned around and rubbed his back until he'd caught his breath, then explained to him about how jumping and dancing and singing and playing guitar used different muscles, and that the muscles for running weren't accustomed to it so they weren't getting any oxygen and were sucking it out of his lungs. Adam didn't even know muscles *needed* oxygen. He worked with a trainer when he was back home, but the trainer never explained things the way Miles did. When they got back to the house, Miles showed him a bunch of anatomy books he had, and they'd looked at them until they got to the sex organs, and then Adam got Miles all hot and breathless for a change.

For someone who claimed he didn't know anything about music, Miles always had something to say when Adam played stuff for him. He seemed to know instinctively what worked and what didn't, particularly the words, probably because he read so much. Adam found himself working harder on the lyrics instead of just tossing stuff off the way he had for so long, figuring no one was really listening to what he was saying under the scream of the guitars. Miles startled him once, when Adam was goofing around playing a riff from an old Dire Straits song, singing the original MTV jingle in a surprisingly sweet falsetto. After that, Adam tried to get him to sing; he didn't have a great voice, but it was pleasant and he hit the notes pretty regularly. But he got embarrassed every single time, even though it was just him and Adam there.

He spent a lot of time working, of course, and Adam didn't mind—he'd sort of invited himself to the lake anyway, hadn't he? Miles did have commissions, and deadlines, and was running a business. But he didn't seem to be bothered if Adam settled on the couch with his laptop and guitars to work on songs while he painted, and Adam found that when he was in the room with Miles, Miles didn't go off into his zombie artist mode where he shut everything else out. He still focused like crazy; Adam could play death metal turned up to eleven, and Miles just kept working. Adam didn't though, because it drove Grace berserk, and *that* bothered Miles.

And they went sailing.

The boat was stored up in one of the mysterious outbuildings near the lodge, its ropes and sails carefully packed against the depredations of weather and mice. Miles showed Adam how to mount the mast once they'd muscled the trailer down the shallow ramp to the boat dock (not the swimming dock by Miles's cottage—this one was further along the lake shore, closer to the actual lodge), and got the boat into the water. Then it was a matter of attaching the sails and doing all the things with the ropes. Adam watched, mostly, or fetched something Miles pointed to with an abstracted grunt, and Miles worked steadily, confidently assembling the piles of ropes and canvas and large wooden pegs ("pins," Miles called them) and bits of chain and hooks and things into a recognizable facsimile of a sailboat.

"No wonder you don't do this much," Adam observed.

Miles looked up at him, flashing one of those quicksilver smiles on his serious face. "It's a lot of work," he admitted, "but the result is worth it. Hand me that, will you?" and he pointed at some other thing Adam had no clue about the purpose of. Adam obeyed, the way he always did. Miles never—or at least, rarely—demanded things, but he had a self-assurance about him that Adam just automatically deferred to. He'd had directors like that, who never had to yell or lose their temper: people just obeyed without thinking. They put their lives in the director's hands and let him take all the responsibility for it. It was like that with Miles. For all of Miles's self-acknowledged social ineptness, when he was in his element, he was completely there.

It was just that when he wasn't in his element, he was completely lost.

He finished whatever it was that he was doing with the sails, and instructed Adam on how to get on board properly, and what to do when he was there, and then he unhooked the rope from the dock, pushed against the wood gently, and the boat slid away and out into the deeper water. He pulled on the ropes, raising the sail, and then the boat leaped—lunging forward smoothly with an increase in speed that made Adam glad Miles had told him where to hang on.

Miles stood, hand on the tiller, his head up, his unruly hair waving in the breeze, and laughed.

Adam fell in love.

Oh, he suspected he'd been on his way since the moment Miles had woken him on the patio that first morning, but up to now it had been a slow, easy ride, learning about each other, growing in friendship and affection. But this? This was a leap, like the sail catching the wind, belling out, shooting the boat off into the deeper water. This was a lunge, a dive, a fucking free fall without a parachute, casting himself into the air with no fear, trusting that something—that Miles—would catch him.

He laughed in joy, just like Miles, and their eyes met and they grinned at each other in perfect amity.

Miles had packed a lunch in the big cooler they'd loaded on board just before they pushed off, and after they'd cruised around the lake for a while, they docked on the far side of the island and tied off the boat. Miles stalked around the land end of the dock, inspecting it and muttering to himself, but finally came back to where Adam was sitting on the dock with his feet in the water and plopped down beside him, pulling his sweaty T-shirt over his head. "There's some damage from last spring's storms," he announced as he took the cold bottle of IPA Adam handed him, "but I think I can fix it myself. Just need to replace a couple of boards." He pulled off his deck shoes and stuck his feet in the water next to Adam's.

"How big is the island?" Adam asked idly.

"Big enough for chipmunks, not big enough for deer. Maybe quarter mile square? Or round, or ovalish. Not big." He sipped his beer. "There's a fire pit, or there was. I think it collapsed a couple years ago. Didn't see much point in fixing it. People used to have picnics there."

"I remember. I think my folks came over here once or twice. Back in the days when they were speaking to each other."

"Guess it was hard when they divorced."

Adam shrugged. "It was all very polite. Dad moved up to Anaheim, so we got to go to Disneyland a lot when we were still kids. Mom stayed in San Diego. We did weekends with Dad, and two weeks in the summer. He worked a lot. Still does."

"Still."

"Yeah, it sucked. But it's okay. We're used to it now, and the folks are pretty civil these days." He leaned back on his elbows and lifted his face to the sky, letting the sun warm it. "I missed this place, though. Seemed like nothing bad could happen here."

"Nothing bad ever has. It's why I live here, I guess."

"Yeah, I can see that."

They sat soaking up the sun a few minutes longer, then Miles surged to his feet. "Come on. Grab the other end of the cooler, okay?"

"Where are we going?"

"There's a sort of overlook up the hill a bit where the old fire pit was. It's a good place for a picnic. Sunny, nice view."

Adam ogled Miles's tan, bare chest, and said, "Nice view right here."

"Funny. Come on."

They put their shoes back on, and Miles draped his T-shirt over the top of the cooler to dry, grabbed a tote bag, and slung it over his shoulder, then they picked up the cooler and hauled it up the slope through the trees to the overlook. Miles had a point; the slightly higher elevation opened up the lake vista, and the view was beautiful. Miles busied himself with setting out the lunch: nothing more complicated than sandwiches and fruit, spread out on the blanket he'd pulled from the tote bag.

Adam, who'd carefully guarded his beer while climbing the slope, sat cross-legged on the end of the blanket, drank his beer, and watched Miles sorting out the sandwiches with his usual absorption. "There," Miles said. "Chicken, beef, turkey."

"Jesus, Miles, it's not a wedding reception. Just how many people did you plan to feed?"

"Just you, but I didn't know what you wanted, so I made a bunch of them. We can eat the rest later."

"Where'd you get the stuff?"

"The lodge. Lisa restocked the kitchen when she found out you were staying."

"When was that?" Adam frowned. "She didn't come to the cottage."

"No, she just brought the stuff and left while we were swimming yesterday. She texted me later. She didn't want to interrupt."

"She's a good sister."

"Yeah." Miles picked up a sandwich and unwrapped it. "I made these last night. I hope they're still good."

"Is that where you were? I woke up, but I figured you were painting."

"I was for a while. Then I thought I'd better get these made so we wouldn't have to do it in the morning."

"I would have helped."

"I know..."

"I would have liked to have helped."

Miles met Adam's gaze. "I know," he said again, and his eyes went soft. "Next time."

"Count on it," Adam said, his voice shaky. He reached for a sandwich, not caring much what kind.

They ate in silence, each polishing off two sandwiches and an apple. Miles packed the rest of the food back into the cooler. Adam picked up the wrappings and apple cores and bundled them together. When he turned to hand them to Miles, Miles got a funny smile on his face and reached out to thumb Adam's cheek. "Mayo."

Adam caught Miles's wrist. "Mine," he said huskily, and licked the mayonnaise from Miles's thumb. Then he licked it again, and Miles pressed it against Adam's lips. Adam let him in, his tongue curling around Miles's thumb, and Miles closed his eyes. After a moment or so, he released it and moved his mouth down to Miles's palm and wrist.

Miles made a sound deep in his throat, one of those Miles noises Adam was coming to love, wordless but so full of meaning. Miles reached for him and he reached back, pushing Miles down onto the blanket and climbing on top of him. Miles laughed. "Pushy much?"

"Yeah," Adam admitted, and ran his hands over Miles's chest, loving the way the hair crisped against his palms. "I love that you have hair on your chest," he said. "I love the way you're hard underneath the skin like this. Girls aren't hard. They're soft and bumpy, and they don't have any hair. Making out with a girl is like, like . . ."

"Like making out with a girl?"

"Mm, yeah." He bent and kissed Miles, feeling Miles wrap his big solid hands in Adam's hair, twisting it around his fingers and anchoring Adam there. Yes, that was right, that was good. Anchored. He sighed and lost himself in Miles's mouth.

Miles pulled him back a little and said, "Lose the shorts."

Adam reached down and unbuttoned his cargo shorts, peeling them down and kicking them away. He hadn't bothered to wear underwear this morning; somehow he suspected they'd end up in this position. Or something similar. He grinned, and Miles raised an eyebrow as he released Adam's hair.

"Something funny?"

"Nope. Dead serious." Adam sat up and pulled off his T-shirt, then set to work on Miles's shorts, shifting so he could work them down Miles's legs. Something crackled in the pocket; he stuck his hand in and pulled out a handful of condoms and pillow packs of lube. "Hm. Prepared, aren't you?"

"You can't say I don't learn from my mistakes." The smug look vanished as Miles's eyes rolled back in his head. "Uhngh . . ."

Laughing, Adam slid down to where he had taken Miles's cock in his hand. He wasn't quite hard yet, but that was easily remedied; he licked Miles, then took him in his mouth, his tongue tracing the rising veins, the soft dome, the slit that, even as Adam's tongue traced it, gave back a taste of Miles. Yep. This was easy. He stretched his lips around him and took him deep, sucking hard and feeling the muscles in Miles's thighs quiver. He felt powerful, making this strong man tremble, the same kind of power he felt performing, at that magical moment when the audience was his.

Miles was his, just as much. But there was nothing of a performance now—this was real and true.

And fucking awesome.

Miles was making those noises again, halfway between a grunt and a whimper. Adam released his one-handed grip on Miles's cock and took him as deep as he could, stifling his gag reflex when Miles bumped against the back of his throat. He put his hands on Miles's thighs as he rode his mouth up and back down, just the tip of his nose brushing the thick pelt at Miles's groin. Then he pulled back, letting Miles pop from his lips, and grabbed a condom and lube.

"Need you," he growled. "Need this."

Miles grunted as Adam rolled the condom down Miles's cock, pausing to cup his balls gently in his fingers. Then he popped the lube and ran his fingers over Miles again, teasing a moment, before straddling Miles's hips. Miles ran his long, strong hands over Adam's thighs and up to his waist, steadying him as Adam eased down.

Full. Anchored. Steadied. Adam gazed down at Miles's face, his cheeks reddened, his mouth flushed and full, his eyes heavy-lidded and hungry. "God," Adam whispered, "Miles . . ." He rocked up, and Miles's hands held him steady as he came down again.

"Ride me," Miles murmured, and Adam did, slow at first, then faster, until Miles caught him and rolled over onto the blanket, hiking Adam's legs over his shoulders and plunging into him, hard and fast. Adam cried out as he lost it, spurting wildly as Miles kept up the heated fucking, his hips snapping against Adam's ass.

When Miles finally came, he threw his head back and let out a long, triumphant howl. Adam shuddered at the fierceness, the wildness of it, feeling thoroughly possessed.

Thoroughly owned.

Miles collapsed next to him, one arm thrown across Adam's chest to pin him there while he caught his breath. Adam was just as breathless, but he wrapped both hands around Miles's arm, holding it against him as if it were a lifeline.

"Okay?" Miles gasped.

"Fuckin' A," Adam wheezed back.

Miles raised his head. His eyes were soft and his smile gentle, as if the madman who'd just possessed Adam had been Adam's imagination. "Me too."

"Yeah." Adam reached up and cupped Miles's cheek. "Totally yeah."

Chapter 12

here was an annoying buzzing sound from the couch. Miles said sharply, "Grace!" but then it occurred to him that she was in her cage; he'd put her in there a while ago when Adam had gone in for a shower and he'd decided to do a little calligraphy. He set down the quill on the pen rest, careful to not let it drip on the vellum, and got up to see what the noise was.

It was Adam's phone. Picking it up, he saw that the little voice-mail icon was lit. He frowned. Adam's phone was almost always with Adam. He tilted his head, listening for the sound of the shower, but heard only silence. One of the things he'd noticed about Adam was that he was always humming, or whistling, or murmuring to himself; usually when Miles disappeared into his art, he'd come out of it to hear Adam's guitar or Adam's voice as he tried out a new song. But there was nothing, just silence.

How long had Miles been working? He glanced out the window—it was still daylight, so not more than a few hours. Where had Adam gone?

He put the phone in his pocket and went looking.

Adam was asleep on the chaise on Miles's patio. His hair was still wet and lay coiled across the cushions like dark snakes; he had on a snug T-shirt and cutoff jeans Miles hadn't seen before, the ragged hems of which rode high on his tanned thighs. Miles's mouth went dry. Who would have thought a pair of cutoffs could be so fucking sexy? He dropped into the chair across from Adam and just stared at

117

him hungrily. Only a few more days, and Adam would have to leave, to go back to L.A., and then Miles would probably never see him again. Doug's words haunted Miles. This last weekend, watching Bobby and Adam bond over technology and barbeque, Miles was sure that Doug had been right. Adam was too social, too charming, too . . . too *everything*. What could someone like Miles offer him? This was just . . . vacation.

But he was beautiful. Phone call forgotten, Miles sat and watched him sleep, the light breeze of the lake teasing the long tendrils of his drying hair, ruffling the ragged threads of the shorts hems. Then he opened his eyes, those beautiful eyes, and smiled sleepily up at him. "Hey," he said, his voice rough with sleep.

It sent a chill through Miles. "Hey."

"Were you ogling me?"

"Who the hell uses the word 'ogling' anymore?"

The smile grew. "Someone who watches too many old movies. Done with your calligy stuff?"

"Stopping point. How long was I working?"

"Couple hours. I took a swim instead of a shower when I realized you'd slid into the zone."

"Sorry." Miles shook his head. "I shouldn't have done that. You've only got three more days and I'm wasting them working . . ."

"Dude. Miles." Adam sat up and reached over to squeeze Miles's thigh gently. "You need to work. I get that. Art to you is like music to me—it's not just a job, it's . . ."

"An adventure?"

Adam laughed at the line from the old commercial for the military. "Something like that. I lose myself in the music sometimes too. Just 'cause I'm on vacation right now doesn't mean I don't get that. Besides, you've spent a lot of time with me this past week, and it's been great. I get that you have to . . . go away sometimes. It's cool."

"We only have three days," Miles repeated.

"This time. There will be other times—" Adam's statement was cut off by Miles's kiss. Miles didn't want to hear the words, because he knew Adam believed them, and if he heard them, then he might believe them too. And they just weren't *true*.

Releasing Adam, he pulled the phone from his pocket and handed it to him. "You have a voice mail."

"Oh, crap. Bill called earlier and I forgot to call him back. Don't move." He grinned at Miles. "I want some more of that, but I really gotta call him, okay? He panics."

"Sure." Miles got up and took a few steps away, burying his hands in his pockets and looking out over the lake. The sun was starting to go down behind the trees on the island; they stood out like black sentinels against the purpling sky. Behind him, he heard Adam's voice, low at first as he greeted his manager, then rising: "Jesus, Bill, I have less than four days, and you have to fuck it up? . . . Yeah, I know it's good press. Christ . . . What? . . . Yeah . . . Yeah," and then his tone fell again as he turned away from Miles. Miles glanced over his shoulder and saw him leaning on the high back of the chaise, his shoulders slumped. He thumbed the phone off and shoved it in the pocket of those cutoffs.

"When do you have to leave?" Miles asked numbly.

Adam turned, and Miles could have wept at the pain in his expression. "It's just overnight. Someone—probably one of the guys— let it slip that I'm staying in the Chicago area, and one of the morning talk shows wants me to guest. It'd be really early—like five a.m.—that I'd tape, so I'd have to stay downtown overnight. Shit. I don't want to do it, but Bill's got his knickers in a twist about me being off his leash so long."

"That doesn't seem normal."

Adam laughed, a tad bitterly. "I'm exaggerating. Bill's got this idea that I should go solo, and he sees this thing as a way of separating me from the band, giving me my own identity, you know? I'll have to go back downtown the night after next, stay over, but then I'll be back here the next morning, probably pretty early, as soon as I'm done taping. So it's only a night." His eyes were pleading for Miles to understand.

One night. *I hate to miss a single minute*, he thought, then kicked himself mentally. What did he call zoning out for hours working on art projects that he really could put off for a few days? He was shutting Adam out then, just as effectively as if he'd gone off the resort. Yeah, it wasn't deliberate, but it still happened. He didn't have any room to complain. "It's just a night," he said, the words coming out like shards of glass.

"Yeah," Adam agreed. "But it's *our* night." He walked over to Miles and slid his arms around Miles's neck. "I hate it. But Bill thinks it's important, and he's never steered us wrong. Plus it's likely to piss off Neil, and that's a plus."

Miles bent his head and rested it on Adam's shoulder. Adam smelled like sunshine and water, and in that one moment Miles knew it was already too late for him. They only had a few days left, and then Adam would be gone. And if Dougie was right, for good. His heart hurt, but he said only, "So. You gonna wear that outfit on TV?"

Adam laughed. "Nah. I got fancy-ass crap in my suitcase in the car. This is just for you."

"Good." Miles slid his hand down the gap in the back of the cutoffs. Adam's body melted automatically against his and he felt a moment of brief triumph. Whatever happened, Adam was his, for now at least.

Chapter 13

here was a brisk knocking on Adam's hotel room door. He frowned. He wasn't due for the interview until tomorrow morning; the producer had called him to tell him they'd arranged for a car to pick him up at 4:30 a.m. He was glad of that; he'd checked into the hotel as Craig Karoshewski, and hadn't really wanted to find his own way to the studio as Adam Craig. With the Morning Show advertising for the past two days that he would be guesting, the paparazzi were likely to be circling. So far, though, no one had copped to his alter ego, so it *probably* wasn't the media.

He got up and went to answer.

"Adam, darling!"

Adam blinked. Evangeline Montcalm, actress, model, and former "girlfriend," lounged in the doorway, looking as perfect as ever.

"Evie? What are you doing here?" He stood back to let her into the room.

She flipped her long, perfectly straight blonde hair over one perfect shoulder, and leaned forward to kiss his cheek. "We're shooting a commercial. I heard you hadn't come back from Chicago, so I called Bill and he gave me your itinerary." Evie dropped onto the suite's sofa, stretching her long, perfect legs out in front of her, and toed off her Louboutins. "Not all of your itinerary, obviously, but he knew about the interview, and where you'd be staying."

"But how did you get the room number?"

"Duh! The label's paying for your room; Bill got it for me. He'd love to see us back together again, you know."

"Yeah, I know. Free publicity for the band and everything."

"The band, nothing," Evie retorted. "You know he wants you to go solo. So do I. I think it would be perfect."

Enough with the "perfect." "I don't think so. Something to drink?"

"What do you have?"

"Beer, wine, various liquors and stuff. Fridge is packed with high end."

"Diet Coke?"

"Still on the hard stuff, huh?"

"You know it." She rolled her head onto the back of the sofa. "I have a party to go to tonight, and it's going to be deadly dull. Want to go?"

"What happened to what's-his-name? Philippe? Pierre? The oil magnate?" Adam found a bottle of Diet Coke in the not-so-minibar and poured it into a glass of ice.

"Thierry, it was coal, and I dumped him." She accepted the glass of cola and sipped it, then went on, "He was making marriage noises, and you know I have sworn off marriage forever. That's why we were so perfect together."

"You and Thierry?"

"No, you and me! You aren't interested in settling down, and I'm one of the few people who know you're gay." She reached over and poked him with her toes. "Aside from the lack of sex, we're perfect."

"Well, the lack of sex is an issue." Adam sat down beside her with a beer.

"Not for me," Evie said morosely. "It's fun at the beginning, but sooner or later it just gets boring. And the idea of being stuck having sex with the same person for the rest of your life?" She shuddered dramatically. "No, thank you."

Adam grinned. He'd been friends with Evie off and on since college; they'd both been in the theater arts program at UCLA years ago, though he'd gone the stage route and she film. A couple of years previously, they'd started "dating"; it was a publicity ploy for her and a smoke screen for him. But the constant media attention had started to grate, and by the time they'd cooked up a spectacular fight that had been captured on camera and spread out over multiple media outlets, they'd been heartily sick of each other.

They'd tried again a year or so later, but that time the fight hadn't been cooked up; it had been so bad that he'd actually moved to get away from the paparazzi, and so had she. They'd lost touch for a while, but he hadn't held a grudge, and apparently neither had she, though they hadn't made any effort to connect again until now.

But Evie was loyal, and never even hinted about Adam's sexual preferences to anyone, and Adam was grateful. He slid an arm around her thin shoulders and squeezed gently. "It's good to see you again, Evie. It's been a long time."

She rubbed her cheek on his shoulder. "Too long," she admitted. "I've been wanting to get in touch with you, but that damn Frenchman was so fucking possessive. I think his hired thugs would have beat the shit out of you."

"He's not going to make a stink now, is he?"

"No. He's not stupid. We had a good and public fight, and then I introduced him to Sally Becker, the new L'Oréal girl, and now they're dating. Of course I sobbed and made a huge fuss." She held out her arm. A diamond bracelet sparkled on her wrist. "I'm very good at making a fuss."

"I remember," Adam said dryly.

"So. I'm footloose and fancy-free, and the party tonight is going to be chock-full of all kinds of people I hate but have to kiss up to if I want to keep working, so how about coming with me and making out in public?"

"If I must, I must."

"You must. Come on. It'll make Bill happy and frustrate your groupies to no end."

"Well, there is that."

"Besides, you didn't have plans, did you?"

"Nope."

"Good. The car is picking us up at nine; wear your club clothes. It'll be fun."

Adam snorted. "I have to be ready for the interview at four-thirty. If I remember correctly, we rarely got home before then when we went clubbing."

"We're not going clubbing, we're going to a stupid party. Don't give me your usual lame excuse about not having anything to wear; I know you."

"Well, yeah, I do have something, I guess. But I gotta be home early, Evie. I'm thirty-one. I can't do this all-night shit anymore."

"We'll be fine. We'll come home early."

"I can't do this shit anymore," Adam moaned.

"Don't sit down!" Evie said frantically. "If you sit down, you'll relax, and if you relax, you'll fall asleep. The car is coming in ten minutes."

"I look like hell. I look like I've been partying all night." He stared at himself in the mirror hung on the wall opposite the bed. Bloodshot eyes stared back. "Oh, my God. I can't go on TV looking like this."

"You'll be fine. I've done *commercials* after a night like this. You have to go through hair and makeup anyway. Here. Take these." She handed him a couple of pills and a glass of water. "They'll perk you up long enough to get through the interview, then you can come back here and crash."

"No." Adam put his face against the mirror and leaned into it, staring into his reddened eyes. "Gotta get back to the lake."

"Nap first, then lake. But *not now*." She pulled him upright. "Take those, and I'll be right back with ice. But *don't sit down*."

Adam swallowed the pills and drank the water, then leaned against the mirror again. "You," he said to his reflection, "are an idiot." He knew he shouldn't have gone out with Evie. They'd done this way too many times for him to have really believed it would be different this time. Turning thirty hadn't slowed Evie down one damn bit. He shouldn't have done it. But it had been a long time since he'd seen Evie, and they always had so much fun together . . .

The door opened again and Evie came in with the ice bucket. Turning on the cold water in the sink, she dumped the ice into the water. "Okay. Here's my trick. Take a deep breath and stick your face in the water."

"Are you *nuts*?"

"No. Seriously. This will take out the puffiness and wake you up. And your eyes won't be as red. And I have drops."

Adam said, "Your knowledge base is way too esoteric."

"What the fuck does that mean?"

"I don't know. The friend I'm staying with talks like that. He said that when I told him he knew the weirdest things."

"Well, talk like that on the show and the hosts will love you."

Adam stared at the frigid water, took a deep breath, and plunged.

The remote was missing. Miles stood in the hallway, his heart pounding, and tried desperately to remember where he'd seen it last. It *should* have been in his bedroom, on the nightstand, where he and Adam had left it two nights ago when they'd watched *The Avengers* on DVD, and had agreed Miles needed a Blu-ray player and a high-def TV. It wasn't there. It wasn't on the dresser, or under the bed, or *in* the bed. Or in the laundry hamper, or the bathroom, or the closet. It wasn't *anywhere*. He quelled his rising hysteria and forced himself to think, which of course had the opposite effect of making his mind go in rapidly expanding circles. He dug in his pocket for his phone (he'd slept in his clothes again, without Adam there to remind him to change—or to give him a reason to go to bed naked) and hit the speed dial. When Lisa's sleepy voice answered, he gasped, "The remote. I can't find the fucking remote!"

When Lisa responded, she sounded wide awake and perfectly calm. "Miles. Stop. Breathe. Don't think. Breathe."

"But—"

"*Breathe.*"

Miles stopped. He breathed. Took a deep breath again. Let it out. "Okay," he said, when his heart had stopped trying to pound its way out of his chest.

"Okay. Now. Stop panicking, it's nonproductive. Where did you see it last?"

"Bedroom. But it's not there. And Adam's going to be on TV, and I want to see it—"

"*Stop panicking.*"

The firm, steady voice stopped him. He breathed again. "Okay."

"Miles, honey—I've got my DVR set up to record it and will download it if you can't find the remote, so you'll see it eventually, okay?"

"Okay. But—"

"Yes, I know. You need to find the remote. It's not in the bathroom?"

"No. I checked. I even looked in the tank."

"Well, if it were in the tank, it wouldn't do you any good anymore anyway." The practical note in Lisa's voice cut through his incipient panic better than her admonitions to breathe had. "How about the kitchen? Maybe one of you carried it in there when you went in for breakfast."

Miles went down the hall to the kitchen and stood looking through the doorway. Grace's cage was still covered, the dishes from yesterday were all washed and put away, and even the last few days' mail was piled neatly on the counter. "It's not here."

"Miles."

"What?"

"Look. God, you are such a man sometimes. Look in the drawers, the cabinets, the fridge."

He started banging open drawers and doors. When he opened the refrigerator door, though, it took a moment of looking at it before he realized the remote was on the top shelf. "Oh. It's here." He dropped onto one of the chairs. "Oh, thank God."

"In the fridge?"

"Yes."

She sighed faintly. "Dad used to do that. Leave the remote in weird places. Are you okay now?"

"Yeah. Thanks."

"Okay. I'm going back to sleep for another twenty before my alarm goes off. Enjoy the show."

"Thanks, Lise."

Her voice was soft as she responded, "Any time, little brother."

He took the remote out of the fridge, put his phone into his pocket, and went back into the bedroom.

"And this morning's special guest, Adam Craig of Black Varen! Welcome, Adam!"

"Thanks, Brenda. It's a real pleasure to be here." Adam was lying through his teeth, which hurt enough from his headache that he thought they might just fall out. That would be something for morning TV, a toothless Adam Craig.

"It's a pleasure to have you, especially with your busy schedule. You and the band just finished a three-month tour, with a sold-out concert at the United Center last week. From all reports, it was a pretty great time! I wish I could have been there."

"Well, Brenda, next time we're in Chicago, just let me know, and I'll make sure you get tickets. You too, Bob!" As if either Barbie or Ken doll would actually show up at anything where they weren't the center of attention. *Catty, Adam.*

"Thanks, Adam. So what's Black Varen working on now?"

"Well, in a couple of days we'll be going back into the studio to start work again on our next CD. I'm really eager to get back to it; we've got a couple of songs that I think are going to be pretty good."

"Are you hoping for a big hit like 'Riot Baby,' Black Varen's most recent hit? It went platinum a few weeks ago, didn't it?"

"Oh, we're always hoping for that. But 'Riot Baby' was a real collaboration between all of us, and I think it shows in the power of the song."

"How do you guys write? Does one person write the words, another the music?"

"Well, usually one of us will come up with a sort of draft of the words and music. Neil Draper, our other guitarist, and I write a lot of the songs, but Chuck and Eddie—our bassist and drummer, respectively—contribute a lot, too."

"Who wrote the first draft of 'Riot Baby'?"

"Oh, that was me. I'd been watching a lot of news about the stuff in the Mideast, and I just started wondering how it affected the ordinary Joe, and some of that came out in the song. But the arrangement, a lot of the music elements, that was all collaborative."

"Rumor has it that you've been invited to become a judge on *American Idol.* Is that true?"

"I haven't heard anything about it." *Oh,* God, *had Bill cooked that up? Shoot me now.* "Not sure I'd do that—it's pretty time-consuming from what I hear. But I'm open to anything."

"What's kept you in Chicago these past couple of weeks? The rest of the band is back in L.A., aren't they?"

"Yeah, all hanging out in Malibu and stuff like that, taking it easy for a bit—touring is tough on everyone." He thought of Miles, waiting for him, and gave the hosts his first genuine smile of the morning.

Miles watched Adam laugh at his own statement. He seemed so relaxed, so easy, as if he did these kinds of things all the time. And hell, for all Miles knew, he did. But when the woman asked "So why aren't you?" to Adam's comment, Miles tensed. He wasn't sure why until Adam smiled and said easily, "I'm from the Chicago area originally. I had a little time after the end of the tour, and it was a good opportunity to catch up with some old friends. People who knew me before Black Varen, you know? It's nice to revisit the past a little." Nothing about Miles, nothing about the resort, nothing that would bring attention to him. He let his breath out.

"And what about the future?" the male host asked.

Adam smiled. "Oh, work. Studio work until next April, when our next tour starts. Maybe play a few local clubs in L.A. just to keep our hands in. Spending some time with family. And of course, looking for that elusive someone, like we all do."

"Speaking of which, we understand that you were seen last night at a couple places, the Smart Bar and Hearts, with a certain lady you've been linked to before. Are things heating up again for you and the lovely Ms. Montcalm?"

Ms. Montcalm. That was the name of the woman Adam had been linked to in the articles Miles had read when he'd looked Adam up. But the articles all said they were over. So why had Adam been out with her last night? He hadn't said anything about going out in his last text the evening before.

"Photos or it didn't happen." Adam grinned. "No, seriously, Evie was in town filming a commercial and we bumped into each other. We go way back, me and Evie. And for the record, those are two of the best clubs I've been to—easily as good as anything in L.A. or New York. We were out kinda late—I was having too good a time."

Miles studied his face. Was he looking a little paler than usual? It was hard to tell with the makeup and the studio lighting. Or maybe he really had had a good time with that Evie person. Whom Adam hadn't bothered to mention the whole time he'd been with Miles, so Miles had figured she was really out of Adam's life. But while Miles couldn't tell if Adam was paler or tired-looking, he could see one thing, and that was the obvious affection in his smile when he talked about the girl.

"But no, Evie and I aren't back together. We were just hanging out. I think she's going back to L.A. today."

There was more, questions about the possibility of Adam getting into acting (Miles snorted; had they done any research on his history before Black Varen? Adam dealt with that one more gently and patiently than Miles would have), what inspired him (mostly generic stuff about friendship and political things), when he thought their next single would be out, and other inanities. All in all, Miles thought Adam did pretty well.

So why wasn't Miles happier about it? Adam had promised him he wouldn't put Miles into the spotlight, and he hadn't, and he'd blown off the questions about the Evie girl. But there was still that note of affection in his voice when he'd talked about her, and that made Miles wonder, a little.

A little more when he got a text about fifteen minutes after the interview was done: *Exhausted. Crashing for a bit. Be home this afternoon, kk?*

Okay, Miles texted back. He hesitated a minute, wanting to say more, but nothing came out, so he just put his phone away again, and went to see about some breakfast.

It was past one when Adam got back. Miles heard Grace start to bark, then stop when the screen door opened and Adam started talking to her. A wry smile tugged at Miles's lips—Adam had taken to Grace like gangbusters, and vice versa. Grace would miss Adam when he left.

His lips tightened as he turned back to the painting he was working on. Grace wasn't alone. But he needed to finish this part before the paint dried; he'd mixed the color specifically and wasn't sure he'd be able to match the shade if he made a fresh batch. Just a bit more . . .

He finished the section, rinsed his brush, then glanced up to see Adam, looking better than he had this morning on the show, leaning against the doorjamb with a grin on his face. The grin faded, though, and Adam said, "What's wrong?"

Nothing, Miles thought, and *Everything.* He tried to smile. "Good interview this morning. I watched." Mentally he kicked himself. Of course he'd watched. Adam was his guest. It would have been impolite not to.

But Adam was grinning again. "Was it? I'm so glad—they said it was, but I was *so* strung out—didn't get *any* sleep last night. My friend Evie was in town, and we went clubbing."

"You said."

"Oh, right. I did. Hell, I don't remember what I said. I was running on autodrive by that point. I didn't sound stupid? Bill said I didn't, but I pay him."

"No." Miles rinsed the brush again.

"So is something wrong? 'Cause I kind of get the impression that there is." He came in and crouched beside Miles's chair, putting a hand on Miles's thigh.

Miles stared down into the beautiful, patient face and thought, *I'm just reminded that you're only temporary. That you'll be gone in a few days, back to that life, back to* your *life, out of mine. Back to people like the interviewers and that Evie girl and the guys in your band. Back to where you belong. And you're going to forget about me, just the way you forgot about that Evie girl while you were here. You never mentioned her at all.* Aloud he said, "I lost the remote."

"You did?"

"But I found it. In the fridge." He rinsed the brush a third time, then set it down. "It was okay."

"Then that's good." Adam stood and put his hand on Miles's cheek. "You know," he said, a teasing note in his voice, "I could really use another nap. Want to join me?"

Miles met his golden, laughing eyes. "Of course," he said, and took Adam's hand.

hat time do you have to leave in the morning?" Miles asked.

Adam, already half-asleep, groaned. "Eleven. The flight's not 'til two, but I have to return the rental. I did the online check-in, but I have to build in time to get through security without blowing my cover. Once I'm through that, I can hang out in the VIP lounge, but security lines at O'Hare are for shit."

"Don't they recognize you? I mean, you have to give them your ID and everything."

Adam rolled over and grinned at him. "My ID says 'A. Craig Karoshewski,' and nobody thinks twice about it. As long as I don't get recognized."

"How do you manage that?"

"I'm an actor, Miles, first and foremost. Did you ever read *Double Star* by Robert Heinlein?"

"No."

"Put it on your list. It's science fiction, so you'll like it. It's a million years old and pretty dated, but the main character is a two-bit actor who's forced to play the president of the universe or something. We had to read it in one of my acting classes. He gives a pretty good description of how to use misdirection to avoid recognition. I use it all the time. When I'm in public or on stage as Adam Craig, I wear heeled boots to change the way I walk, I wear costumey clothing, sometimes makeup; I stand differently, more cocky and stiff. As Craig Karoshewski, I wear sneakers, ordinary clothes, those glasses, and stand kind of slouched. I channel the straights I know. I might get the 'do you know you kind of look like Adam Craig' comments, but only on rare occasions do I get fingered." He shot Miles another grin. "The guys in airport security don't even blink."

"What about your hair?"

"I wash it and towel dry it and don't use conditioner. It's a fuzzball. Adam Craig has these long, dramatic locks. Craig Karoshewski has ordinary long guy-hair."

Miles ran his fingers over the sleek dark strands. "I can't imagine these fuzzy."

"Wait 'til tomorrow morning." Adam stretched. "God, I'm going to miss sleeping with you."

"Just sleeping?" Miles asked.

"No, not just sleeping." Adam reached up and brushed Miles's cheek with his fingers. "Fucking. And talking. And watching old movies. And listening to Grace make weird comments. And swimming."

"You can't swim in November," Miles said. "The weather's for shit, then. Cold. And it usually snows Thanksgiving weekend."

Adam's smile faded. "You don't want me to come back?"

"No! Jesus, no. But if you can't . . . I get it." Miles lay back, staring at the ceiling.

"I'm coming back," Adam said quietly. "As long as you want me to. I won't forget."

Miles gave him a brief, humorless smile. "It's okay."

"No, it isn't. Miles, I want to come back. I like you—a lot. I want to see you again."

"Shhh." Miles shifted over him, kissing him hard. "Don't talk about it. I know. I like you too."

"Good, then that's settled."

"Shut up," Miles said.

"Can't help it. My older brother told me that's how he knew I was gay; I talked more than any other guy he knew. I don't think that's necessarily a trait of gay guys, but maybe of theater arts majors. I'm very verbal. Auditory, too—I do better hearing my lines than I do reading them. Ditto for lyrics. I'm an auditory learner." He grinned up at Miles, who was staring at him blankly. "I'd guess you're more of a visual learner."

"You really need to shut up now."

The grin grew larger. "Make me."

"Speechless?" Miles said.

"Yeah. Try." Adam chuckled. "Betcha can't."

Miles regarded him with a dark eye. Then he sat up and reached for the supplies on the nightstand. Adam watched with interest. "Sex is good," he said, "but I bet I can still talk through sex."

"You usually do," Miles said, then greased up his fingers. Instead of going for Adam, though, he reached behind himself.

Adam sat up, startled. "What the fuck . . . Miles?"

Miles gave him a wicked grin. Adam fell silent, watching Miles with his mouth open and nothing coming out. When Miles reached with his free hand for the condom and tossed it onto Adam's chest, Adam let out a long, wordless sigh before grabbing up the packet and tearing it open with his teeth, fumbling it on. Miles chuckled and straddled Adam, curling his fingers around Adam's cock. "Unngh," Adam said, and closed his eyes.

"Told you," Miles gritted out as he eased himself carefully down. "Speechless."

"Unngh," Adam agreed. He held himself still until Miles was all the way down, then reached up to rub the lines on Miles's face.

"I'm okay," Miles said. He raised himself on his knees, shifted position, and came down again, this time with a little gasp of arousal. "Fuck, that's good. I didn't know . . . It kind of hurts, but in a good way . . . I mean, I've read that it feels good, and you seem to like it, but fuck . . ."

"Unngh," Adam said.

"I've used a dildo," Miles admitted, raising himself up again, "but you feel different."

Adam reached up and stopped him. "Miles—shut up and fuck me, okay?"

Miles grinned and obliged.

The bathroom door opened and Adam came out, scrubbing his head with a towel. His hair wasn't quite a fuzzball, Miles thought, lying in bed and watching Adam, but it was certainly drier than usual and less sleek. It was still beautiful, though. Miles wasn't a portraitist by a long shot, but seeing Adam standing there in nothing but a towel made him wish he were.

"I didn't take pictures," he said.

Adam paused and glanced at him. "Did you want to?"

"Doug said to. He might have been joking, though."

"Probably. He strikes me as a leg-puller from way back." Adam pulled on a pair of dark-red Jockeys, then stepped into his jeans. Buttoning them up, he said, "We've got a couple of minutes before I hit the road, if you want to."

"Want to what?"

"Take pictures. Not of what I'm sure Doug meant for you to take pictures of, but if you want a picture . . . If you have a photo printer I could even autograph it for you." He grinned at Miles. "I'll sign it, 'To Miles, the best fuck I ever had. Love, Adam Craig.' Does that work for you?"

Is that all I am, a fuck? Miles thought, but only smiled thinly at Adam. "I fixed coffee. Did you want breakfast before you leave?"

"Nah, I'll get lunch at the airport. You doin' okay?"

"Yeah. A little sore, but not bad." He rolled over onto his stomach and rested his head on his hands. Staring at the headboard, he said, "The whole prostate thing—I can see that being good. And I suppose you get used to the stretching. Bobby likes it. And you do."

"But you're not crazy about it." Adam sat on the bed and rubbed a hand over Miles's bare shoulder. "It's cool, Miles. To each his own and all that. Nobody says you have to switch-hit, you know."

Miles shrugged. Adam said, "You're thinking it wasn't good enough for me again, aren't you? You gotta stop that and remember that with guys in general, any sex that ends with *someone* coming is good sex, and sex that ends with *everybody* coming is great sex."

"Then I guess it was great sex." Miles rolled over, grinning, and pulled Adam down into a kiss.

A few minutes later, Adam raised his head. "Well, so much for the couple of minutes we had. No pictures for you. I'll send you some promo shots for Doug and Bobby, okay? And you, of course—if you want one."

"Sure," Miles said. "Visual, remember?"

"I remember." Adam kissed him again. "I'll remember everything."

Miles followed Adam out to the gate in the Jeep and unlocked the gate so Adam could drive over the chain. Adam put the car in park and got out, walking around to where Miles stood relocking the chain. "See you in November?" he asked.

Miles nodded. He wanted to say something, but as usual, when he really needed to talk, nothing came out. So he just nodded again. Adam leaned forward and kissed him softly. "I'll email you when I get home. And you get to work on that calligy-thing, okay? 'Cause I really do want it."

Miles nodded. Adam kissed him again, then got back into the car and drove off, waving. Miles waved until Adam went around the corner and disappeared.

"Great," he muttered to himself. "Nothing like seeing the best thing ever drive off because you're too fucking messed up to go with him." Not that he really could go with him, anyway—he had too many commissions pending to just drop everything. But it would have been nice to think that maybe he could fly out and visit Adam sometime, see the studio where he worked, see where he lived, see *something* other than the lake and the woods that were his entire world. He stared down at the chain as if it were the chain holding him here instead of his own fucking madness, and gave it a shove to set it wildly swinging.

On the far swing, he stepped past the post that marked the edge of the property line and stood there until the chain thwapped him in the shins. There. He was off the property. And it wasn't so bad, was it? He started counting in his head, and thirty-three seconds later stepped back over the line, sweat beading on his forehead and his breath fast and harsh in his ears. "Fuck," he swore, kicking the post, then turned and walked back to the Jeep.

Chapter 15

To: miles@milescaldwelldesigns.com
From: aceydeucey@premierrecordings.com

Just got your email. In studio all day. We're really doing some good stuff. Haven't seen the guys this energized in a long time. Bill says the new material is doing it. Have you to thank for that. The design looks AWESOME. I like the Latin in the main part of the music staves—do you know Latin or do you have a translator? Or is it just made up? Looks cool. I can't believe you're so far along with it. Adam

To: aceydeucey@premierrecordings.com
From: miles@milescaldwelldesigns.com

It's the first verse and chorus. I know a Latin scholar who translates for me. It's not as far along as it might look; this is a colored-pencil draft so that I can work out color placement and tone. I haven't started the actual piece yet; I work out the details ahead of time and use this cartoon for reference. M.

To: miles@milescaldwelldesigns.com
From: aceydeucey@premierrecordings.com

Funny you calling that a cartoon. Makes me think of Bugs Bunny.

To: aceydeucey@premierrecordings.com
From: miles@milescaldwelldesigns.com

That's what it's called.

To: miles@milescaldwelldesigns.com
From: aceydeucey@premierrecordings.com

I get that. It's still funny. What's the bottom part where the words to the song are going to go called?

To: aceydeucey@premierrecordings.com
From: miles@milescaldwelldesigns.com

"The bottom part where the words are going to go."

To: miles@milescaldwelldesigns.com
From: aceydeucey@premierrecordings.com

Smartass.

To: aceydeucey@premierrecordings.com
From: miles@milescaldwelldesigns.com

It's not just my ass that's smart.

To: miles@milescaldwelldesigns.com
From: aceydeucey@premierrecordings.com

No, but it's one of my favorite parts.

Adam hit send, grinning. He could almost see Miles reading that and flushing in embarrassment. He waited a minute, but there wasn't a response. Not a surprise; he'd figured out that when he made a joke like that, Miles wasn't quick to answer. But he didn't think Miles was mad; he was just being Miles.

He missed him. It had been three days since he'd come home, and the first two had been filled with work, to the point where he'd come home to his condo every night and fallen into bed.

Today hadn't been that grueling; for one thing, it was Saturday, and Eddie and Neil had been hungover this morning and late to arrive. Chuck had been there, but focused more on his date tonight than the music he was learning. So they'd just gone over what they'd already practiced, and laid down a few vocal tracks, then left early, about 4:30.

Adam had done some grocery shopping to fill the fridge that had been empty during his absence on the tour, and now had an entire evening to fill. He checked his other emails to see if anyone had anything going on, but one of the problems with touring was that people tended to forget when he was home. He sighed and shook his head. Maybe a movie . . . But that made him think of Miles, and lying together in Miles's big bed, watching DVDs, and arguing about things like alternate endings to *Casablanca* and which was the best screwball comedy of all time (Miles insisted it was *Bringing Up Baby*, while Adam was firmly in the *My Man Godfrey* camp). And eating popcorn at two a.m. and weird bacon and questionable eggs for breakfast and sometimes supper . . . It was hard. He missed Miles, missed him like his absence was a hole in his heart.

Nothing felt right, sounded right, tasted right. When he heard a joke or someone said something particularly stupid, he found himself looking beside him for Miles, to share the joke with him. But Miles wasn't there.

Wouldn't be there. Ever. Even if Adam could go back to Indian Lake, they could only be together there. And Adam's life was here.

Even if his heart was at the lake.

Miles hadn't quite known how to respond to Adam's last email, so he did what he usually did—ignored it. At least while he worked on transferring the design from the cartoon. And then he'd gotten absorbed in doing the inking of the calligraphy on the actual piece. He'd chosen the finest lamb vellum he could get; it was soft as tissue paper and required an especially light hand, as well as absolute concentration, to avoid damaging the surface.

That had taken him most of the rest of the day, and then while his premade gesso buttons were soaking in preparation for the gilding, he finished scraping the verdigris off the copper plate and tossed out the ammonia and washed the pan. By the time he finished that, the gesso was ready to use, and he started painting the first layer on the spots where the gold would go.

When he drifted out of his art fugue, Grace was sitting on the edge of his slant board, her head tucked under her wing. "What time is it?" he asked her. She didn't respond, so he knew she was really sleeping and not just dozing. Late, then. It had been dark for hours, so that was no clue, and he couldn't find the clock again, and his watch was—somewhere.

He put his hand up and nudged Grace's feet gently; without taking her head from beneath her wing, she stepped onto his hand, and stayed immobile while he carried her into the kitchen to her cage. She roused momentarily when he opened the cage door, long enough to hop onto her perch inside, but then went back to sleep. Miles checked to make sure she had enough water, then tossed the cover over the cage.

When that was done, he went to bed; there was nothing else he could do on the piece until the gesso set, anyway. He'd have to remember to respond to Adam's email in the morning.

He dreamed about Adam that night. It was one of those horrible nightmares where he wasn't sure if he was remembering the crash or his subconscious was just filling in arbitrary details, but he was driving, and Adam was sitting in the passenger seat. He wasn't watching his driving, he was looking at Adam. Beyond Adam, out the car window, the landscape was changing from fields to woods to cityscapes, and the cities were Moscow and London and Venice and a dozen others he recognized from movies and travel magazines. Adam was talking, as usual, but Miles couldn't understand him, and as Miles leaned closer to hear him, he saw beyond, outside the window, the front grill of an enormous, outsized Kenworth semi, headed right for them. He tried to scream, to draw Adam's attention to it, but Adam just gazed out the windshield, his mouth moving and nothing coming out.

And then they were spinning around, upside down, right side up, horizontally like a top, just spinning and spinning until everything exploded apart into a maelstrom of sparks like fireworks. Miles screamed Adam's name, but Adam was gone.

He sat up, sweat pouring down his body and tears pouring down his face and his heart pounding like a kettledrum. "Fuck," he breathed, and put his head in his hands.

It took him a while to get back to sleep, but eventually he did, and woke sometime midmorning to Grace talking to herself under the cage cover. After he'd fed her, he sat down at his computer and opened his email account. There were a couple of new emails, but none from Adam.

There was, however, a Google Alert for "Adam Craig"; he'd set it up the evening Adam had left, though he wasn't quite sure why. When he opened the email, there were half a dozen links to articles which, as far as Miles could see, were about his erstwhile lover and the woman named Evie. The one that caught his eye, though, was the headline: "Adam and Evie, Together Again—Is Third Time the Charm?" He clicked on it without thinking.

A page from an entertainment blog came up on his monitor, a large photograph of Adam with the Evie woman at some party or other. The background was dark and the people behind them pale blurry blobs, but Adam and his date, as tall as Adam in her stilettos, were clear in the foreground. He had his arms linked around her hips, she had hers draped around his neck, and they were laughing at each other affectionately. The story under the headline read, "On-again off-again romance is on again, apparently, as supermodel and actress

Evangeline Montcalm showed up at Club 51 with former fiancé and stud rocker Adam Craig in tow—"

"Rocker." Miles snorted at the memory of Adam's disdain for the term.

"Fresh on the heels of her breakup with coal magnate Thierry Fortier, Our Miss Evie seems to have landed back in the arms of her One True Love. The pair spent the whole evening in each other's pocket, dining, dancing, and drinking at Club 51 before heading out together. Later that evening, they were discovered in the bar at the Four Seasons Hotel, tête-à-tête in the corner. Has love blossomed again for the Dynamic Duo?"

Miles stopped reading at that point. The photo was too distracting. He supposed the woman was what passed for beautiful in Hollywood—too tall, too skinny, and too blonde—but it was the expression on both her and Adam's faces that was the most damning. They looked . . . delighted. Adam's expression, in fact, was exactly the same as the one he wore when he looked at Miles.

He clicked the "x" to close the link, feeling sick. It was bullshit, then, wasn't it? Adam had been gone less than a week and he'd already hooked up with his former girlfriend. No—former fiancée. Which meant that at some point in the past, Adam had had a current fiancée. Which he'd carefully managed to leave out of his conversation with Miles about the girl. What had he said? Something about him occasionally having sex with women just to keep his cover? A "fiancée" seemed like a whole lot of sex with a woman. Adam had acted like it had never been like that with the Evie girl, or anyone, for that matter, but if they'd actually been engaged, wouldn't he have *had* to?

So if that was bullshit, what else was bullshit? Did Adam even *want* the calligraphy piece? He seemed really enthusiastic about it—but then he'd seemed really certain when he said he didn't like fucking women. He'd acted so into Miles—but then he *said* he'd majored in theater. Maybe he'd been acting all along. Maybe he was just an opportunist. Maybe he was one of those people who could figure out a person's buttons on first meeting them, like a con artist could. He sure as shit knew what buttons to push with Miles. Miles had thought it was just them finding so much in common. But then again, Miles didn't know jack shit about other people. Hell, he even still misunderstood Doug and Bobby, and he'd known them for years. How could he begin to understand someone like Adam, who was so extroverted, so clever, so . . . perfect.

He walked outside to sit on the patio. The flagstones were cold on his bare feet, despite the warm breeze. *He* felt cold, but from the inside, as if he were coming down with something. Yeah, something, like blatant stupidity. But being with Adam hadn't seemed stupid—it had felt warm and right and amazing. Was he that fucked up that he'd mistaken opportunism for enthusiasm? Had Adam's interest in Miles just been an act? He'd said he didn't get fucked very often anymore. Had he just been using Miles to get an itch scratched? Miles sucked in a breath and tried to calm himself down. Maybe Adam wasn't an opportunist, just a nice guy. A nice guy who liked to fuck. Was that all he'd been interested in? Miles's head spun. He didn't know what to think. He didn't know what to feel. All he knew was that Adam was gone, he was alone, and probably always would be.

This was stupid. *He* was stupid. Mooning over a chance-met stranger was stupid. The only thing between him and Adam was the piece he was working on. He needed to separate the art from the emotion. He needed to get over this, get back to work, to the one thing he'd always been sure of. The art. The sooner he finished the commission, the sooner he could get back to his regularly scheduled life and forget all about Adam Craig of "Adam and Evie" fame.

And he wanted that. God, he wanted that. Forgetting wasn't something he ever wanted, but right now? He'd take it.

Doug had warned him. He'd been stupid not to listen.

Chapter 16

nd I thought after that, I'd buy a truckload of dry ice and dump it in the lake to make it a year-round ice-skating rink."

"Uh-huh," Miles said, then, "What?"

"You haven't heard a word I said, have you. Miles, we need to make a decision about the resort. We can't neglect it like this—"

"We aren't neglecting it. We're doing the renovations you wanted—"

"No, we're doing the renovations *you* wanted. *I* want to renovate the whole resort, not just the, the infrastructure."

Miles snorted. "'Infrastructure'? It's the septic system. You make it sound like the Loop Deep Tunnel project."

"Exactly my point! It's hardly renovations. It's basic maintenance. This building needs work, and if we're going to fix it up, we need to do a real job of it, not the piddly little penny-ante shit we've been doing all these years. We can't afford *not* to renovate."

"The trust . . ." Miles's throat had gotten oddly tight.

"The trust is fine, but some of our other investments got hit really hard by the recession, honey." She must have noticed his discomfort, because her voice got soft and gentle. "We can afford the renovations I want if we work fast, but what we can't afford is to let the resort get any more run-down. If it keeps on the way it's been going, in a year or two it'll be in the kind of shape that really will cost us a fortune to fix." She reached across the table and put her hand on Miles's wrist. "We fix things now, while they're fixable, or we'll have to look at selling down the road. I know you don't want that."

Miles stared at her, his head pounding. Sell the resort? Sell his home out from underneath him? Maybe he could stay on—God knew he couldn't *leave* . . . but he knew better. Knew that this property was extraordinarily valuable—their taxes were high enough—and that any buyer would want to build more than just a dinky resort. They would want income property, property they could parcel off and sell to rich suburbanites. He thought about living surrounded by McMansions, with motorboats and Ski-Doos on the lake all summer, and felt sick. "It can't last," he said numbly.

Lisa, as usual, seemed to know what he meant. "No, it can't last forever, honey. Things change. But we don't have to sell just yet, and there are ways to work around it."

"The resort."

"We could reopen the resort, yeah." She rubbed her fingers over the back of his hand. "Or we could put some real money into it, and turn it into an event site. We're close enough to the city to make that workable, and far enough away that people will feel that they're getting a break."

"Event site—what is that?"

"For events, you know. Weddings. Corporate shindigs. High-end events. With the right modernization and marketing, we could charge good money for them, and have a tight control on the frequency. The real estate market still sucks, but the corporate event market is starting to pick up again." She leaned forward, her eyes excited. "Weekends only, Miles. You'd still have all week to recuperate. This place is so beautiful, and it's been *dead*. It needs to live again."

Miles regarded her animated face, then around himself, trying to see the place through her eyes. It *was* beautiful; the dining room they sat in overlooked the lake, and the honey pine of the wall panels was ornamented with graceful, sinuous leaf carvings that echoed the outdoors. According to Lisa, the room could easily hold seventy-five people, the patio beyond another hundred, and the pocket doors at one end could open to the resort's great room opposite. He could see upwards of two hundred people milling through these rooms, with waiters moving among them, trays of champagne flutes in hand. There would be flowers on the round tables that right now were stacked against the wall, and music.

Just on the weekends. The weeks would be quiet, and peaceful. But the resort wouldn't be this haunted place anymore, populated only by ghosts Miles didn't recognize. "I guess it would work," he said slowly. "I guess you're right . . ."

"I am right," she said with a grin.

"What do we do?"

"I need to talk to a couple of contractors, and maybe an architect," she said happily. "We can probably start a lot of the inside work over the winter, when there isn't such a demand for builders. There's a renovator I worked with on a trust case; I'll see if he's willing to give me an estimate." She went on talking about costs, and estimates, and timeframes, and Miles sat and watched the autumn sun glinting off the lake.

To: miles@milescaldwelldesigns.com
From: aceydeucey@premierrecordings.com

Hey, M. Long time no hear from. How's the calligy-thing going?

To: aceydeucey@premierrecordings.com
From: miles@milescaldwelldesigns.com

Fine.

To: miles@milescaldwelldesigns.com
From: aceydeucey@premierrecordings.com

Busy? It's been kind of crazy here. Days just fly by. Looking forward to seeing it when it's done.

To: miles@milescaldwelldesigns.com
From: aceydeucey@premierrecordings.com

Miles? You there?

To: miles@milescaldwelldesigns.com
From: aceydeucey@premierrecordings.com

Miles?

Adam waited a while, staring at the monitor and willing a response. He'd sent the comment about how busy he was yesterday afternoon, and the first follow-up this morning. Now it was nine at night, and he was supposed to pick up Evie to go to the after-party for some movie premiere or another. And if it was nine here, it was eleven in the Midwest, so maybe Miles had gone to bed or something. Or was wrapped up in his art, in his usual inimitable fashion. Still, before, he'd managed to get back to him. More than just the curt "Fine" he'd gotten earlier.

Curt. Was it curt? Or was it just Miles? Was Adam stupid for reading anything more into it? Miles's social ineptness translated to his emails as well, and it was probably dumb to think that it was anything but that. Just because it had been nearly three days since Miles had sent the last update, and he'd been sending them daily. Which was why Adam had sent the first email to begin with. He rubbed his forehead. Damn it—he didn't want to deal with a headache when he had a long evening ahead of him.

There was a knock on the door, and Adam closed the lid of his laptop before getting up to answer it. Evie stood in the hall, barefoot, with her Jimmy Choos hanging from her fingers. "Hey, I was ready early and thought it was stupid to wait for you to come get me. I mean, I live a floor away from you. You look pretty."

"Thanks." Adam leaned forward to kiss her cheek. "Armani. Is this thing gonna be as big a drag as I think it is?"

"Aren't they usually? Be of good cheer, though, loverboy. There's another party I think you'll like better at Scorpio. We just need to make the rounds at the movie thing and then we'll head over there. The studio sent a limo for the evening so we don't even have to worry about a cab."

"Great," Adam said.

"You okay? You seem sort of distracted."

"Yeah. Hang on just a minute, okay? I need to text someone." He picked up the phone that was lying on the coffee table and pulled up Miles's number, texting, *Strtg to worry—u ok?*

A second later the phone buzzed. *Fn. Bsy. Y?*

Jst chkg. TTYL.

K

Adam breathed a sigh of relief.

Evie said, "So is he okay?"

"Yeah ... What?"

"Whoever you texted. You were distracted—worried? And now you're not. I figured it was the guy you met while you were in Chicago."

"How did you know I met a guy in Chicago?"

She shrugged. "I don't know. Maybe because you haven't checked out a single guy's ass once on any of our dates? Maybe because every once in a while you get this dopey smile on your face like you're thinking of something sweet? Maybe because I think you're in luuuuuuve?"

"You're mental," Adam said automatically, then blinked.

Was he? That was just crazy talk, wasn't it? After all, he hadn't thought of Miles more than a couple times a day, and okay, maybe he did tend to smile a bit thinking of him, because he *liked* Miles, and there weren't a lot of people who he liked. Not *liked* liked, like Miles. But he had been worried about him when he hadn't heard from him; they'd emailed practically every day. Okay, usually a couple of times a day. And he hadn't really noticed any other guy—it wasn't like he was some horndog out for a pickup every single moment of the day.

Except that before he went to Chicago, he kind of had been. He hadn't acted on it, of course—couldn't pick up anyone, not and stay so firmly closeted—but he'd looked. However, in the three weeks since he'd met Miles, he'd kind of lost his interest in ass. Strike that—he'd stop being interested in ass the day he died. But he was more interested in Miles.

He rubbed his forehead. "Shit," he muttered.

Evie patted his shoulder. "It's okay, honey. You'll get over it—I always do. Come on, the limo's waiting."

The party was okay, and a couple of producers made noises like they'd be interested in having Adam read for a couple of guest parts on some TV shows, which he wouldn't mind, and one actually was talking about a movie role, which he would love. But at these things it was mostly all talk, so Adam gave them Bill's card and told them to follow up with him, and immediately forgot the producers' names. The headache was starting to come on gangbusters by the time they'd been there two hours, so when Evie suggested heading over to Scorpio, he said he thought he might go home instead.

"No, you can't! I can't go to Scorpio alone, not after Thierry. He'll probably be there, and he'll get all smug and pompous and vile." Evie slid her arm up his and leaned into him. "Come on, honey. Just for a little while?"

"Only if there's aspirin in the car," Adam said.

She smiled wickedly. "I've got something much better than aspirin," she purred. "Come on."

In the car, she opened the tiny bag she carried and pulled out a couple of bright green tablets. "E?" His brows went up. "Evie—I didn't know you cared."

She laughed and handed him the bottle of champagne she'd liberated from the party they'd just left. "There are flutes in the arm there." She indicated the side of the limo, and he pulled them out and handed them to her while he wrangled the champagne.

"I'm gonna be so fucked up in the morning," he said with a sigh, "but this is the only way I'm gonna get through another night with you, party girl."

"Damn straight, loverboy." They clinked glasses and downed the Ecstasy in tandem, the way they always had, and leaned back against the soft leather seats as their driver took them on to the next party.

And the next.

And the next.

By the time Adam woke up in his condo the next day, he couldn't remember how many parties he and Evie had hit, or how many drinks, or who he'd flirted with—but it didn't matter, because chances were no one else did, either. He'd been pleasantly buzzed when he'd gotten home somewhere around four in the morning; the E had worn off hours before that, but by then he'd been fried by the champagne from the limo, and the martinis and dancing at Scorpio, and the gin and tonics—and dancing—at Nexus, and some other shit they were passing out at L'Exchange which he didn't remember ever hearing about before but it had sounded good . . . He lay on his back, staring up at the ceiling and wondering why his head felt like it belonged to a stranger.

Something moved beside him, but he was too numb to react other than to glance over at his bed partner. Evie. Thank God. She raised her head, her hair hanging in her bloodshot, bleary eyes, said, "Unngh?" to him, and dropped her head back down on the pillow.

"Told you," he rasped, his voice sounding like seventeen-year locusts. "Fucked up."

"Unngh." This one was muffled by the pillow. "Ntimezit?"

"What?"

"What. Time. Is. It?"

"Oh." Adam essayed a raising of his thirty-pound head and fumbled for his cell phone. "Eleven twenty-eight."

"Oh, *fuck*," Evie said, sitting straight up.

Adam sat up, too, realizing he was supposed to have been at the studio an hour ago. He echoed, "Oh, fuck. I'm late!"

"Me too!"

They stared blankly at each other. Adam said, "I hope you mean that in the 'I'm late for an appointment' sense and not the 'I might be pregnant' sense."

"Don't be an idiot." She ran her hands through her tangled blonde mane. It didn't help. "I'm supposed to be having lunch with David Edelstein about a part in some TV pilot—at *noon*!"

"Where's your phone?"

"In my bag . . . Where the hell is my bag?"

They found it in the living room on the coffee table, between the beer bottles. Evie stared at them a moment. "Did we drink all of this?"

"I guess so," Adam said.

"No wonder I feel like hell. Beer always makes me sick."

Adam snorted. "And popping every bit of shit someone gave you last night didn't?"

"Shut up." She sank down on his couch and put her head in her hands.

"Darling Evie." Adam took the miniscule purse from her hands, extracting the cell phone. "Did you forget the cardinal rule of success?"

"'Don't be late for lunch with powerful Hollywood producers'?"

"'Fake it 'til you make it.'" He scrolled through the list of contacts. "Edelstein?"

She nodded and watched him while he waited for the call to go through.

Adam tossed his head back, put a hand on his hip, and said into the phone, "Hello? Is this Mr. Edelstein's secretary?" He made his voice high and breathless. "This is Evangeline Montcalm's *personal* assistant. Ms. Montcalm is *terribly* sorry, but she's still *tied up* in a meeting with another *producer*—oh, no, I'm sorry, she *specifically* told me not to tell *anyone*—yes, I'm *terribly* sorry. Would it be possible for Mr. Edelstein to *forgive* her and perhaps meet at one? I know it's a *terrible* inconvenience, but Ms. Montcalm would be *ever* so grateful . . ." He covered the phone with his hand and said in his normal voice, "You may have to sleep with him to get out of this one, sweetie." Then back to the phone, "Of *course* I'll hold. It's my *life*, darling, waiting on hold!" He tittered effeminately.

Evie rolled her eyes, and he stuck his tongue out at her.

"Oh, *thank* you, darling! I was so *worried*. You know how she gets! Well, all right, perhaps you don't, but *trust* me, you don't want to!"

Evie's eyebrows were somewhere up under her bangs and she was making mean faces at him. He stifled a chuckle.

"Thank you, darling. I'll let her know. Ta!" He closed the phone and tossed it to her. "You owe me."

"Owe you? You practically pimped me out to a guy old enough to be my grandfather!"

"But you'll still get the lunch and probably the part," Adam said reasonably.

"That's not the only part I'll probably get," she grumbled.

"I'll make you some coffee before you go home. At least you don't have to go far."

"No, thank God. I was so right to buy in this building. And I will love you forever if you make me coffee while I try to clean up a little."

"Don't kiss me—you probably have morning breath."

"Bitch. Why do I waste my time with you? You won't even fuck me."

"Because you love me."

"True."

"Look at it this way," Adam said, "if anyone sees you leaving my place at this hour wearing the same shit you had on last night, it can only be good for both our reps, right?"

"Yeah, yeah, yeah."

"So it doesn't matter if I fucked you or not. Everyone will think I did."

"What about the boyfriend?"

He froze. "Boyfriend?" No. Miles wouldn't see. Miles didn't watch TV or read newspapers or magazines. Let alone surf the internet . . . did he? He tried to remember. He had a website, but did he surf . . . no. No. He hadn't even known who Adam was, or who Black Varen was. "He won't know. He doesn't follow any of the gossip sites. And even if he did, he wouldn't believe it." But even as he said it, he wondered. Miles was so . . . different. He wasn't sure if he really understood his thought processes. Would it bother Miles? "Besides, he's not my boyfriend. He's just Miles. And he . . . well, he's not my boyfriend."

Why *would* it bother Miles? It wasn't like the guy had asked for his hand in marriage or anything ridiculous like that.

She snorted. "Ever since Chicago, it's been 'Miles' this and 'Miles' that. Last night you were especially bad. Adam honey, you have got it bad for him."

"Shit. Did anyone hear?" He didn't remember. What had he said?

She patted his shoulder. "Don't worry. You were just raving about 'this artist I met.' Going on and on about what a genius artist he is and something about gold and crap like that. After about five minutes people's eyes were glazing over." She patted him again. "Now go make me some coffee, loverboy, while I brush my teeth and try to look presentable."

he UPS truck was just pulling up to the gate when Miles arrived in the Jeep. He waved at the guy in the brown shorts—what was his name again? He was newer; Miles's old UPS guy had retired about six months ago. Bill? Phil? Something like that—and went around to the back of the Jeep to pull out the crate. Bill or Phil backed the brown truck up to the chain, hopped out, and climbed over the chain to help Miles wrestle the crate over to the truck. "Big sucker," Phil—the name was on his shirt—said. "Goin' where?"

"L.A.," Miles replied absently.

"You ship all over the place, doncha? Art, right? You paint or something?"

"Yeah. Paint." It was close enough.

"One of the guys used to carry for a big gallery downtown." Phil lifted the crate into the truck, settling it so that it wouldn't shift in transit. "He used to talk about some huge shit he had to haul around. Yours are pretty small, compared to that."

"Yeah."

"Hard to make a living at art, I heard."

"You heard right." Miles took the electronic thing UPS used nowadays and signed his name with the stylus, then handed it back. "Gets harder every day."

"I hear you." Phil closed the truck and secured the door. "Thanks. See ya, Mr. Caldwell."

Miles waved vaguely and watched as Phil climbed back into the truck and drove away, with Adam's music in the back. He'd finished it nearly a week ago, but had dragged his feet about framing and shipping it, even though it had been ready for that for days. Some of it was the usual reluctance to admit that he was done—he almost never felt like a piece was done, really. But some of it was the sneaking suspicion that once he'd finished, once he'd shipped the thing, there wouldn't be any more connection between him and Adam. *They* would be done.

He shook his head. Who was he fooling? There had never been a "they."

But the piece was beautiful, one of Miles's best yet. He'd incorporated several different styles into the design, but kept it mostly late fourteenth century Italian, with an inhabited initial that showed the girl of Adam's song staring into a mirror while the boy looked on, helpless and ignored. He'd used his smallest brush, a 30/0 sable, to paint the faces. He wasn't a portraitist by any stretch of the imagination, but the boy had Adam's face. Miles had taken extreme close-up photographs of the details for his portfolio, as he always did, and had spent a long time last night staring at the one of the initial.

It was done. That was all there was to it—it was done. Miles got back into the Jeep and drove slowly back to the cottage.

Grace was sitting on her perch when he came into the kitchen; he held out his arm absently to let her climb onto it and carried her into the living room. The day had gone gray and soft, and although he usually didn't mind the mistier days that sometimes hit before Indian summer, today it bothered him. He didn't like to think that the summer was gone completely, that soon it would be winter and he'd be even more isolated than usual. He made a mental note to call the service that kept the drive plowed to make sure they had him on their roster for this year, and to call the furnace people while he was at it. Lisa was working on the contractors, but didn't expect them to start until after the holidays. If Adam came at Thanksgiving . . .

Gah. He set Grace on the drawing board before dropping onto the sofa. What was he thinking? Adam wasn't coming for Thanksgiving. Even though he still texted or emailed Miles at least a couple of times a week, there was nothing in them to speak of anything other than casual friendship. And that was okay, wasn't it? He didn't want anything more from Adam than that. Dear God, he didn't, did he?

Work. He needed work. He had a couple more commissions after Adam's, but they weren't due for months yet; he needed to study the requests and research the proper style for them, but he didn't want to do that now. Besides, he wasn't ready to shift gears into a new calligraphy project. He usually wasn't after finishing a commission; he'd leaped right into Adam's after the last one because he'd been so excited about it. But that only meant he was even more burnt out than usual now. He needed something that would distract him, but something removed from his usual work. Running, his fallback occupation, was out—the rain of the last few days and the fallen leaves meant the trails would be slippery and dangerous. Maybe sorting out his stock of supplies?

He was pretty organized, at least with his art supplies, but there was a box shoved away under the shelving unit that held stuff he'd needed to go through. He wasn't even sure what was in there—it had been underneath the bookshelf since he'd moved in. That would keep him busy for a while, and get his mind off the strange sense of loss he was feeling.

The box was jammed under the shelves, the flaps only folded over the overflowing contents, so that they caught on the underside of the shelf. It took him a minute to work the box out; he set it on the floor and flipped back the flaps. Paint-stained boxes of pastels, oil paints, acrylics, watercolors; dried bottles of turpentine and linseed oil; worn-out paintbrushes, their bristles stiff with paint; palettes of dried colors, one with a palette knife still stuck to it; all were piled on a stack of large pads of newsprint, cold-press watercolor paper, and stretched but unprepared canvases. A life of painting in that box, and all of it unfamiliar to Miles. He sat back on his heels and regarded the detritus, feeling even more lost than he had before.

Picking through the stack of boxes, he found a couple of unopened packages of charcoal and charcoal pencils and set them aside. Some of the oil paints were still good—he could feel the contents squishing inside—but the acrylics and watercolors were solid rock. He began to methodically sort through the stuff, sorting the total losses from the salvageable.

The latter pile ended up being pretty small: the charcoal pencils, a few tubes of oil paint, a small bottle of linseed oil, a handful of unused brushes. The newsprint was mostly still good, though turning brown at the edges; he spent a few minutes flipping through the first few pages and looking at the rough sketches there. They were good, interesting, but not his style. It took a moment for him to realize that he'd done them, a long time ago. At least the guy he'd been then had done them. His first instinct was to pull out the pages and throw them away, but he resisted the urge, and just set the pad on the "keep" pile. The stretched canvases, too. He wasn't sure what he was going to do with them, but it wouldn't take much to get them gessoed and ready to use.

The rest of the stuff he hauled out to the garbage, and when he came back in, he stared at the pile of kept stuff a long time before picking up the newsprint pad and the box of charcoal.

"Adam. Hey, Adam!"

"What?" Adam put down the electric guitar he was messing with and looked up at Eddie, who'd gone to the front of the studio building to get a Coke. He was holding the Coke, but his attention was all on Adam. "What?"

"Got a package. A big sucker."

"Not as big as mine." Neil grabbed his crotch. Chuck laughed. Eddie just rolled his eyes.

"Seriously, dude. It's huge. The UPS guy just dropped it off."

Package? Shit! "Miles," he gasped, and headed for the door. Eddie stepped out of his way and followed him down the corridor.

The box was in the reception area, leaning up against the orange plastic guest chairs bolted to the wall. It was about three feet tall and two wide, and a good eight inches deep. Adam grabbed it and looked at the shipping label. Yep, it was from Miles—he'd had him send the package to the studio rather than his condo since he was usually here during the day. His heart pounded. His painting. It was his goddamned painting. "You got scissors?" he asked Jan, the receptionist, his voice rasping.

"Box cutter," she said. "Possibly crowbar—that corner where it's torn, it looks like a wood crate underneath the paper. Scissors ain't gonna cut it, if you'll pardon the expression." She came around the desk and handed him a box cutter. He sliced carefully through the heavy brown paper.

There was a wooden box underneath; not a crate, its surface was smooth and finished in a light maple. A heavy hasp decorated one side, the kind that you turned to line up the pegs to open. Adam turned the hasp and opened the box. "Oh," he said softly.

"Holy shit," Eddie said. "What fucking museum did you rob?"

"Oh my God." That was Jan. "Adam, that thing is gorgeous! Where did you get it?"

Adam didn't answer. He couldn't. Instead, he ran his finger lightly over the silky mahogany of the frame, feeling the rise of the simple shell pattern carved into the side and staring at the beautiful, beautiful page beneath the glass and triple mat. The paper—parchment, Adam remembered—was a creamy ivory, the lettering stark black amid the brightly colored vines and leaves. The musical notation of the first verse and chorus was black squares, in a kind of old-fashioned style, rather than the round notes Adam was used to seeing, and the Latin words beneath were in blocky Gothic script. Beneath that, in smaller red Gothic letters, lighter and more airy, were the English words of the song.

He wasn't sure what the heavily decorated first letter of the Latin text was supposed to be, but it was round and had tiny people painted inside it. Adam bent to look closer, and saw a minuscule woman sitting at a vanity, her attention on her reflection, and behind that, deeper in the mirror, a fainter reflection of a man watching her, his expression lost and longing. "He looks like you," Jan breathed over his shoulder. Beneath that little vignette was a man sitting at a slant-top desk, writing; he had the same face. An abandoned guitar lay at his feet; it couldn't have been more than a half an inch long, but Adam could count the individual frets on the neck, exactly the same number as on a standard guitar.

The whole thing was done in blues and greens with splashes of crimson and purple. And gold. Gold that caught even the crappy fluorescent light in the reception area and turned it into magic. It glowed, and in its glitter, set the vivid colors in the piece glowing, too. "Illumination," Adam said softly, reverently. "My God, Miles."

"Who's Miles? The only Miles I know is Miles Davis."

Adam replied to Eddie without looking up. "Guy I met in Chicago, when I went walkabout. Artist. His stuff is beautiful. I ordered this . . . but I sure as shit didn't think it would end up looking like this."

"Musta cost you a fortune," Eddie said.

Adam blinked, then reached for the paper. "Was there a packing slip? An invoice? Did you see anything?" he asked Jan. She shook her head.

"Maybe in the box," Eddie suggested.

Carefully lifting the frame out of the box, Adam looked beneath it. The box was lined in fabric, but there was no invoice there, either, and the back of the frame was covered with kraft paper. "No," he said. "I guess Miles'll be emailing me with the cost. But man—I don't care what it costs. I'd pay a million bucks for this."

"Good thing you got a million bucks," Eddie observed.

Adam ignored him, lost in the painting.

"So what do you think?" Adam asked.

Evie stared at the piece, hanging over the side table in the place that once held the mirror. "Wow. Just . . . wow. He's incredible, Adam."

"Yeah." He was wearing a stupid, proud smile, he knew it; could feel it curling his lips as if he were the one who'd painted the page. "It like takes over the whole room, in a good way. I think I need to redecorate."

"No," she said. "I think the room is fine just the way it is—your furniture's sort of minimalist and the frame is, too, so the focus is on the content, on the actual art. But it's in the wrong place. It should be over there, by the chair, where it can be seen from any spot in the room. Get rid of that hideous oil painting"—she pointed at the abstract that had come with the condo that Adam had been meaning to dump but hadn't yet—"and move this there. Put the mirror back here where it's useful."

Adam had forgotten that Evie not only was a model, she also had a minor in art and knew about stuff like that. She sounded really smart and confident talking like that; if she ever decided to dump the entertainment world, she could probably make a decent living as a decorator or something. Studying the wall she pointed to, Adam nodded. "Yeah, you're right. That painting's too big for that wall,

anyway, and I always hated it. I'll need help to take it down, though—
the mirror was easy, so I could move that myself. That's why I put this
here."

She kicked off her Louboutins. "Come on, let's move it. Dorian
knows a gallery owner that sells crap like that painting, so you can get
rid of it."

"Wait a minute." Adam pulled out his phone and checked for
messages. Nothing. He punched in Miles's number and left another
message for him. "I don't know where Miles is, and he didn't include
the invoice. He's probably working on another project; he doesn't
always answer his phone."

"You sound worried."

"I am, kinda. He usually answers back within at least a day or so,
and it's been two days." Adam chewed his lip.

"Well, this isn't the first time you've had to wait for him."

"No, that's true. I guess I could call his sister, if I had her number.
Which I don't."

"Didn't you say she's a lawyer?"

"Uh-huh."

"Duh. Google her, moron. But move the painting first, while I've
got my shoes off."

The phone rang once, twice, then: "Lisa Caldwell." Her voice was
brisk and professional.

Adam, expecting voice mail or a receptionist or something,
stuttered, "Um, Lisa? This is Adam Craig... Karoshewski?"

"I know who you are." This time the voice was amused. "How are
you, Adam?"

"Good, good. Listen, is Miles okay?"

She hesitated, then asked, "Is there a reason why he shouldn't be?"

"God, I hope not. No. I've just been leaving messages for him for
a couple of days, and he isn't answering my texts or my emails, either.
He's usually pretty good at getting back to me after a day or so, but
it's been ... shit, it's been since Friday, and while most people do go
out over the weekends, Miles kind of doesn't, does he, and I was just

getting kind of worried . . . He sent the calligraphy I'd commissioned, but he didn't include an invoice, and I didn't know how much to send or anything—"

"Adam."

He stopped.

"I talked to him Thursday, and he was fine. He said he was working on a new project. That's probably what it is—you know how involved he gets."

"Yeah, that's what I figured." Adam sighed in relief. "I did want to talk to him, though I guess if he's not in a hurry for the payment, I can give it to him when I come out after Thanksgiving."

"You're coming out at Thanksgiving?"

"Well, not the day of, but that weekend, yeah. I was planning to, anyway. Didn't Miles say anything about it?"

"No, he didn't. That's strange."

Adam was . . . hurt. Disappointed. Though, knowing Miles, he probably just forgot to tell Lisa. But if he'd forgotten about Adam—well, that hurt. "Well, it's still a month off. I don't even have my plane ticket yet."

"I'll check with Miles and make sure he gets back to you. It'll be in the next day or so for sure—I've got a meeting with some beneficiaries out your way at the end of the week, so I'll have him call you before I leave."

"Thanks. Hey—you're coming to L.A.?"

"Yes, Thursday."

"Will you have time for lunch? I'd love to see you."

There was a moment of silence, then Lisa answered, her voice gone Valley. "What, have lunch with *Adam Craig* of *Black Varen*? Ohmigod! That would be so *awesome*!" Then laughter, and her normal voice again. "I just freaked out my secretary. Yeah, that would be great. Friday?"

"Yeah. Lemme give you my cell number." He rattled it off, confirmed that she'd call when she got into town, and hung up.

"Sure," Evie said from the couch, "make lunch dates with women who aren't me."

"It'll add to my mystique."

"So, did the boyfriend forget about Thanksgiving?"

"With Miles, who knows." He flopped down beside her. "I don't know, Evie. Am I just setting myself up? What if Miles isn't into me? I mean, I thought he was. I thought he really liked me. He's not at all chatty, but I kinda thought that was just him. But maybe he just isn't interested?"

"Maybe you need to get off your ass and go see him yourself instead of whining like a seventh grader?"

"I would," Adam said, ignoring the insult, "but I'm committed to this week in the studio. We're mixing vocals. And on Thursday we're meeting with Bill to set out the touring schedule for next year. And the promos for the new album. And I don't give a shit about it because all I really want to do is drop everything and fly back to Chicago." He rolled his head against the leather of the couch.

"God, you are so gone it's ridiculous," Evie said. "You're worse than any girl I ever knew."

"I know why stalkers do what they do," Adam moaned.

"You need to get laid."

He raised his head and gave her an accusatory look.

"Not by me, dork. By the boyfriend. Tell Bill and the others that you'll be back next week and you can do all that stuff then. And fly out on the red-eye to Chicago so you're in Miles's arms for breakfast."

"I can't do that. It's irresponsible."

"You're a fucking rock star. You're allowed to be irresponsible."

"Besides, what if he doesn't want me there? I'll wait 'til he calls. Then maybe I'll go out there next week. Depending on what Lisa says."

She shook her head.

Chapter 18

iles! Miles?"

He blinked, focused on the painting in front of him, blinked again, then looked up at Lisa, framed in the doorway. "Oh. Lise. Shit, it's not Sunday already, is it?"

"No, it's Tuesday. What are you . . . Oh. Oh, Miles."

Embarrassed, he turned the easel away from her suddenly bright eyes. "What? So I'm trying out some other medium for a change. Nobody said I had to stick with illumination."

"No, of course not." She walked past him and stood staring at the painting on the easel. Then she looked around, took in the scattered charcoal drawings, the figure studies, the color studies, then back at the painting. "It's beautiful. *He's* beautiful."

"I can't get the eyes right," Miles said. He set the palette, its oil paints streaked and smeared across its surface, on his calligraphy desk. The slant had been set true horizontal, and was scattered with paint tubes, brushes, rags, and bottles of turpentine and linseed oil. "I can't get the color. Everything looks muddy."

"You haven't painted a portrait since art school, and haven't worked in oils since the accident."

"No." Miles felt himself flush. "I found them when I was cleaning up, and just wondered how it would feel . . . I'm out of practice. I figured these were mine, but it's been a hella long time. And my arm hurts."

She frowned. "What do you mean?"

He made a swooping gesture with his right arm, something he vaguely remembered as a loosening-up technique. He'd filled half the newsprint pad with wild, wide strokes like this, trying to recapture the muscle memory of large-scale drawing. His arm still ached, though not as bad as it had the day after he'd found the newsprint and paints and had started work with them. "I did a painting of Grace, first," he said vaguely, gesturing over at the stack of canvases leaning against the bookshelves. Then he frowned as something niggled at his memory.

"I cleaned her cage for you," Lisa said, as if she were reading his mind. "She was sitting on top of it whining about 'stinky pot,' and rightly so. It stank. If you're going to work like this, Miles, you should set a reminder on your phone or something. At least you remembered to feed her, and she has water. You remembered that much."

"Right. Yes. I fed her this morning? I think." He looked back at the painting, wondering if he mixed a little gesso—not the gilding kind, the oil-painting kind—with burnt umber, if that would get the clear amber light that reflected in the eyes and turned them gold. There was a jar of gesso on the drafting table; he opened it and poured some onto the palette, then daubed a bit of the umber into the puddle. There—that was close, anyway. He frowned and touched the brush to the eyes in the painting. Almost there . . . Maybe a tiny hint of ochre, also mixed with the gesso . . . Maybe some real gold, shell gold . . .?

"Miles."

He glanced up, surprised. Right. Lisa was here.

"You painted a landscape?"

"Well, a lake-scape, anyway." He scratched his ear with the brush handle. "I was doing some practice work. Color studies."

"You have something very like this at my house." She was standing with her back to him, studying the painting on the floor. Her voice sounded funny.

"Do I?"

"Yes. It's not exactly the same, but it's still your style. Would you like to see it?"

He went cold inside. One of *those*. "Uh . . . No. No, I don't think so. I don't need to." He glanced at the lake-scape. It wasn't particularly good, but he'd just been trying out some of the colors, anyway. "It's nothing, just a color study. I'm just . . . I don't know. Playing."

"Play is good." She turned and smiled at him. Her cheeks were wet, and she wiped them with the sleeve of her sweater.

Guilt was not a new feeling where Lisa was involved. She missed her brother, the old one, and he knew it. But he just wasn't that guy anymore—didn't even know him. He'd come to know and love Lisa over the past dozen years, but that was more because she was so determined to love him and care for him that he'd finally buckled under. Besides, sometimes it was reassuring to have someone who knew what he'd been through, like Doug and Bobby. Someone who understood, most of the time. "You want coffee?"

"No, I'm good. When was the last time you ate?"

"I don't know. I think today sometime."

"You should eat." She moved to the pile of charcoal drawings and sifted through them. They were crap, but she never had criticized his work. "He called me."

"What?"

"Adam." She gestured at the drawings. "He's been trying to get ahold of you, and started to get worried."

"Oh." He turned away and stuck the paintbrush in the turpentine, rinsing it carefully before setting it in the wire holder to dry.

"Miles, why didn't you tell me he was coming for Thanksgiving?"

Miles blinked. "He's not."

"Well, not for Thanksgiving, but he said he's planning to come that weekend, and you knew about it. Why didn't you say anything?"

Oh. Not good. Adam was still planning on coming? Shit, shit, shit. He shook his head, and something hit him in the back. He realized he'd backed up into the bookcase. "No, he can't. He said he was, but that was then, and he's got a girlfriend, and he's just a friend. No, he's not coming. I'm not ready for him."

Her face was worried. "Miles?"

"He can't come. Call him. Tell him he can't come."

"Okay . . . I'll call him and tell him you don't want him to come. But I don't understand, Miles. Can you explain it to me? Why don't you want him to come? I thought you liked him. I thought . . ." She waved her hand at the painting. "I thought you *liked* him."

I do. Miles shook his head. "It's no good. That was then."

She took his hand, gently, as if he were going to run away from her. "Come on, let's have some coffee, and you can tell me why it's no good."

He shook his head again, but followed her obediently into the kitchen.

She had picked through the refrigerator and managed to put together enough stuff for sandwiches, and made him sit down and eat. Sitting across from him, she watched him with sad, steady eyes, and when he'd finished his sandwich, she said, "Okay, what's going on? Why don't you want Adam to come back?"

He took a sip of coffee and wiped his mouth with the back of his hand. "He's bi, you know. He sleeps with women, sometimes. He told me he does. It helps him keep his cover."

"Keeps him closeted, you mean," Lisa said dryly.

"Well, yeah, but he has to be. He'd probably get death threats if he came out or something. Anyway. He's gotten back together with his ex-girlfriend. Evie something."

"Evangeline Montcalm. She's a model." Lisa nodded. "I've seen the news stories. Kind of hard to avoid them, especially with all the expectancy about the new album. So?"

He blinked. "So . . . so he's back together with his ex-girlfriend. That kind of says it all there. He's moved on."

"So would it be so hard to just be friends with him? He's still texting you or emailing you—that tells me that he still wants to keep the connection open."

Miles shook his head. "No—if he's serious about this girl, he shouldn't want to come back here. The only thing we had was sex—and don't think it isn't squicking me out talking to my sister about sex. But the only reason he would want to come is to have sex with me and I know it's just because he knows I won't tell anyone—I don't *know* anyone—and he can have sex with me and get that part of his life while he's having straight sex with the Evie girl, and I can't let myself be *used* like that, like he just wants me for the gay sex stuff"—*like I use Bobby,* he thought in self-disgust—"and I can't, I can't . . ." He was short of breath; he pushed at the table to slide his chair away, and she reached out and put her hand on his.

"Miles, honey . . ."

"I can't, Lise."

"I know, honey." Lisa sighed and squeezed his hand. "I'm not pressuring you to see him if you really don't want to, but are you sure? It seemed like you guys had a lot in common, what with the old movies and stuff."

"I read an article—" Miles swallowed painfully. "—that said that they were practically engaged, that the gossips were saying they're aiming for a Christmas wedding..."

"Fuck the gossips. What does Adam say?"

"I haven't asked him."

"Maybe you should."

To his acute embarrassment, Miles felt his eyes fill. "I can't," he said again, numbly. "If he said he was gonna marry her, then it would be real. I can't do real, Lise. I can't."

"Oh my God." Lisa's voice was soft and shattered. "You're in love with him."

The tears spilled over. Miles put his head down on the table and let them come.

After a while he began to be aware of small sounds: Grace on her perch cracking sunflower seeds, water running in the sink, the metallic scrape of skillet on stove grate. And smells—scrambled eggs, cheese, bacon. He looked up and Lisa handed him a box of tissues.

"Clean up—dinner's ready."

"Sorry."

"It's okay."

They ate in silence. When they were finished, Lisa put the plates in the dishwasher and turned it on, then sat down across from Miles again. "You need to talk to Adam. He thinks he's coming here for Thanksgiving. If you don't want him to come, you need to tell him."

"I can't tell him." Miles thought the eggs might be backing up on him. "I can't talk to him, Lise. I'll call him and I'll get all, all, you know, stupid, and he'll just think I'm an idiot or something. And then he'll ask why, and I can't—" He started hyperventilating.

Lisa calmly got up and got his inhaler from the kitchen drawer where he kept his meds and gave it to him. He took three puffs, and when his breath settled down again, he set the inhaler on the table in front of him. Pushing it around in circles, he said miserably, "I can't explain it to him. I won't know how."

"Then email him. You can write, can't you?"

"I *tried*. Everything sounded stupid. I mean, I didn't try to write anything about Thanksgiving, I just tried to ask him about her, but it got all accusatory or whiny and pathetic." He shuddered. "Or like a business letter. I'm good with business letters. Maybe I should write one of those, like you do. The party of the first part and all."

"I don't think Adam would appreciate that." Lisa's voice was dry.

"Maybe I won't say anything, and if he comes, I'll, I'll just go camping until he goes away."

"Miles—it'll be *November*."

"I've camped in November before."

"And what? I'll have to entertain him?"

"Would you?"

She rolled her eyes. "No. Seriously. You can't tell him?"

"Not intelligibly." Miles rubbed his head. Panic attacks, even when staved off with the albuterol in the inhaler, tended to leave headaches behind. At least he hadn't puked this time—that happened every once in a while. And wouldn't Adam just find *that* attractive? He wanted to cry again, but it seemed like he didn't have enough energy.

"Okay. I'll tell Adam you don't want to see him again, but it's gonna cost you."

He frowned, confused. "What?"

"I want a year of your life."

"What?"

"A year of your life. For one year, you are going to see a therapist at least twice a week. You promise me that, and I'll tell Adam you don't want to see him—for a year."

"A *year*?"

"Is that about the year of therapy, or the year of not seeing Adam?"

Miles thought. "I don't know. Either. Both."

"The therapist I have in mind isn't like the ones we went to after the accident. I met her through some pro bono work I was doing for animal shelters. She's good, and she'll make house calls out here. If after a year you want to continue—and I think you will—maybe your progress will let you go to her office once in a while. But you can't stay like this, Miles. It's been twelve years since the accident, and you haven't had any seizures or anything in a decade—just panic attacks, and those we can work on. I worry about you, Miles. I don't want to have to keep worrying like this. It's not fair."

He deflated. "A *year*. Seriously, Lise? A *year*?"

"Yeah. Every day to start with, which means you have to be a little more organized as far as your time is concerned. No more working all night and sleeping all day. On the other hand, if you agree to this, I'll tell Adam."

"That I don't want to see him for a year. Why a year? Why not, just, I don't know, that I don't want to see him at all?"

"You don't want that, do you? Really?"

"I . . . Shit, Lise. I don't know. I do, but I don't. It's like, if I were a different person, maybe, yeah, I'd want to see him again. Because he's worth a better person."

"Sometimes I'd like to smack you, Miles." Lisa reached across the table and gripped his hand in hers. "No one in the world is good enough to deserve you. But you do have . . . issues. No doubt of that."

"He doesn't need to deal with my issues."

"Then don't you think maybe you should?"

He glanced up at her, arrested. "You mean the therapy?"

"I mean the therapy. Yeah, you've got issues that you think are going to come between you and Adam. They might. You might be right. But isn't it worth *trying*? Fixing them?"

He stared at her earnest expression, hope blooming.

"Because if he's really into you—which I kind of think he is—he'll wait. And nothing will happen with the Montcalm chick. If he doesn't wait, then you'll at least know the truth. You'll know he wasn't worth the effort, and you'll have only lost a year, instead of wondering forever if it might have worked out."

"Okay . . . You're a good negotiator, Lise."

"It's my life too. I can't be happy until I know you're happy—and you haven't been happy for such a long time."

"It hasn't been fair to you, has it? All this, this *drama*?" He waved his free hand.

She got up and came around the table, bending to kiss his cheek. "A year, Miles. Give me a year, and it will all be fair. You've fought me over this for a decade, but isn't Adam—the *possibility* of Adam?—worth it?"

Taking a deep breath, Miles said, "Okay."

Chapter 19

enedetto's was quiet, and dark, and Adam got a table for them toward the back, away from the windows. He'd given Lisa the address when she'd called that morning, but he found himself fidgeting as he waited, rearranging the salt shakers and experimenting with proportions of oil to parmesan to bread, tearing off bits of bread and dunking them in the oil before rolling them in the shredded parmesan, then leaving them decorating the small bread plate like dead soldiers. The waiter brought him a carafe of a very nice table wine, but he turned down a plate of antipasti. After a few minutes, the waiter came by again and took away his bread plate with a stern look, so Adam poured himself a glass of the wine and fidgeted with that for a while.

But Lisa was right on time, and he rose to give her a hug before pulling out her chair for her. "Wow, a gentleman," she said, laughing. "Isn't that against your rock star rules or something?"

"I hate that 'rock star' crap," he admitted. "I like the business, I like the attention, and of course I like the money, but so-called rock stars aren't any better than anyone else, except at one thing, and that's performing. There are so many better artists out there, better writers, better composers, better musicians, but it's all about the theater. Get the theater right and that's all there is to it. We get the theater right. But I'll tell you, we ain't stars of nothin'. We're decent musicians, but if we hadn't been in the right place at the right time, the rest of them would all be session guys and I'd still be doing theater-in-the-round someplace."

"You sound a bit like those well-known actors who say they hate publicity but you see them at every opportunity putting themselves out there." Lisa shook her head when he offered her the wine. "Can we get a beer here?"

"*Thank* you." He held up his hand. When he ordered two Peroni, the waiter's disapproving expression got more disapproving, but when Lisa smiled at him, his face cleared and he nodded, vanishing toward the back. "I don't think he likes me," Adam said.

"What made you pick this place?"

"Oh, I eat here all the time. It's quiet, they keep out the paparazzi, and I went to college with Louie."

"Who's Louie?"

"The waiter." Adam grinned at her. "He actually owns the place. Luigi, but we always called him Louie. He was my roommate for a couple of years. I introduced him to his wife."

"And he doesn't like you?"

"I love the bastard," Luigi said, and set a pair of sweating bottles on the table. "But he doesn't appreciate food. Wasted a perfectly good slice of fresh bread just now, playing with it."

"Well, if you didn't treat me like a total stranger every time I come here, I wouldn't have to work so hard to get your attention."

"You don't want my attention, not with a beautiful lady sitting here with you."

Adam snorted. "Ease up, Louie. She's just a friend, and she knows about me."

"You have no sense of self-preservation. I can't believe you still get away with being closeted—I never met anyone gayer than you."

"Rudy."

"Okay, Rudy. But you're a close second."

Lisa was watching the byplay with a grin on her face. "I like you," she said to Luigi. "Keep giving him shit."

"It's my purpose in life, *signorina*." He took the carafe and wineglasses away.

When he came back, they ordered, then solemnly clicked bottle necks and sipped at the beer in silence. When Lisa finally spoke, she sounded unhappy.

"I have a message from Miles, and I'm not sure how you're going to take it."

Adam's gut hurt. "He doesn't want to see me anymore, does he." It wasn't a question—the look on Lisa's face said it all. "Why?"

She shook her head. "It's not quite absolute—he's agreed to limit it to one year. If you're still interested in picking up with him next fall, he'll consider it."

"What? Why?"

Sighing, she went on, "He thinks you're just . . . well, that you're really invested in the girl you're seeing—"

"*Evie*? Jesus, Lisa, she's like my fucking *sister*. We're friends, is all."

"Yeah, well, he's reading all the gossip sites talking about you and her and how you're practically engaged, and you *are* living together—"

"We're not living together! Where did he get that idea?"

"There have been pictures of you both going into the same building, together and separately . . ."

"Oh, Christ on a crutch. We live in the same building."

"He doesn't know that—he thinks you're planning on marrying her and keeping him as your dirty little secret."

There was a roaring in Adam's ears and his vision went gray for a moment. When he could speak, he stuttered, "He thinks I'm like *that*?"

She reached across and caught his arm. "No. No, listen, Adam. You have to understand—you have to understand Miles and where he's coming from. He's not . . . he's not *hateful*. He's just . . . scared."

Luigi came up with their entrées then, balancing the big tray. In a low voice, he asked, "You guys okay?"

"Yeah," Adam managed. He took a swig of beer and avoided looking at Lisa while Luigi set their plates before them. He stared at the entrée, wondering what the hell he'd ordered.

"Anything else?"

"Another round." Lisa indicated their bottles. Luigi nodded curtly, then went away again.

"He doesn't think much of me, does he." He wasn't referring to Luigi, but Lisa seemed to know what he meant. "Guess it's par for the course—no one really takes me seriously."

"'Seriously'? Jesus, Adam, I think he's in love with you, and he's scared shitless."

A faint hint of hope bloomed in Adam's chest. "In love?"

"Yeah. Look, what do you know about what happened to Miles?"

"Almost nothing. I know something happened, because I remember him from when I was a kid, and he's completely different. I just don't know why or how." He poked at the penne pasta, but his attention was all on Lisa.

"He was in the accident that killed my parents," Lisa said. "He was driving, but it was absolutely not his fault—I want to make that clear up front. They were doing everything right, but some drunk ran a light and smashed into the passenger side. Dad was riding in the front seat, Mom right behind him. They were killed instantly. Michael was thrown against the driver's side window; he didn't have a lot of injuries, but they were all to his head. He was in a coma for a month."

"Jesus," Adam said. His throat was dry, so he took a sip of beer. It might as well have been water. "Is that why he's sort of . . ." He waggled his fingers, not sure how to describe it.

"Sort of what?" Lisa demanded hotly.

"Well, don't get mad at me," Adam said, "but he kind of reminds me of my nephew. He's autistic, but high functioning—what they used to call Asperger's, but I guess they don't anymore. Anyway, bright and intelligent and he talks and everything, not like the stereotype of the autistic kid rocking in a corner and all, but Ryan is really distractible and has issues with focus. Miles reminds me of him sometimes."

Lisa sighed. "Yeah. I can see that."

"I thought maybe the injuries messed up something in his head like that."

"They messed up something. He doesn't have any memory of before the accident."

"I've heard that sometimes happens," Adam said. "People don't remember the hour or so before—"

"He doesn't remember *anything*," Lisa corrected. "Anything at all. Nothing about his life up to then."

Adam blinked. "Wow. Amnesia? I thought that only happened in books and soap operas—"

"This is *nothing* like books or soap operas!" Lisa snapped. She stabbed at her plate of pasta, her fingers white around the fork. "It's not a joke, it's not fictional. My brother Michael *died* in that car crash, just as dead as my parents. I *lost* him. And instead I get this, this *stranger* wearing Michael's face." She caught her breath and visibly fought back tears. "You didn't really know Michael before. God, he was . . . was *delightful*. Funny and charming and outgoing and *smart*. He had so many friends, and was so talented. My parents were so proud when he got his MFA from the School of the Art Institute. He was in both the *Tribune* and the *Sun-Times* as one of the rising stars in the local art world."

"At least he still has that." Adam's heart was breaking.

She shook her head. "He was a *painter*. His paintings were huge, spectacular, colorful things full of life and energy, not this, this *copying*. That's all he does now, copy the way things were done five hundred years ago, as if reconnecting with someone else's history makes up for lacking his own. This would have bored Michael to tears. *Miles* is obsessed with it." Rubbing her eyes, she went on wearily, "So instead of my lively, charming, social Michael, I have this stranger who looks like him, who's bitter and surly and antisocial and neurotic. And I can't walk away from him. He *needs* me."

"Do you *want* to walk away from him?" Adam asked worriedly.

She shook her head. "God, no, of course not. I love him. Still love him, even if he isn't my brother Michael anymore."

"He *is* your brother Michael. He's maybe changed, but Lise, he's *still* funny and charming. He's not bitter or surly. Yeah, he gets cranky. We all get cranky. But he's still . . . I don't know. He's still the sweetest man I've ever met. And smart, and clever, and I—"

"You didn't know him before. You can't possibly—"

"I did know him," Adam interrupted. "Before, I mean. He didn't know me, but I knew him, back when we were kids. He must have been about fifteen the last summer we were there. I vaguely remembered him from years earlier, but that summer . . . It was the summer I realized I was gay, and I had the most enormous crush on him. I remember him the way you do—outgoing and laughing and messing around with his friends. I wondered why he had changed so much."

"He changed completely. Oh, every once in a while I get a glimpse of Michael—something will amuse him and he'll laugh just like he did then, or he'll get enthusiastic about something, and he'll start rattling on about it and it'll be Michael again. But when he's done, he goes quiet again." She twirled her fork in her angel hair, moodily watching it slide off the tines. "He doesn't choose to be like he is. He isn't full of self-pity or anything. He gets frustrated sometimes, and that makes him bitter and, and . . ."

"Cranky," Adam supplied with a smile.

"Cranky. Yes."

They both ate quietly. Adam didn't know about Lisa, but he didn't have much appetite anymore. Finally, when Luigi had removed their plates and brought coffee, Adam asked, "So after the accident he went to the resort and wouldn't leave anymore?"

"Oh no. No, after the accident he went through therapy because being in the coma that long, his muscles atrophied, and the brain injuries messed up his nervous system signals, so they needed to work on that, too. They had to teach him how to do stuff all over again. A lot of basic stuff he remembered, like walking and tying his shoes and brushing his teeth and stuff. But he had to learn to read and write all over again."

"Oh, God."

"That's how he got into the calligraphy; one of the therapists suggested it to help his hand-eye coordination. The reading he picked up really quickly; the neurologist said he probably hadn't actually forgotten how to read, he'd just forgotten how to make the connection between the print and words. Once he was able to straighten that out, he was able to read fine."

"The Vargarian books," Adam said.

"Yes. They were actually mine, originally; I gave them to him while he was still in rehab. He was there for about fifteen months; then he came home and lived with me." She took a drink of coffee, then set the cup down carefully, as if it would tip over if she weren't cautious with it. "It was horrible, you know, bringing him home to the house we grew up in. He walked around like a lost soul, trying to remember things. Once I came home and found him sitting on the couch crying over a picture of our parents. I got kind of excited thinking he remembered them and was grieving, but he was crying over the fact that he didn't remember them, and they looked like such nice people." She was crying now; Adam handed her his napkin and she held it to her eyes until she stopped. His own eyes burned. Finally, she took a breath and went on. "It was really hard, but we were making it. He was sketching again and taking some art classes as a refresher, and one of his teachers was trying to get him a job as an assistant curator at a small local gallery. He didn't have to have a job; my parents had left us well enough off, and I have a decent income, and the settlement from the accident was enormous, but we both agreed he should have something of his own, for his own self-esteem.

"Some of his friends couldn't deal with the change in him and the fact that they no longer had a shared history, but some of them sucked it up and dealt with it and him. His friends Doug and Bobby were two of them; they'd known him since high school."

"I met them," Adam said. "They were okay. They treated Miles like he was just like anybody else."

"It was hard for them, too. They had to adjust to the changes just as much as I did. And there were a lot of changes—his personality, his attitudes. He won't even look at any of the paintings he'd done before the accident—says they're someone else's and he doesn't want to see them."

"So what happened?"

She frowned. "What?"

"You said he was taking art classes, was up for a job, and all that? How did he end up turning into this hermit?"

Lisa didn't answer right way. She started turning the bottle around and around in her hands. Finally, she said, "He had a seizure—at least that's what the doctors think happened—he had two more after that, so it makes sense. He doesn't have them any more—they were apparently due to the initial brain damage, and whatever was causing them healed up eventually. But the first time . . . He was on a bus on his way home—he hadn't started driving again yet—and he passed out. By the time the paramedics got there, he was conscious and freaking out. He didn't know where he was or how he'd gotten there. He didn't know who he was, though that time he remembered after a few hours. It messed him up; he started to be afraid to leave home, or go anywhere alone.

"Then the next time he was in an accident . . ."

"'Next time'?" Adam echoed, feeling sick. "He was in *another* one?"

"A minor one. Barely more than a fender bender. But the same scenario—someone running a red light. He wasn't driving that time, and the other driver just clipped the front of the car, but even though he doesn't actually remember the first accident, *something* must have clicked, because he just freaked out. He got out of the car and wouldn't get in it again; he walked home all the way from Riverside in the middle of the night.

"I thought he was okay the next morning; we had planned on going out to the lake to make sure everything was closed up for winter, and he got in the car okay, and we made it out to the lake without any mishaps. He hadn't been there for nearly two years, since before the accident, but for some reason, the place felt familiar to him. He said he didn't remember anything about it, but that it felt like home to him. And he didn't want to leave."

"I don't blame him," Adam said with a smile. "It feels like home to me, too."

She managed to smile back. "Yeah, it does, doesn't it? Anyway, he moved into the caretaker's cottage; the old caretaker wanted to retire to Florida, so it worked out okay. I worried a lot at the beginning about the seizures, but he hadn't had one in a year or so, and hasn't had one since, so that was okay. We used to stay in the lodge when we went as a family up there during the winter to ski and ice-fish, but for one person it was too much. Neither of us knew enough about hotel management—I had my job downtown, and Miles couldn't handle running the lodge. So we decided to close the resort permanently. Miles moved there and never left.

"I ended up selling the house, since Miles never came there anymore, and got a smaller place a few blocks away. It was easier for me—the memories were just too much for me to deal with. The profit was put into a trust for Miles; ownership of the resort is in the same trust, so he doesn't have to worry about maintenance or upkeep or taxes or anything. That's all taken care of through the trust. Any money he makes from his calligraphy is his own, but everything else is taken care of by the trust."

"So, what happened to Miles's—excuse me, Michael's paintings? I didn't see them at the cottage. Did they get bought or something?"

"No. I've got them at my house. Miles hates them, because he doesn't remember painting them, and they upset him. But he won't give permission to sell them, either. So they're stored at my house."

She brooded a moment. "Not the safest place to keep them, but he doesn't want anyone to see them. Though they're good enough for any gallery. And last week he started experimenting with more of the same style. Working in the oils he used to. I suspect you might have had something to do with it. I hope he keeps it up—what he's done is just beautiful."

"I'd like to see them sometime," Adam said softly.

She shook her head. "You'd have to get his permission first. And he won't give it."

"Not if he won't talk to me. Lise—can't you talk to him for me? Tell him I really do want to see him? That it's not just—you know. Not just a dirty little secret."

"Adam . . ." Lisa sighed. "I feel like Cyrano. Look, I'll try, but Miles's mind is made up. He's a stubborn bastard, and he's got it in his head that it will hurt him less if he just cuts it off now. I mean, he won't leave the resort, and you have to be on the road for so much of the time, and you're not exactly"—her voice dropped—"*out*, now, are you?"

"No. And right now," he sighed, "I can't be. Not until the new album is released and the tour's over. Not for at least another year. I've talked to Bill, and I think I'm going to end up leaving the group anyway, but I need to establish myself as a solo artist if I'm going to stay in music." He took another sip of beer. "I don't know if I want to do that—what I'd *really* like is to go back into musical theater. Bill screams when I say that, but I think I can maybe get into some bigger show just on the basis of my name, you know? That would be okay. I can prove myself then. But not 'til the tour's over. I owe the guys that much." His heart ached, and he knew he looked like a puppy when he met Lisa's sympathetic eyes. "Maybe after that? Maybe a year is a good idea. But to have *no* contact with Miles? That'll be brutal. I'm not going to forget him—do you think he'll forget me?"

"My brother . . ." Lisa started, stopped, then started again, "Miles is a good guy, but he's very . . . self-defensive, if you know what I mean. He's afraid to get hurt, and he knows that of anyone, you're the one who could hurt him the worst."

"I wouldn't!"

"I know you wouldn't want to. God, what a fucking mess. Just . . . just let him be for a bit, Adam. Give him time. Get done what you need to get done, then call me, and I'll see if he's ready to see you." Her voice turned gentle. "But don't be surprised if he still won't. He's very good at protecting himself, and right now, he's protecting himself against you."

There was prickling at the back of his nose. Fuck. He was *not* going to cry in public. Damn Miles anyway—he had no idea why the cranky hermit bastard was so important to him, why it *mattered*, but it did. He did.

He knew Lisa was right—Miles was stubborn.

But so was he. He wasn't sure yet what he was going to do, or even, really, *why* Miles was acting this way. But he was going to figure it out.

Chapter 20

To: miles@milescaldwelldesigns.com
From: aceydeucey@premierrecordings.com

Was good to see Lisa again Thursday. Guess her business went well—she was done when she got to the restaurant for lunch. Went to Benedettos—it's a little Italian joint nobody knows about. Good food and no paparazzi. She said you're painting in oils again. Good to hear. Did I tell you I put the painting up where I can see it from my couch? I sit there and look at it. My friend Evie helped me get it up there—it was a lot bigger than I expected. Two man job. Or whatever. Looks great. Wish you could see it.

To: miles@milescaldwelldesigns.com
From: aceydeucey@premierrecordings.com

I was hoping you'd get back to me about Thanksgiving. I know Lisa said you didn't want me to come but I'm coming anyway. I'll just get a hotel room in Gurnee or someplace. I still want to see you.

To: aceydeucey@premierrecordings.com
From: miles@milescaldwelldesigns.com

Don't come. No point.

To: miles@milescaldwelldesigns.com
From: aceydeucey@premierrecordings.com

WHY?

Adam hit send and waited, his heart aching. He'd sent the first email four days ago, with no response, and when he'd finally broken down and followed up, he got *this*? A sort of bone-deep misery had settled in him since Lisa's visit; he'd been angry and hurt and determined to outwait Miles, but he'd never been terribly good at deferring things. He wanted—no, *needed*—to know why Miles was backing off like this. Lisa's explanation made sense, but couldn't Miles see that they were good together?

But Miles didn't answer. Adam tried calling, but it went straight to voice mail. Tried texting, but got no response. So he switched to emailing Lisa, who told him Miles was fine, and Adam should just be patient.

Adam tried. He wrote songs—which he uniformly hated. Rehearsed with the band—and lost his temper with them over and over again. "Dated" Evie—who told him point-blank that one more evening with him being so fucking morose and she would ditch him in public again. Did interviews—and couldn't believe afterward that the interviewer believed the fake-ass persona he presented. Partied, trying hard to find a momentary amnesia of his own in the noise and the dancing, the sweaty bodies and the haze of drink and pills. And at night, he dreamed of Miles.

The dreams always started out innocuous: he'd be walking down the street with Miles, their hands linked, not talking, just walking. Then something weird would happen—someone would come up to them and start yelling, or guitars would start flying past, or geese would chase them (really? geese?), or something equally strange. Once it was Neil, grown to the size of an apartment building, reaching down and picking up Miles and eating him. That almost made sense: Neil was as serious a homophobe as he was a druggie, and would sometimes ride Adam for being bi. Adam had always suspected that Neil was in serious denial. Maybe in Adam's dream, "eating" Miles was dreamspeak for something a little more complex.

But once . . . Oh, once it was the best dream ever. Adam was walking through a landscape of green and blue and gold—real gold that glittered like, well, gold—that was full of twisty, knotted vines spiked with pointy ivy leaves and odd little flowers. It was the illuminated manuscript of Adam's song, and there was music playing, and the notes were dancing like something out of *Alice in Wonderland*. Adam danced through the notes, feeling absurdly happy, but he wasn't content to stay among them when that large round door beckoned just at the top of the page: the illuminated initial, outlined in gold and black, decorated with white filigree, with a little scene he couldn't quite make out in the center of it all.

So he danced through the notes, and as he approached the door, it swung open and Miles was there, his hair long and over his shoulders, ivy twisting in it and down around one arm, like some forest king. He was nude, his tall, strong body straight and proud, looking at Adam with eyes like the sky and a faint smile, as if Adam were a worshipper and Miles his god. Adam danced up to him, and Miles put his hand on Adam's shoulder, and Adam's clothes melted away until he was as naked as Miles. The ivy grew and spread over Adam, and linked them together, drawing him into Miles's arms.

Miles bent and kissed Adam's throat, and color spread from the spot over Adam, red and blue and green and gold and purple, bright jewel splashes in the shapes of flowers and trees and animals and birds. His cock, flaring upright, turned blue as if tattooed with the image of a peacock, with the tail spread across his chest. Feathers in every color grew along his arms, and Miles laughed his low, rich laugh.

"Miles," Adam said, and the sound came out as music.

Miles laughed again and pulled him back into his arms, kissing his throat once more, and it was then that Adam realized that great butterfly wings had grown from Miles's back. They flexed and fluttered, and Miles and Adam rose from the ivy-strewn parchment, bound together by the vines. Over Miles's shoulder, Adam saw the illuminated door, and the painting in the center was of two men, one with butterfly wings, the other with a peacock's tail, wrapped in a kiss.

Adam woke hard and hungry, and he had barely curled his fingers around his cock before he was coming, his back arching and a deep groan tearing itself from his throat. It seemed to go on for minutes, and he thought afterward that he might have actually blacked out from the intensity. He fell back asleep almost immediately, and woke to damp, sticky sheets and his hand still clutching his cock like a little boy.

But most of the dreams with Miles in them weren't that good. Even some of the simplest of them would start out well but end up with Miles being torn from Adam's arms. Once he turned to kiss Miles, and it was Evie. He woke from that one sweating.

Between the dreams and the general unhappiness, he wasn't sleeping all that well. He'd managed to score some Valium, but it made him groggy and even more crabby. Some of the stuff Evie gave him worked a little better, and sometimes drinking would help. But then he was hungover, and that didn't work out too well.

A few days before Thanksgiving, Bill got sick of Adam's sullenness, Neil's attitude, and the others' inability to focus, and told them all to take some time off. Adam, with nothing better to do, went to San Diego and his mother's house, where he moped around some more until she got out of him what he was bugged about.

She was sympathetic. His older brother, less so.

"Seriously, dude? You still got the hots for Mike Caldwell? Dude, I thought you were over that at about fourteen." Eric shook his head as he opened the refrigerator door. "Ma, is there any strawberry jelly?"

"No, just grape. Eric, have a little sympathy for Adam."

"Adam doesn't need my sympathy. He needs a kick in the ass. How can you make PBJs without strawberry jelly?"

"Strawberry jelly in PBJs is an abomination," Adam said morosely. "PBJs need to be made with grape jelly. And smooth peanut butter."

"You're sick. Completely sick."

"Don't you have your own home to go to? What, did Melanie throw you out? *Again?*"

"Eat shit and die, gayboy."

"Eric."

"Sorry, Ma, but he's such a loser. Look at him, all droopy. What, it's not good enough to have a zillion bucks and be all famous and shit? You want to be happy, too?"

"I deserve happy," Adam said, stung. "Everyone deserves happy."

"Sure. But very few people get it. So stop feeling sorry for yourself."

"I *don't* feel sorry for myself. I'm just . . . I dunno, depressed or something."

"You're not depressed. You're feeling sorry for yourself."

"He has a point," Adam's mother said. "You should do something to get yourself out of this funk."

"I'll be happier if he goes home. What's he doing here anyway?"

"I came by to get the stuff Ma picked up for Melanie to make the salad for Thursday. *I* have a legitimate reason to be here. I'm not just freeloading off Ma because I feel sorry for myself."

Adam gave him a glare. Eric crossed one eye at him. "Ew," Adam said. "That is fuckin' gross."

"It's why he does it," Ma said.

"Look, douche bag—"

"Adam!"

"—did *I* stomp all over you when Mel threw you out three months before the wedding for extreme douchebaggery?"

"*Adam!*"

"No, you didn't, but you smirked a lot."

"That's my responsibility as younger brother. So shut the fuck up, okay?"

"Ma's right. You should do something."

"What?"

"How the fuck should I know? I'm not gay."

"I'm more than just gay, you know. I have a *life*."

"Yeah, yeah, rock star theater grad composer bullshit ad nauseam. You're so smart, you figure it out."

"Write him a song, Adam." Ma handed Adam a plate of PBJs. "And not one like that last song with the hos and bitches in it."

"It was *ironic*." Adam picked up a sandwich.

"Well, it wasn't *nice*. Write him a nice song."

"Black Varen doesn't do *nice*."

"Well, you're not Black Varen."

"I am, sorta."

"Sorta doesn't count. You're a nice boy. I'm not crazy about that Evie girl you hang around with, but *you're* a nice boy."

"Oh, crap, Ma, remind me to never let you be interviewed. I'm supposed to be edgy."

Eric snorted. "You should get an Oscar for that one. You're about as edgy as asparagus."

"Fuck you."

"Dream on, gayboy."

"All right, that's *quite* enough. Adam, go to your room and write that nice boy a *nice* song. Don't come out until you have something you can play me. Eric, go down in the basement and get the sausage out of the freezer—it needs to thaw overnight in the fridge or else you're not having your favorite stuffing. *Capiche?*"

"Slavedriver," Eric said, but headed for the basement door.

"Ma . . ." Adam whined.

"Go." She turned and pointed toward the kitchen door with the oven mitt. Adam sighed loudly, then moped off toward his bedroom, where he flopped on the bed and stared at the ceiling.

Eric is such a dick. How could Doug have had a crush on him all those years ago? Thinking of Doug started him thinking of Miles—like he could *stop* thinking about Miles—and how he would probably side with Eric, just to give Adam shit. He smiled faintly to himself. Yeah, Miles probably would give him shit. And rightly so—he was acting like a total mope. But dammit, he *missed* Miles. Missed even his curt texts, his rambling phone conversations—he remembered one where Miles had tried to explain how to cure goatskin for parchment, with Adam wondering the whole time why the hell someone would *want* to.

The thing had devolved into Miles talking about scraping off gobs of fat and soaking the skin in poop and all kinds of really gross shit, until Adam had begged him to stop. Chuck had been talking about his fat ex-girlfriend a day or two later and didn't get it when Adam fell apart laughing. Well, he wouldn't. But that was how it was. Someone or something would get Adam thinking about how Miles would react to shit, and then Adam would be laughing or otherwise responding inappropriately. Or someone would stroll by and would have shaggy light brown hair, or would walk like Miles, or have some mannerism like Miles, and Adam would think for a second that it *was* Miles, until rationality reminded him that Miles never left the resort. For a guy who never left his home, Miles was everywhere. Seemed like every place Adam went, he saw Miles's face.

I see your face . . . every place . . .
He could work with that. He got up and pulled out his laptop.

Chapter 21

he shrink wasn't anything like Miles had expected, nothing like the ones he'd had to deal with in the years after the accident. She was younger, for one thing, with curly black hair, a sweet face and voice, dressed in a soft woolly thing instead of the suits his previous therapists had all worn. And when she saw Grace, her face went all mushy and delighted, which of course made Miles like her, when he'd been determined not to. "Oh, she's *beautiful*," cooed the shrink, whom Lisa introduced as Harper.

"Harper does animal rescue work," Lisa said. "How many dogs are you fostering now?"

"Four," Harper said absently, her attention on Grace. "And three cats." She gave Miles a very un-shrink-like grin. "How big is her vocabulary?"

"Four hundred words and probably another hundred distinct sounds," Miles said. He reached into the cage, and Grace stepped onto his hand. She put her beak to his nose in a birdie kiss. "Love me?" Miles murmured.

He expected her to reply with Lisa's standard "Love you!" but instead Adam's voice came out. "You're one hot cootchie papa!"

"Shit," Miles said.

Harper and Lisa broke up in laughter. "That's Adam," Lisa said. "Miles's friend."

"Adam," Grace said, then started humming what Miles realized after a moment was "Is It Okay If I Call You Mine" from *Fame*. The song Adam had been playing in the kitchen when Miles had forgotten he was there. The song she'd taken to humming every time someone mentioned Adam's name. "Shit," Miles said again. "I'm gonna have to send her home with you, Lise, if she keeps this up."

"Why do you feel that way?" Harper asked.

He shrugged. "I dunno. The song." He set Grace on his shoulder, and she bit his ear gently. "You want something to drink?"

"Got any sweet tea?" Lisa asked, and stuck her head in his refrigerator. "Miles, what *is* this? It smells like rotten eggs."

He glanced over her shoulder. "Glair. It *is* rotten eggs. But I ran out of clove oil to add to it to make it smell tolerable. Oh, and bottles for it. That's why it's in the fridge."

"That's disgusting."

"Is that for your art?" Harper asked.

"Yeah. It's a medium for powdered pigments. The kind of paint you use is all really the same—dry pigments mixed in a wet medium. If you use oil, it becomes oil paint. If you use a water soluble medium, like glair or gum arabic, it becomes watercolors. If you use an acrylic base, it's acrylics. But the pigments are the same. I use genuine period pigments whenever possible."

"Even the poisonous ones, so be careful what you eat and drink around here."

"I'm careful," Miles said defensively.

"Most of the time. And you do watch out for Grace, I'll give you that."

"African Greys are very inquisitive birds," Harper said, but not in a way that sounded like she was criticizing Miles. She held out a hand to Grace, moving slowly. Miles approved.

He was surprised to find himself liking her—it had been a long time since he'd had to interact with any women other than Lisa, unless he counted vague memories of the hospitals and his life after the accident and before the resort. But Harper gave off such a sense of restfulness that he found himself relaxing in her company. And she seemed to know Lisa pretty well—well enough for them to exchange mirthful glances at his expense.

He didn't mind.

Lisa had found a couple of bottles of Coke and was passing them around. "These *are* Coke, right? Not some bizarro concoction?"

"Coke. Not even opened. And relatively new so they shouldn't be flat yet." He gestured for Harper to sit down at the table, which he'd cleared off when Lisa had called to say they were coming.

"So." Harper cracked the seal of the Coke bottle and let the trapped air hiss out. "Lisa tells me you have issues you want some help with."

"Nice way to say I'm batshit insane," Miles said.

"You are *not* insane," Lisa sniffed.

"Come on, Lise. I'm agoraphobic, reclusive, obsessive-compulsive, attention-deficit-ed or however you say that, batshit."

"So which one are you concerned about?" Harper's question was easy and amused.

He frowned. "Agoraphobic?"

"Sure?"

"Yeah, I know I'm agoraphobic. I've read the literature. Yeah, I go outside, but not off the grounds."

"Why?"

"Because I freak out every time I try!" Miles was starting to sweat. Had he thought he liked this harpy? Because he was starting to change his mind.

"Why do you think that is?"

"I don't know! Don't you think if I knew I'd *do* something about it?"

She smiled, which pissed Miles off more, but her voice was soft when she said, "I think you probably don't know what you know, Miles. That's a big part of the purpose of therapy—to work through whatever secrets we're keeping from ourselves. We all have hang-ups, we all have issues. It's just that something about yours is affecting the way you live, and if it bothers you, then we'll work on it."

Something in her words struck a chord. The incipient panic faded back.

"I'm not promising miracles. I'm not even promising that a year from now you'll be able to walk off the grounds without a second thought. But we will figure out what it is that's keeping you here, and we'll try to find ways to work around it."

Miles dropped down into the chair opposite. "I don't know where to start."

Lisa stood behind him and squeezed his shoulder.

"That's okay," Harper said gently. "I do."

 here had been a light snow earlier that day, and some of it stuck, a crisp white rime on the brown grass of the lawn. Ice was beginning to form along the shallows of the lake, and it caught the waning afternoon sun and sent sparks into the chill Thanksgiving sky.

Behind him, Miles could hear the sound of preparations in the lodge kitchen, Lisa talking to Doug about the pies that would need to go into the oven as soon as she'd taken the turkey out. There were murmurs of other voices, too, a couple Lisa knew from work. Their families lived in different parts of the country, and one of them was involved with a big enough case that they weren't able to take the time to fly to either one's family home for the holiday, so Lisa had invited them to share with them.

It was okay with Miles—they were using the lodge, so he didn't care who was there, and they seemed pleasant enough. He'd done the social thing a while, then escaped to the lounge and the windows looking down toward the lake. But he thought he'd managed pretty well in talking to them: he hadn't said anything weird or overtly stupid, he'd been courteous and welcoming, and as soon as he could, he'd encouraged the shift of the conversation to the case that the woman was so involved with. That got all three lawyers talking about the case in generic, nonspecific terms (something about ethics and client confidentiality, and all kinds of esoteric lawyerly stuff), and since it was an intellectual property issue, Doug was swept up in the conversation, as his website design business had to deal with copyright issues all the time. That was Miles's cue to sneak out of the kitchen and to someplace quiet where he could readjust after the social moments.

Miles had been worried that the two lawyers would be assholes, but then realized Lisa wouldn't bring anyone around who would piss him off. And Doug seemed to like them, so that was good. Bobby, as usual, was working quietly on the tossed salad when Miles had left, but it wasn't a surprise when Miles felt his big, solid presence behind him while he stared out at the fading afternoon.

"You okay?"

Miles nodded. "Yeah. They're all right."

"Seem to be." Bobby put his hands on Miles's shoulders; Miles leaned back against him, feeling the comfort that always seemed to emanate from his friend. Bobby was quiet and dependable and nonjudgmental. And solid. Miles sometimes wondered if things— if *he*—had been different, whether he and Bobby would have fallen in love all those years ago, instead of Doug and Bobby. But then, he wouldn't have remembered it anyway, and that would have only hurt Bobby.

He thought instead of what it would be like if he and *Doug* had fallen for each other, and snorted a laugh. At Bobby's inquiring noise, Miles just said, "Me and Doug."

"That would be . . . *interesting*," Bobby said diplomatically. They stood there a few minutes, and then Bobby added, "Doug's been doing some work for Adam."

Miles tensed. Bobby apparently noted it, because he asked softly, "Does that bother you?"

"No." It didn't, really, not the "some work for Adam" part. But the name—the mention of him . . . "It doesn't matter. I'm glad Doug's getting some work from him."

"We were kind of surprised. Black Varen's website looked fine to me, but Adam said that they've been having some problems with the site manager or administrator or whatever the hell, and he and Bill wanted a better site anyway. I guess he had talked to Doug when he was out here this summer. Doug was kind of disappointed when Adam told him he wasn't coming out this weekend after all."

"Get in line," Miles muttered.

There was a moment of silence behind him, then Bobby asked curiously, "I thought Adam said you'd told him not to come."

"I did."

"Oh."

"Yeah, I told him not to come out. I don't want to see him anymore."

"Oh." A faint sound, not quite a sigh, more of an exhale. "Want to talk about it?"

Miles shook his head.

Bobby looped his arms around Miles's waist and rested his cheek against Miles's head. Miles wasn't short, but Bobby was just that little bit taller that he could do that. Quietly, Bobby said, "Doug and I took separate cars, so if you want me to stay afterward, I could."

Miles shook his head.

"Does this have something to do with what Adam said when he was here? Because I do love you, you know."

"Yeah." Miles's throat was tight. "It's all kinda . . . I don't know." He did know—he wasn't sure how, or why, but suddenly this whole thing with Bobby didn't feel right anymore. He supposed it probably was because of Adam, and that once he was over Adam, once Adam was out of his blood, that he'd go back to the same old arrangement.

Except somehow, he knew he wouldn't. That being with Bobby, who was in love with someone else, wouldn't be enough anymore. That they'd always be friends, always love each other the way they did, but now that Miles knew what it was to *love* someone, just *fucking* wasn't going to be enough. Not ever again. He turned in Bobby's arms and buried his face in Bobby's clean-smelling shirt, in the familiar warmth and scent and solidity of his friend, and broke down.

Through his tears, he was vaguely aware of another voice, of Bobby's rumbling in his chest, but Bobby never moved, never shifted, just stood and held Miles safe.

Chapter 23

 he email came the Saturday after Thanksgiving, on a day Adam would have been there if Miles hadn't fucked up royally and told him not to come out. He tried not to think of it as he was working on his current commission, but the tedious coloring of the Celtic knotwork on the piece let his mind wander too much. It was all tiny little patches of solid color, like paint-by-numbers kits he'd seen online. As long as he had the cartoon with the color placement next to him and he was careful to follow it exactly, he didn't have to pay too much attention to it, and the Celtic style didn't use enough gold to make him too terribly excited about the piece. The yellow bits, like what he was working on now, were lead tin yellow, which was more accurate for the ninth-century style. Still, it was a good commission, reasonable text, and he was mildly pleased with the design he'd come up with, though of course it was never good enough to really satisfy him. He thought he vaguely remembered someone saying that artists were always their own worst critics.

Be that as it may, although the design was complex, the execution was kind of boring. He noted the next placement of the lead tin yellow on the cartoon, dipped his squirrel-hair brush into the mussel shell he was using as a paint pan, and carefully filled in the diamond shape. He was cautious not to touch the stuff, and was glad it was fairly pleasant out today so that he could open one of the French windows to let air circulate, because the lead was toxic. "Not as bad as orpiment. That's made from arsenic," he said aloud, as if he were talking to someone, and in his head Adam's voice came back, that lovely voice that always had a hint of laughter in the background: "Cool? Is it traceable? I got a few people I'd love to use it on ..."

Miles smiled faintly to himself. That sounded just like Adam.

His laptop dinged with a message in his inbox, but he ignored it for now. He needed to finish the yellow bits before he took the break he'd been promising himself for the last two hours. *Finish the yellow*, he thought, *and then go for a run and shake the Adam-thoughts out of my head.*

His inbox dinged again as he was washing out the brush and setting it in its holder to dry. He wiped his fingers on a rag and opened the laptop, going to his mailbox. There were five emails there: one from Doug, wanting to know if he was busy Sunday or not, as there was a game on TV; one from Lisa, forwarding a second thank-you from the Addisons, the couple who had come for Thanksgiving dinner, and three from Adam. Miles sighed. His telling Adam not to come this weekend had apparently not put the other man off; he still regularly emailed and texted. Miles never answered Adam, and felt guilty about that, but he was still glad to get the emails.

The first email had just a link, but the subject line was "Calligraphy thing I found yesterday," and the link text was for a museum in Baltimore. When Miles clicked on it, it brought up the catalog site for a recent exhibit. He bookmarked the site and went back to Adam's emails.

The second email's subject line was "Admit it, you miss my ass," and it held a picture Adam had apparently taken with his cell phone in a mirror. He was naked, his back to the mirror, and he was looking coquettishly over his shoulder with one hand raised with the cell phone. The lighting was excellent—the curve of Adam's exquisite ass caught the light beautifully. Before the subject sank in, Miles was impressed with the quality of the picture; then he could only goggle helplessly at the sight of Adam's beautiful butt. "God," he groaned, then right-clicked on the picture and saved it to his hard drive.

The next one from Adam was a video file. For some reason, it made Miles nervous, but he opened it anyway.

The initial image was of a wide leather armchair, empty, with a low table beside it. There was something on the table but Miles couldn't quite make it out. Then Adam came into the picture and sat in the chair. "Jeez, I hope this comes out," Adam said with a grin. "I've never done this before—I mean, yeah, I've shot videos before but I'm usually the one on the other side of the camera. I've never done a solo shot, but I guess this is kind of private, so having a camera operator on the other side would kinda be stupid. Anyway." He reached up and started to unbutton the flannel shirt he had on.

Slowly. His eyes on the camera so Miles felt like they were meeting his through the screen, Adam flicked open each button. "So I was thinkin' the other day that maybe we're going about this all wrong, Miles. I know you said you didn't want to see me for another year, but you know, seeing me and *seeing* me are like maybe two different things? Like, you don't want me actually there, but hey, thanks to the miracle of modern technology, you can . . . watch." He grinned. He'd finished unbuttoning the shirt and it lay open, hints of his bare chest peeking through. With a soft sigh, he reached up and pushed the shirt aside, running his fingers over his chest.

Miles's mouth went dry.

"I think of you." Adam's voice had gone low and dreamy. "I think of you at times like now, when I'm touching myself, imagining it's you touching me. You have great hands, Miles, an artist's hands, strong and sweet. God, it feels so good . . ."

Miles grabbed the laptop and scrambled for the bedroom, dropping it on the unmade bed and rummaging in the bedside table, shoving aside the condoms and his favorite dildo in his search for lube. Adam's fingers were stroking his nipples now; his eyes were half-closed and his lips already flushing with arousal. "God, Miles, the way you touch me."

Miles peeled out of his jeans and dropped onto the bed beside the laptop. "Fuck," he groaned.

Adam smiled as if he could hear Miles. "I hope Lisa's not there with you. I think we need to be alone for this. I can't wait to get you alone, Miles. I can't wait to touch you like this." His hand slid up his throat and jaw, and he pulled one finger into his mouth, sucking on it. "Oh, God, Miles . . ."

The words were meaningless. Miles was rapt, watching the way Adam's fingers stroked over his body, watching the way his skin flushed darker, the way his nipples hardened.

Watching the way his cock filled beneath the worn denim of the jeans he wore, in echo of the thickening in Miles's as he touched himself the way Adam was, his fingers on his nipples, in his mouth, as if Adam were leading the way.

Adam was talking, but Miles didn't hear it. He watched as Adam got up, unbuttoned the jeans, then turned to slide them down over his hips. His bare ass was to the camera, and Adam glanced back over his shoulder and gave him the same flirtatious look as in the still shot. Then he wiggled his butt, and turned around to sit back down in the leather chair. His cock was fully hard, curved up to touch his belly just below his navel. "Are you naked, Miles?" Adam whispered.

"Yes," Miles groaned.

"I hope you are. I hope you're there, ready to fuck me. I need you to fuck me, Miles. You don't know how much I need it." Adam rubbed his thumb over the broad head of his cock and then over his lips, leaving them shiny. Then he sucked on a couple of fingers and trailed them down the center of his chest and beneath his balls. "Mmm . . . that's good. Touch me, Miles. No—wait. We need lube for this." He reached over to the table and picked up the bottle, pouring it over his fingers, then glanced at the camera, his grin wicked. "Oh, not a good enough view for you? We can fix that . . ."

And he shifted lower in the chair and spread his legs, hooking one over each of the chair's arms and giving Miles a perfect view of his ass. He rubbed the lube between his fingers and started long, firm strokes on his cock.

Miles fumbled for his lube and echoed Adam's movements, taking his cock in his hand and stroking it, but his attention was on Adam, on his long-fingered musician's hands moving on his shaft, the neatly trimmed patch of dark hair surrounding his round, shaven balls, and—Miles swallowed hard as Adam's fingers dipped lower, teasing the little hole, sliding in and out, deeper and deeper on each stroke. Miles moaned and reached for his own opening, thrusting two fingers in and whimpering in pleasure.

"Oh, this isn't enough," Adam said, his usually smooth voice gone harsh and raspy. "Not enough. I need you to fuck me, Miles. God, I need it."

Miles's mouth went dry as Adam reached out and caught up the other thing on the table, which Miles now saw was a long, thick, flesh-colored dildo. Adam coated it with lube, then put the head right at his opening. Looking Miles in the eyes, he pushed the dildo slowly into himself.

Miles watched Adam's eyes close and his mouth, full and flushed with his arousal, drop open. He took his own fingers from his ass and curled them around his cock, stroking himself two-handed as he watched Adam fuck himself with the dildo. "Yeah," Adam moaned. "Fuck me, Miles . . ."

Torn between the need to close his own eyes and get lost in his fantasy, and the absolutely overriding need to watch Adam, Miles lay with his eyes slitted, his hands working his cock hard. Adam was moaning wordlessly now, the toy rocking back and forth, sweat streaming down his lean, tanned chest. Miles licked sweat off his own lip and pretended it was Adam's, pretended it was Adam's tight body he was pumping into, pretended he could feel Adam's hands on him.

"Oh, God, *fuck me, Miles!*" Adam cried out, and climaxed, come spurting over his belly and chest and even a few drops on his mouth. He licked it off his lips, and the sight of it was enough to make Miles come too. He lay panting, shuddering in aftershocks, then rolled over into the piled-up sheets but didn't take his eyes off the laptop screen.

It took a few minutes for Adam to pull himself together, but finally he sighed and eased the toy out, tossing it to the floor. "Holy shit, Miles," he said faintly. "It's better with you in my imagination than it is with a lot of guys in real life."

"Yeah," Miles said, forgetting that Adam couldn't hear him.

"But I still wish I was there with you." He stretched languorously, like a cat, and a rush of revived arousal ran through Miles at the sight. "If you change your mind—let me know. 'Cause I'm really starting to miss you."

"Miss you too." Miles reached out to touch the laptop screen.

Adam smiled ruefully at the camera, then the screen went dark and the framing email came back up. Miles closed the laptop, then buried his face in his pillow. He'd promised Lisa a year, and knew she was right, knew if he begged Adam to come back he would, but somewhere in his mind he'd always wonder if Adam was serious. And in a year, if Adam did return, Miles would be better. He knew he wouldn't be *well*, but he'd be better. And Adam deserved a better Miles, not the one he was now.

But that video tempted him so badly. He missed Adam like the pain of an amputation. He held the pillow to his face and tried to imagine that he could still smell Adam in the linen as he had last summer. But all he smelled was fabric softener and his own sweat.

hree days. Three fucking days, and not a word from Miles.

Adam finished laying down the harmony vocal track to the song they were working on, holding the last note until the engineer signaled for him to quit. "Good job," Chuck said over the intercom from his perch on the mixing panel beside the engineer. "Sounds great."

Taking the headphones off, Adam dropped them on the chair beside him and ran his hands through his hair. Three fucking days, and not a peep. Nothing. He'd poured himself into that little porn video, and *nothing*. He'd been patient, but after a day or two, he'd sent a follow-up text, just a *Hi, how are ya?* Nothing.

And now he was getting angry. He was tempted to take the calligraphy piece Miles had done for him to an appraiser, get an estimate of the value, and send the motherfucker a check for that amount, with a note saying "Fuck off." For a whole five minutes he reveled blackly in the fury that Miles would feel getting that. It would be a pale echo of the hurt and rage Adam was feeling right now, but it would be enough to know Miles was hurt.

Assuming that it *would* hurt Miles. That Miles even cared.

Fuck. Misery washed over Adam and he picked up the headphones, sagging into the chair. "You okay, Adam?" Chuck asked, his voice echoing in the studio.

Adam gave him a weary thumbs-up, then raked his free hand through his hair again. The door to the studio opened, and Chuck came in. "Seriously, dude? You look wrecked. Girlfriend troubles? You looked pretty tight at L'Exchange last night."

"Were we there?" Adam asked.

"Yeah. With a bunch of clothes-hangers from the Fashion Week runways. Those girls do *not* look human. Compared to them, your girl is fat."

Adam snorted. "His girl." Right. As far as the world was concerned, Evie was his girl. Adam and Evie. "I just got shit on my mind."

"This have to do with the couple of weeks you took off in Chicago?"

Adam froze. "What?"

Shrugging, Chuck said, "I dunno. It just seems like you've been kind of off since you came back from there. I mean, we were all pretty wiped after ten weeks on that fucking bus, and bein' able to fly home was a nice perk, but we've all gotten over it. You're still fucked up."

"I got shit on my mind."

"You met somebody, didn't you?"

The breath whooshed out of Adam's chest, and he stared blankly at Chuck. "What?"

"You met somebody. Somebody rocked your world, and you don't know how to deal with it." Chuck went and picked up his bass, settling on a corner of one of the amps. "That's why you came home and picked up with Miss Evie again. She's easy and don't ask much of you. Who was she? Some chick you met after the concert?" At Adam's head shake, he chuckled. "Come on, theater boy. I know the signs. You look just like my sister did when she met the guy she ended up ..." He trailed off, staring at Adam. "Holy fuck."

"What?"

Chuck checked out the closed door, then the engineer's booth. The engineer had his back to them as he messed around with one of the boards. When Chuck spoke, his voice was low so as not to be overheard. "It's a guy, isn't it?"

Adam felt the blood drain from his face. "I don't know what you're talking about."

"Dude, come on. I know you swing both ways. Ain't no way you're gonna get that look on your face for a *chick*. Not with Our Miss Evie—or whatever the hell the internet calls her these days—in the running."

"Do not fucking even joke about something like that," Adam said furiously. "Neil barely tolerates me as it is, and he thinks the bisexual thing is an act, that I'm doing it to get attention. He thinks with Ray gone that he should be in charge of this group and he thinks I'm keeping him from it."

"Varen's a democracy and Neil fucking knows it. We're all equal partners." Chuck shook his head. "He can't do anything about you."

"Yeah, except make my life a living hell. And leak it to the press."

"He's not that stupid," Chuck said. "He knows that it would be Varen on the line—"

"Yeah, but if there's enough blowback, he'd have an excuse to get rid of me."

"Counterproductive. You're the face of Varen, and if you go down, we all go down."

"Maybe. But I'll bet Neil doesn't see it that way."

"Neil's head is so far up his ass he can lick his own tonsils. It's too bad—he didn't used to be this way. He doesn't handle the shit as well as you do, and it shows."

"What do you mean?"

"You know. You guys are both partiers, but you handle it better. Eddie drinks too much, but he manages it."

Adam shook his head. "What do you mean, 'you're both partiers'? Neil's a fucking cokehead, Chuck!"

The bassist held his hands up. "Easy, dude. I'm not making accusations. But you do have a sort of . . . well, we won't call it a problem, because I haven't seen it fuck you up the way that it does Neil. But you do like the 'ceuts, that's obvious."

"I don't . . . it's not . . ." Adam blew out a breath. "It's not *like* that, Chuck. It's not like I need the shit, it's just recreational."

"Yeah." Chuck was suddenly sober. "It's just recreational until you end up like Ray. I worry, Adam. I worry about you, and I worry about Neil, and I worry about Eddie. You might have the rep as the den mother around here, and that's cool—you know how to negotiate, you know what works, you know how to do the whole presentation thing. You're smart, and you're educated, and you think big picture. I'm just a bassist. But I'm standing back there watching you guys, and I'm worried." He played a few notes on the bass, moodily plucking the guitar's strings. "Sometimes I think it would be a good thing if Varen did implode. I wonder sometimes if it isn't just pulling us down the wrong track, y'know?"

There didn't seem to be much to say to that. Adam fiddled a moment or two with the headset, then there was a rap at the door, and Eddie and Neil came in.

"It was a boneheaded play! He didn't have anybody in the open. He shoulda just carried the fucking ball."

"Martinez was there! He was open!"

"Yeah, for about two seconds before he got sacked. Jesus, Neil, have you got *any* brain cells left?"

"Fuck you." Neil looked at Adam and added, "And fuck you too."

"Me? What the fuck for?"

"Being alive." Neil went for his guitar.

"Fuck off, prick."

"Children, children," the engineer said over the speakers.

Adam sighed. It was going to be a long afternoon.

Dear Adam.

No. *Hey, Adam.*

No, that didn't sound right either. Miles sighed and put his finger on the backspace key. It didn't go far: just the same nine spaces he'd been trying to fill for the last three days. God, that video was hot—he'd watched it four or five times already—and he was in awe of the fact that Adam was that confident, that sure of himself that he could pour himself into something like that and mean it only for Miles. If the music thing ever dried up, he could make a fortune doing online porn.

Except it wasn't porn, not really. It was . . . it was . . . Miles swallowed. If he didn't know better, he would think it was . . . *love.* The look in Adam's eyes when he said he missed Miles. The way he put himself out there—for God's sake, he was *naked.* Talk about vulnerable. And Miles could only stare at the blank email he'd been staring at for three days, and could say *nothing.*

What could he say? "Nice video"? Well, it was, but he didn't think Adam would appreciate that. Maybe he would. Maybe that's all Miles needed to do, to validate Adam, to recognize the effort. But "nice video" didn't seem to be the right words. "Great video"? "Awesome video"?

"*I love you*"?

Miles rubbed his forehead and closed the laptop on the blank, accusatory screen. He took his phone out of his pocket and went to the text messages. The last one was Adam's, of course. Just *Still alive?* and a colon-parenthesis for a smiley. Text. Texts were easier. He took a deep breath and typed, *Yes. Thanx for video. It was good*, and pressed Send.

"Good"? *Christ, Miles!*

Hastily, he typed a second text. *You know what I mean. Sorry.*

Then a third. *Miss you.*

Then he shut the phone off and tossed it on the couch. He couldn't do this. Why was Adam wasting his time on a loser like Miles? He took a deep breath, then another, and when he stopped shaking, he went and sat in the shower until all the hot water was gone.

Miss you.

Adam let out the breath he'd sucked in at the sight of the first, unhopeful text. "Good" was so *not* good. "Good" was . . . horrible. But then the second text came, and he thought of Miles, wordless, confused Miles, and thought maybe, just maybe, he did know what Miles meant, which was, of course, not what anyone else would have meant. The *Sorry* was so very Miles. And then, after an agonizing few moments, that *Miss you.*

He saved the texts, then picked up his guitar again and started to work.

Chapter 25

Do you know what I mean when I say I miss you?
It's not just the good-bye in the last time I kissed you
When I see your face in the windows that I pass
Though you're far away and not behind the glass
Missing you isn't just a feeling in the way my life shakes out
I'm one big regret and no one knows what that's all about

Do you know what I mean when I say I miss you?
I would give anything to see you again
To hear the whisper of your voice, to feel the touch of your skin
I would give anything, my life, my dreams, my fate
But the thing I want the most to give is the one thing you won't take

Do you know what I mean when I say I miss you?
Do you know what this hole in my chest signifies?
I'm standing in the rain, my heart in my hands
Just waiting for you to know what I mean
What I mean when I say I miss you.

Adam finished playing and laid his hand over the strings of the guitar, stilling them. Bill said, "Damn, that's good."

"What the fuck was that?" Neil sniped. "That was a pussy song if ever I heard one."

"Shut up, asshole," Eddie shot back. "We gotta have a ballad on the album. We always have a ballad. That's like a power ballad. Something like from a Broadway show or something."

"Oh, fuck," Neil said. "There goes the great theater guy, singing fucking power ballads."

"Dude," Chuck sighed wearily, "chicks fuckin' *love* power ballads. You're gonna be swimming in pussy when they hear this."

"Neil doesn't care about swimming in pussy," Adam said nastily. "All he cares about is scoring some blow, and power ballads don't score blow, do they, Neil?"

"Fuck you. You don't care about pussy, all you want is dick," Neil spat. "Band's gone fuckin' downhill since you joined. We used to play *real* music, real metal, not this pop shit. We used to be a *metal* band, not this crap. It's like how Mick Fleetwood *destroyed* Fleetwood Mac when he hired Buckingham and those chicks."

"Yeah, destroyed the band to the tune of a couple zillion bucks," Chuck pointed out. "And, hello? How many metal bands you know play the fucking United Center, let alone the L.A. Coliseum?"

"Coliseum doesn't count—we were part of a festival."

"Yeah, of the top acts in music, dickhead. How many metal bands were there? I'll tell you, since you can't fucking count—*one*. Us."

"We ain't a fucking metal band, unless you count tin foil as metal!"

"Cut it out, guys," Bill said. "Adam, the song's good. Work with Chuck on the arrangement. Neil, you done with that one song you've been working on? We need three more songs to make this thing worth buying, otherwise it's not worth pressing any CDs."

"CDs are bullshit anyway," Eddie interjected. "Everything's digital now. We should just release one or two songs at a time instead of waiting for a whole CD's worth."

"Except that sort of means you'd be touring all fucking year," Bill pointed out. "And people'll get used to you coming out with a song a month and start to not pay attention. This way each CD's an event, and you get the promo going without having to work at it."

"Oh. That makes sense."

"That's why he's the manager," Adam said.

Neil said, "Hey, Adam—with you and Bill, who fucks who?"

"You fuck donkeys," Adam retorted.

"Jesus, I feel like a fucking kindergarten teacher here. Neil, cut it out. Chuck, what do you think?"

Chuck mused a moment, then said, "I think we should do two versions."

"Seriously?" Eddie said, intrigued. "Why?"

"One arrangement, power ballad style, for the theater geek in Adam. The second one with a harder edge—" He played a hard bass line that made Neil sit up and pay attention. "—that picks up the minor key and plays it into a sort of accusation, you know? The first one is somebody missing the girl, the second is the guy totally pissed off because she's just not getting it."

"You're fucking brilliant," Eddie said. "Seriously, dude, you are fucking brilliant."

Adam was doubtful, but the idea of a challenge kind of appealed to him. He started thinking of arrangements that might work. But then Neil picked up his guitar and started throwing out chords, and after about two minutes of that he couldn't think at all anymore. "Shit," he called over the noise of Chuck and Neil. "I'm goin' out for a smoke."

He closed the studio door behind him and waved at Jan down the hall as he headed for the back entrance. There was a little patio there, shaded by a couple of palms and cooled by a tiny fountain in the corner in the shape of a waterfall. He sat down on the lip of the fountain and lit up. Edgy. It needed to be edgy, but it needed to be clean, too—needed to have the feeling behind it. Yeah, maybe the guy was pissed because the lover was so *thick*, but he was really in love, too, and that made him all the madder. Because the lover just didn't get it. He didn't understand how much Adam loved him. He was pushing him away because he didn't understand, and Adam didn't understand how Miles could *do* that, how Miles could be so cold as to keep Adam away like this . . .

He stopped and took the cigarette out of his mouth, staring at the cherry-red end. *Fuck*. He was putting Miles back into the song again, when he'd tried so hard to keep him out, to keep the "lover" generic. But it couldn't be generic, not and be real. So yeah, Chuck was right—there was anger there, because there had been anger on the inside when Adam was writing it. He'd just toned it down because it was for Miles, and Miles *couldn't* understand.

He finished his cigarette and ground it into concrete of the fountain's edge. Yeah, he thought, he knew where he could change the tone of the song, how to read the lyrics so that they were angry.

Because he *was* angry. He just hadn't acknowledged it before. But he was.

Carrying that anger like the tool it was going to be, he went back into the studio.

And stopped.

His laptop was open, but no one was paying attention to the video playing. At least no one was actually watching—Neil was standing in front of it, gesturing wildly at the screen.

"Do you fucking see? Jesus Christ, the guy films a fucking porn video for his fucking *boyfriend*. I am not fucking playing in a band with a goddamn *homo*!"

"*What the fuck?*" Adam stormed over and slammed the laptop closed. "What the fuck are you doing, dickhead? That's my goddamn personal business!"

"He was looking for the music for the song," Eddie said apologetically. "We didn't realize you had that video on there, but it said 'for Miles,' and he said, 'ain't that the guy that did the painting thing,' and opened it before we could stop him. Then we—hell, we were curious to see what you were doing, and then it was, 'oh God, my eyes' sort of thing, and Neil went ballistic."

"Shut the fuck up!" Neil yelled. "That is not the fucking point! The fucking point is that you've been *lying* to us the whole time, you fucking faggot! You're not bi, you're fucking *gay*. *You fuck guys.*"

"Yeah!" Adam yelled back. "That's part of being bi, you moron! And this is news, how? I mean, shit, you're always giving me grief about it—"

"But I didn't *know*, did I? You weren't doing fucking pornos. So what, you gonna post this on YouTube and make Black Varen a fucking laughingstock? You gonna fuck us over? Fuck this. Fuck you. I want you out of this fucking band today. Bill—tell him to get the fuck out."

Bill shook his head. "Sorry, Neil—that has to be a unanimous decision of the remaining band members. Says so in all your contracts. So. Guys—does Adam go?"

"Fuck no." Chuck snorted.

"Prick!"

"Eddie?"

Eddie's face twisted. "I don't like that he's a homo, but I don't wanna go back to playing in dives and opening for boy bands anymore. We done good since Adam came on board. And he's okay— it ain't like he flaunts it, except on stage, and you know that's part of the act. I guess, I mean, I think I can work with him. It's gross, but he's okay, you know."

"No, he ain't!" Neil was livid now, his face scarlet with rage. "He's gonna ruin everything for us. If it gets out, we're fucking screwed."

"So we don't *let* it get out," Eddie said reasonably. "We just keep our mouths shut. Nobody has to know."

"*I* know." Neil ground his teeth and glared at Adam. "Fine. He stays. But things are going to change around here, starting with that fucking song. It's out. We can do the hard rock version we were working on, but the ballad is out."

Adam caught Bill's glance, and nodded quietly. If it took catering to Neil's hysteria to keep things together, he'd just have to cater to Neil's hysteria. It would only be for a while. They could keep it quiet for a while.

In the end, though, it was Neil who fucked it up. Somehow, stoned or high or drunk or something, he let it slip to someone, who took it right to the media. The first Adam heard of it was a phone call from Bill a week before Christmas, warning him that he'd been getting phone calls from reporters all afternoon, wanting to know if it was true that Adam Craig of Black Varen was gay.

ou can't stay brooding in here," Evie said sharply. "You've got to go out and let people know you're above all this crap."

"He did it on purpose. I know he did it on purpose. He even told them about Miles, out of pure evil. Thank God he didn't know his last name. And I don't believe he slipped." That was what a supposedly repentant Neil had told Bill. "He did it on purpose."

"Of course he did, even if he was stoned at the time," Evie shot back. "He fucked himself over too, but he's too stupid to realize it. So come on. You can't let the harpies win, and if you stay home licking your wounds, they win. Everyone will see it as confirmation that you're gay."

"Fuck it, Evie!" Adam roared. "I *am* gay!"

"No, you're not. You're *bi*. Everyone who's anyone knows that, that—"

"That nothing. I'm gay. I'm not bi, I don't *like* fucking women. Shit, Evie, the only girl worth having sex with is you, and I don't even *want* to have sex with you. It's bad enough I have to date some chick once or twice a year so Bill's happy. I can't do this anymore. What am I supposed to do, go out and get drunk and pick up some skank that I can fuck in public to prove that I'm not queer?"

"No. You and I are going to go out clubbing, and we're gonna act as if nothing has happened. Someone asks, you just laugh and blow them off."

"What if they ask about Miles?"

She brushed his hair back off his face. "Then you say 'Who?' as if you had no idea of what they were talking about."

"No."

"Adam—"

"Evie, I'm not gonna pretend Miles doesn't exist. He *matters*, Evie. I can't do that. It will kill me."

"Fine, then you say he's a friend. You don't have to go into details—the people you meet clubbing aren't exactly Barbara Walters. We'll just go and dance and pretend nothing's wrong, just the way we always do. Because you're a better actor than this. Got it?"

"I don't want to go."

"Too bad." She tugged him to his feet—she was surprisingly strong for such a waiflike creature—and shook him. "Come on. You need a shower. I'll pick out your clothes. Smoke a joint while you're in the bathroom—you'll feel better. I just hope you don't have that skunky-smelling pot."

"No, I hate that crap." Adam shook his head. "I need a Valium."

"You can have half. I don't want you falling asleep."

"I won't fall asleep."

"No, you won't, because I'm only letting you have half. Come on, Adam, honey, you gotta keep your shit together, at least for a couple of hours. Long enough for people to see that you're fine."

"I'm not fine."

"Then fake it 'til you make it, remember?" She shoved him in the direction of the bathroom. "Go. Shower and make yourself pretty. Add some glitter and guyliner. Play the game, right? You're better than Neil ever will be."

He hesitated at the door to the bathroom. "Evie?"

"What?"

"Thanks for this. Thanks for being my friend."

"Don't sound so terminal, Adam—you're freaking me out."

"Oh, I'm not terminal. But I have to warn you—I'm done with the closet. I'll play it this way tonight, because you're right, and to spite that asshole Neil, but I'm quitting Black Varen. I can't live like this anymore."

"You can't live like this? Or you can't live without Miles?"

"I have to prove I'm for real. Miles doesn't deal with fakery."

"Are you sure? Because quitting the band is a pretty big step, just for a guy."

Adam shook his head and smiled faintly. "Miles isn't just a guy. And I've been thinking about it for a while. Neil's crap just kind of pushed the schedule forward a bit. I don't know quite what I'm going to do, but I know I can't fake it anymore."

"Fine. Whatevs. But know this—I am telling everyone that you're bi, because I am *so* not going down in history as your beard, okay? If you want, we can have a screaming fight at the end of the evening and I'll say loud and long that you only wanted me for sex, okay? Because a girl has her pride."

He stared at her a moment, then started to laugh. Somewhere deep in the laughter, it turned to tears, and he stood in the hallway for what seemed like forever, Evie's arms wrapped around him and his face buried in her thin shoulder. Finally, he drew back, pretending to wipe his nose on her dress until, laughing, she shoved him into the bathroom.

Black leather. And chains—not shiny new poser chains, but real ones, pitted and tarnished. The jacket he'd had in the back of his closet forever—a holdover from some play sometime, found in a Goodwill store—was just the ticket, battered and tough-looking. It made his shoulders look wider, and his slim build bulkier. A too-tight black silk T-shirt emphasized the muscles energetic performances and hauling equipment had given him. Tight black jeans, because leather pants would have been wussy. And the Docs, heeled and thick-soled, adding an extra inch and a half to his six-foot height, to make him stand out among the notoriously short entertainment crowd that was their audience tonight.

Evie was the pale princess in a silver bustier and flirty white skirt. She wouldn't have been Evie without the stilettos, but they were lower than usual, to contrast with his height, and all silver straps, dainty and delicate. Her pale hair was up and she wore glittering diamond earrings in the shape of flowers. She fit nicely under his arm, curled up in his protective shelter.

They were nothing if not theater kids, after all.

Their arrival at the first party was pure theater, him stalking in with his arm draped around Evie's shoulder. The greetings were curious and cautious, but when someone got up the nerve to ask about Neil's statements, Adam laughed. "He's just jealous," he yelled over the noise of the crowd, and pulled Evie into his arms, palming her ass through the silk skirt.

Into his shoulder, she hissed, "You are so paying for that."

He said loudly, "Later, baby, later," and the people around them joined in his laughter.

At another party, a girl he'd dated briefly a few years ago came up to him on her boyfriend's arm. "Neil Draper's full of shit, Adam, honey! And I'll tell anybody so."

"Pammie, sweetheart," Adam said, kissing her hand and shaking her boyfriend's in a manly fashion, "you're a doll, and if anyone asks, a perfect lady."

After they'd gone away, Evie started making gagging noises, and he pinched her ass. "Cut it out. She's ammunition."

Not everyone was that accommodating. There were comments, and whispers, and while Adam and Evie deflected the former, they could do nothing about the latter. They hit party after party, club after club, until they were both exhausted. "I'm done," Adam said in the cab on the way to the last party on their list, a private one at L'Exchange, the current hottest spot on the Hollywood map. "Can't we skip this one?"

"No," Evie said. "This is the hardest one yet, Adam. This is the one Jesse Fantorelli's giving for his artists. You have to be there. And so do the rest of the guys. You gotta hang in for this one—people are gonna be watching you and Neil like hawks."

"Oh, fuck. Neil." Of course—Fantorelli was the CEO of Black Varen's label. He was screwed. He was so screwed. He and Neil had been working together for the last couple of weeks in a sort of armed truce, but facing each other in public, in a place where people would be jumping on Neil's statements like monkeys on a trampoline, would be a nightmare. It would be easier if he knew how Neil was going to handle it, but he suspected the guitarist would be feeling defensive, and that would make him nasty. He sighed. "Fuck."

"It's gonna be okay. Jesse's always got coke at these parties—do a line and you'll feel fine. We only need to get through meeting the guys, you put Neil in his place, and then we leave. Twenty minutes, tops."

"I can't do this, Evie."

"Fuck. Okay. Here's a Valium, that'll numb you down, then do the coke for the energy, 'kay? I'd give you E, but people have flipped out mixing that with coke, and you need to be at the top of your game."

"Fuck."

"Fake it 'til you make it, remember?"

He dry-swallowed the Valium and followed her out of the cab.

"There's my sweethearts!" Jesse Fantorelli's voice boomed out over the thumping beat of the house music. The club was packed, even if it was a private party, and the noise was horrendous, with people screaming to be heard over the music and over other people screaming. Evie dragged Adam over to Jesse and shrieked, "We need quiet!"

Jesse nodded and started to bull his way through the crowd. Adam and Evie followed him to one of the private rooms, where he shut the door behind him. The sound was still loud, but muffled, and they could at least hear each other. "How you doin', Adam?" Jesse asked.

"Dealin' with the bullshit," Evie answered for him. "He's wrecked, Jess. It's been bullshit for hours."

"I figured. Couple people said they saw you guys making the rounds."

"What's the word?"

"You're doin' good. People pretty much think Neil Draper's a dick, anyway, and everyone knows Adam's never made a big deal out of being bi, even if he's never been seen with anybody but a girl. They think Draper's just making a mountain out of a molehill."

"Why," Adam said to no one in particular, "is it okay for me to fuck a guy if I'm bi, but not if I'm gay?"

Jesse winced. "Don't say the 'g' word, sweetheart. You can say you're bi all you want, as long as you only date girls. Jim Morrison was bi but you never saw him with anything but girls. That's what matters, not what you say you are."

"That sucks." Adam dropped into one of the chairs in the room and folded his arms across his chest. "And you say 'anything but girls' like there's a wide choice of options. And besides, Morrison's dead."

"Oh, look. You're so cute when you sulk—*not*," Evie sniped. "Give him a line, Jesse—he needs to perk up. We haven't run into any of the rest of the band tonight yet, but I'm sure they'll be here."

"They are," Jesse said. "They're up on the balcony level in one of the roped-off sections. Chuck and Eddie have their girlfriends with them, but Neil's here alone. Bill's here too."

"Evie, I'll pay you twenty grand to go up and stab Neil with your stiletto."

"Sorry, toots. I'm wearing the four-inch ones tonight—they'll never make it past the sternum."

"Shit."

"Jesse, take care of him, will you?" Evie shook her head. "We need to get this over with."

They were heading for the stairs to the second-floorbalcony level when they came face to face with Neil. Both Neil and Adam stopped dead, and the people around them went suddenly quiet, only the thump of the music for background noise. "Neil," Adam said, the Valium and the coke giving his voice an artificial serenity he didn't feel.

"Yeah. Hey."

Adam cocked an eyebrow. "Having a good time?"

"Sure. Fine. You?"

"Of course."

"Neil," Evie said.

"Evie."

"Hey, Adam," someone called from the crowd. It was too dark to see who. "Is it true what Neil says? Are you gay?"

"As gay as Jim Morrison," Adam called back.

"Was Jim Morrison gay?" someone else asked.

A third person said, "No fucking way was Morrison gay," and then an argument broke out. Over the fight, Adam yelled, "He was fucking bi, just like I am, you fucking nitwits!"

"Is that an announcement?"

"Oh, for Christ's sake," Neil shouted. "Bi, gay, what difference? You like dick!"

"Not yours!"

"Fuck you!"

"Not even for money, asshole!" Oddly, Adam was starting to enjoy this. Like before a performance, the coke gave him a false sense of invulnerability, and, facing Neil, he didn't much care anymore what anyone thought of him. He was done, Black Varen was done, the whole thing was over, and he didn't give a flying fuck. The only things he cared about were Miles, and not hurting Evie. So even though he knew he was really gay, not bi, he knew it would hurt her and her image if he said that. But he was done. "Hey, Neil, you know what a homophobe is?"

"Of course I know what it is, faggot."

"It's someone who's afraid that they're gay. Are you afraid you're gay, Neil?"

"Fuck you! Fuck you and your skinny fucking beard there, too!"

Wham! Evie hauled off and smacked him, not the sissy-girl slap her princess outfit would predict, but a good, solid open-handed blow that sent him staggering. "I'm not a fucking beard, asswipe!" she screamed. "And you're only jealous 'cause you *wish* Adam would fuck you!"

Neil tried for a drunken swing at her, but cooler heads prevailed, and bystanders grabbed both of his arms, hauling him back away from her. Adam got right up in his face and snarled, "Don't you touch my girlfriend, fucker, or I will *break* you."

"Whoa! Whoa!" Bill was suddenly there between them, shoving them apart. Adam backed up a pace and grabbed Evie, holding her tight. She was shaking with fury. "What the fuck is going on here, guys?"

"Neil is a fucking asswipe who's hiding the fact that he wants Adam to fuck him, but Adam has too much goddamned taste!" Evie shouted.

"Shut *up*, you fucking bitch!" Neil screamed back.

"You *both* shut up!" Bill yelled over them. He turned to Adam. "What the fuck is going on, Adam?"

"Neil's usual bullshit," Adam said, enjoying himself. "Called Evie a beard, and she slapped him. Damn near knocked him off his pins. Baby girl smacks him, and he can't even stand up."

"Cut it out." Bill pointed a finger at him. "Jesus Christ, kindergartners. Fucking kindergartners. You guys have got to calm down."

"No, we really don't," Adam said. "Because I quit. Neil can have the band. I'm done."

Again a wash of silence over the immediate area, like water on a beach. Adam thought of the lake, and Miles, and smiled to himself.

"You can't quit," Bill said. "Not yet."

"Yeah, I can. Just did." He looked past Bill to Neil, who'd gone expressionless. "Band's yours, Draper. Just like it was before I came on board. Enjoy your new career. I hear One Direction's looking for an opener."

"Fuck you," Neil said furiously. "Fuck you. I'll show you!"

Adam leaned forward and met his eyes. Then slowly, deliberately, he put his finger against the side of his nose, closing one nostril, and took a long, slow sniff. Then he grinned and walked away, Evie at his side.

"That was kind of hypocritical." Evie grinned. "Considering you just did that yourself."

"Everyone does it once in a while," Adam said dismissively. "Neil's got a habit. I don't. I need a drink. Come on, let's find the fucking bar in here."

The events of a moment before ran through the crowd faster than he and Evie did, so by the time they reached the ebony length of counter, Adam was getting pats on the back and questions like, "Are you really leaving Varen?" And then the one he'd been hoping for: "Is it true Neil's in love with you?" That one left him laughing long and hard, and if the laughter had an edge of hysteria, no one seemed to notice.

The rest of the evening was a blur of sound and lights and faces, flashing white and brown in the crowd. Voices speaking words Adam gradually lost all understanding of. He was patted, poked, prodded, kissed, hugged, stroked. He danced. He drank. He schmoozed. He promised to call people he didn't know, and stared blankly at people he did. Somewhere along the line he lost Evie, found Bill, danced with Chuck's girlfriend, danced with Chuck, lost them both, lost Bill.

Found Eddie, who dragged him into a quiet corner away from the dance floor and the bar, tucked away not too far from the bathrooms (where, Adam thought, he himself might have gotten a blowjob tonight from Sally Becker, Evie's friend, but he wasn't sure if it had actually been her or just someone he thought was her. He'd have to ask Evie tomorrow). "Dude," Eddie said, shoving him down into an overstuffed leather chair and dropping in its partner, "I am so fucked up. Are you really leaving Varen?"

"Yeah. It ain't gonna be any good anymore." Adam leaned his head back against the chair and threw a leg over the arm. "Neil's fucked it up for good. And it don't matter how much damage control I did tonight or Bill will do tomorrow—the band's fucked with half its fans. Maybe this will be good for the album, but the band's done."

"Fuck," Eddie sighed.

"Yeah. Sorry."

"Hey, ain't your fault. You were born gay—Neil had to practice bein' a dick. I saw Evie punch him earlier from upstairs. That was a fuckin' great punch."

"Wasn't even a punch," Adam said sleepily. "Open-handed slap. She's got a lot of power for such a skinny little thing."

"She's pretty. You're lucky, if you take advantage of it. If not— well, you're just stupid." Eddie grinned at him to take the sting out of the insult.

"Yeah, well, shit happens." Adam rubbed his cheek against the soft leather of the chair. He was really comfortable here. Maybe he'd just go to sleep and let the party go on without him.

"Sure does." Eddie waved down a waitress carrying a tray of beers and snagged two, handing the second to Adam. "Hey, don't fall asleep on me."

"Where's your girlfriend du jour?"

"Du what?"

"Never mind. Where is she?"

"Dancing or something. Seriously, dude, don't fall asleep. I only got outta dancing because I said I was gonna go talk to you."

"Mmm," Adam said.

"Look, here. I got some shit give you a buzz, keep you awake, okay? They're great. I took one earlier and it's better than coke, I tell you. Even Neil says so." He handed Adam a couple of green pills. "Wake you right up."

Adam took the pills. Eddie shook a couple out of the little plastic bag into his own palm, then swallowed them, chasing them with a swig of beer. Adam followed suit. "What is it?"

"Hell if I know. Friend of Jesse's gave 'em to us upstairs."

Adam closed his eyes and took another drink of the beer, then rested his head back again. After a few minutes, he started to feel a warm buzz in his blood, not unlike the buzz from coke, but without the nasal burn and head rush he sometimes got. "Sweet," he murmured.

"Yeah. Oh, there's Bethany. I'm goin'. See you later."

"Later," Adam said.

"There you are," Evie said. He opened his eyes. She was bright— bright silver, bright white against the black backdrop of the club. She sparkled. He liked that she sparkled. It made him feel good—excited and happy.

"Hey," he said. "You're bright."

"You're either drunk or stoned, I don't know which."

"Yeah, but I feel great." He gave her a wide grin. "I feel like dancing. Come on!" He caught her wrist and dragged her onto the packed dance floor.

He wished for a moment it was Miles he was dancing with. Then he thought of cranky, misanthropic Miles braving the dance floor to be with him, and laughed.

"What are you laughing about?" Evie yelled over the music.

He just shook his head, caught her in his arms, and danced.

Chapter 27

isa set the thick manila folder on the table and poured herself a cup of coffee. "Okay," she said, "are you sure you want to do this?"

"Yeah." Miles prodded the folder with one finger as if it were a snapping turtle. "There's no point in putting it off. Harper says . . ."

"Harper says what?"

"Well, she kind of doesn't say anything about it." Miles scrubbed his hands through his hair in frustration. "But somehow or other she got me to admit that I'm ready to look at this shit."

"She's sneaky like that," Lisa agreed. "But you said more than just look at it. Are you serious about having a show?"

"No. But I am serious about putting them up for sale. They're not mine anymore, Lise."

"You've been doing more in that style lately, so they're still yours. Or maybe yours again."

"Don't confuse me." Miles took a breath, then flipped over the cover of the folder. An eight-by-ten-inch glossy photo of a landscape stared up at him. The colors were wild and vibrant, the style Expressionistic.

"That one is twenty-four by thirty-six overall," Lisa said. "Most of them are that size or larger, though there are one or two portraits that are sixteen by twenty."

"Who of?"

He must have looked as sick and scared as he felt, because she said quickly, "One's of Doug. The other was of someone I don't know—I think you did it as part of a class, because there's a label on it with your name and 'Figure Study 401' on it. Nothing . . . nothing scary."

He nodded, and flipped it over to see the next one. They went on through the stack, Miles pulling out ones he wanted to think about before selling, and Lisa taking the ones he was ready to let go of. The Figure Study 401 piece went in that pile; the one of Doug went into a much smaller third stack of paintings Miles definitely didn't want to sell.

The sell stack was larger than the others, and Lisa looked pleased. "I think we can do well with these," she said in satisfaction.

"Whatever. Take those, and I'll let you know about the others. There were one or two I kind of liked. The one of the lake . . ."

"What?" she asked when he didn't go on.

"I thought Adam might like it."

"Oh. He probably would. He really likes it here. He said it sort of felt like home." She cocked her head and regarded him thoughtfully. "Are you going to last out the year before asking him to come back?"

"I don't know." Miles stacked the pictures, aligned them on one end, tapped them on the table, then turned them and tapped again.

Lisa took the photos away from him and put them on top of the refrigerator.

"What if he doesn't want to come back?" Miles asked. The words hurt.

"Then he doesn't." Lisa sat back down and took his hands. "Sometimes people don't come back, Miles. Sometimes the good-bye you say is the last one."

"Like them. Your parents." He swallowed hard. "Like Michael."

Her eyes were wet. "Yes. Like our parents. Like Michael. I've got you, though, and that helps."

"I'm sorry you lost them. I wish . . . I wish I could make you forget them, too, so you didn't hurt so much."

"Forgetting didn't help you, did it?"

"Aw shit, Lise." He drew her hand up and held it against his forehead. "No, not really."

"Either way, it sucks. But I think—I *think*—I'd rather have the memories, and the pain, than to be . . ."

"Empty," Miles said.

"Are you empty?"

"Sometimes. Grace, the art—it helps." He sighed. "Doug, Bobby, you." Then a deep breath, and a slow exhale. "Adam."

"Then ask him back, Miles."

"What if he doesn't want to come? It's not a year yet. Or what if he just wants—"

"Don't say he just wants sex, Miles. You should have seen him when I talked to him. That's not what it's about."

"Okay. Okay. I'll email him, right now."

She got up and went into the living room, returning a minute later with his laptop. "Here. Do it now, before you chicken out."

He laughed, and opened the laptop, pressing the button to start it up. Lisa patted his shoulder and busied herself making more coffee. "You need to get on Peapod," she said over her shoulder. "You're nearly out of coffee and filters. Did you want me to start a list so you can do that too while you're online?"

"Sure."

The laptop finished booting up, and immediately chimed that his email had a Google Alert. Idly, he flicked open the email program and then the email. There were no less than seven alerts, which surprised the hell out of him—he'd checked it late last night and there hadn't been anything. Frowning, he clicked on the first item.

"Drug Deaths at Nightclub! Six people are known dead, including two from the rock band Black Varen . . ."

From somewhere in his quirky memory a vision swam up, of Adam, prancing around Miles's living room, singing about a girl named Elsie, who'd died of too much drink and drugs, but died happy. And how, when Adam went, he was going just like that girl . . .

"Miles! Miles! Oh, God, Miles, talk to me!"

He blinked. Lisa was crouched on the floor beside his chair, hanging onto his hand, a look of absolute panic on her face. "What?" His throat hurt.

"Oh God, thank God. I didn't think you'd ever stop making that horrible sound. What is going on?"

He was dizzy, confused and lost and somehow terrified, but he didn't know why. Had he had another seizure? Oh, God, please not that, not after so long. The laptop chimed, and he looked at it, and realization poured back in. "Adam," he croaked. "Adam . . ."

There was the sound of machines beeping, and rubber soles squeaking, and the rustle of paper like pages being turned. Adam opened one eye against the brightness and closed it immediately. "Uh?" he said, and his voice sounded raspy and raw.

"I imagine you're thirsty." It was a man's voice, vaguely familiar. "But I don't think they'll let you have anything to drink for a while yet."

Adam blinked, and peered at the guy in the chair beside the bed. He looked vaguely familiar, too, but Adam wasn't quite sure where he'd met him before. "Uh?" he rasped again.

"Robert Halloway. We met at Miles's place."

"You're Bobby," Adam said. At least he tried to—his lips were so dry he could barely manage the words. He thought maybe it sounded more like "Wu Wowwy."

"Yep. I'm here as official representative of the Associated Enablers of Miles Caldwell, Medical Division. I was chosen because I'm the one most likely to be able to pick through the medical jargon they'll hit me with. And by the way, since your mother has power of attorney in the case of your disability, she gave me the okay to talk to your doctors." He held up his fingers in the Boy Scout salute. "By my oath as a real live doctor, I swear to keep it all confidential."

"What happened? Why am I here? Why are you here?"

"You don't remember, do you?" Bobby got up and went through another door, which Adam assumed was the bathroom. He came back with a wet washcloth, and blotted Adam's lips with it. "Better?"

"Uh-huh. What happened?"

"What do you remember?"

Adam shook his head. "Dancing with Evie. Feeling sick—dizzy. Puking on some chick's boots. They were purple tooled leather. I remember her screaming. That's about it."

"Well, that's about the time you passed out. You've been in a coma for three days. Apparently you took something that didn't agree with you, although it could have been worse."

"Worse?"

"Well, you're alive, and coherent. Which is more than one can say for your bandmates Neil and Eddie." His face got very sober. "I'm sorry about that."

"What happened to them?"

"They didn't make it. Along with four other people at that party. The cops are waiting for you to wake up so that they can interview you—you're apparently one of only a few people who survived whatever shit it was you took."

Evie . . . "Jesus! *Evie!*"

"Ms. Montcalm is fine," Bobby said reassuringly. "She didn't participate, luckily for you. When you passed out, she immediately started CPR. She deserves a medal for that."

Adam lay back on the thin hospital pillows and stared up at the ceiling. Jesus. Eddie dead. Neil dead. He felt bad, even about Neil—he'd been a dick, but he'd been part of Adam's life for the last five years. Nobody deserved that. "Shit," he said, his throat half-closed with tears.

He thought about Eddie and how he'd stood up for Adam, even reluctantly, in the face of Neil's accusations. He thought about Neil and how lately he'd seemed to be honestly trying to get along despite his feelings about Adam. Thought about happier times, like when they'd won the Grammy and stood on that stage together, all of them linked with their success and their joy in making music.

Because when it all came down to it, it was always about the music. And Neil and Eddie had gone silent.

"Shit," he said again, and this time there was no room for sound around the tears.

When he woke up next, Bobby was gone. Instead, a haggard-looking Evie was sitting in the visitor's chair, her hands twisted in her lap. She wasn't looking at him; her attention was on the screen of one of the medical monitors, watching his blood pressure or oxygen levels or something like that change numbers. She wasn't wearing makeup and her hair was just dragged back into a ponytail; she was wearing jeans and a USC sweatshirt. "Jesus, Evie," he said, and his voice wasn't as hoarse as before, which made him feel oddly good. "At the very least wear a UCLA sweatshirt."

"Adam!" She leapt from the chair and flung herself at him. "Bobby said you were going to be okay, but you looked like shit, and oh my God, I thought you were dead, and all I could think of was that I talked you into going to that fucking party, and how was I gonna face your mom and Eric and Miles, who I haven't even *met* yet . . ."

"Easy!" Adam brought up one arm and put it around her shoulders, and she promptly collapsed on his chest and burst into tears. "Ow," he said, because his chest fucking *hurt*. "Ow. Jesus, Evie, ease up—my chest hurts like a bitch!"

"They did the paddles and shit, and I think they pumped your stomach or something. I don't know. I think you almost died." She leaned back on the bed beside him and took his hand in hers. "I'm so sorry," she said, her eyes big and sad and repentant.

"Don't be stupid, Evie. I went to that party with open eyes, just like every other party we've gone to, and I took that shit, you didn't force it on me. I'm just fucking lucky you were there. Bobby told me you did CPR when I went down."

"I was so scared. People were freaking out, and you were just lying there, and I couldn't have stood it if my best friend . . ." Evie's voice ran out, and she started to cry again.

Adam patted her back, then something occurred to him. "Did Bobby talk to Miles?"

"Yeah." Evie sniffled. "He called him a couple hours ago. Told him you were going to be okay. I guess his sister and his shrink were with him; Bobby talked to both of them because Miles apparently went catatonic or something when Bobby gave him the news."

"Not quite," Bobby said from the doorway. "He just couldn't talk. You know how Miles gets."

"Yeah." Adam swallowed painfully. "Does he . . . can I call him?"

"Later, when you're feeling better," Bobby said. "Probably a better idea than a videoconference at this point. You look like shit."

"Thanks. Always good for my ego."

"We try. Your family's here. Your mom was sitting with you awhile but then your nephew seemed to have a bit of a panic attack, and she went to take him for a walk."

"Ryan?" Adam shook his head. "He hates hospitals. Too much stimulus or something."

"So in a couple of minutes, I'm going to go down there and let them know they can come up. Your regular doctor is talking to your manager about what they can say in a statement to the press. And then, afterward, they're going to come in and talk to you about what happened."

"I don't remember what happened."

Bobby folded his arms and looked as menacing as a pretty blue-eyed blond could. "Not about the event. About what led up to it. Specifically, your drug habit."

Adam blinked, stung. "I don't have a drug habit!"

Evie made a small, squeaky sound. He turned and looked at her defensively. "What? I don't."

"Let me rephrase that," Bobby said. "I will grant you that you are not an addict, from what I can see and from what Miles has told me. But you—and your girl there, so don't look so innocent, chicky—have a habit of indulging in far too many recreational pharmaceuticals. *This* I have gotten from talking to your family and your friends. You were fucking lucky this time, butthead, and it's time you grew up and decide if you want to be Adam Craig or fucking Neil Draper. Alive or dead. And if you are going to be anything to my best bud Miles, you damn well better choose the first option."

"Miles doesn't want me." The words were like knives in his aching throat.

Bobby hooted. "You are such a fucking idiot. Miles *sent* me here, asshole. He said he doesn't want you going like Elsie, whoever the hell Elsie is. If he could, he would have been on the next flight out. Of course, that's not possible, because this isn't a romance novel where his disability disappears the moment you need him. But because he *is* a romantic, he sent me. He fucking loves you, and you'd better fucking decide whether or not you love him. And if you do, you're going into therapy, *capiche*? If for no other reason than Miles deserves a mentally healthy relationship with someone who doesn't use drugs to manage stress." He cast a baleful glance at Evie. "And so are you."

"Me?"

"Yes. Because Adam cares about you, and if he has to go through it, so do you."

Evie sighed.

Adam said, "I suppose you know exactly how I do this, too. Betty Ford?"

"Yes and no. Yeah, you'll do at least six weeks there, inpatient, but after that I've got an outpatient program not too far from Miles's place that I can get you into. *If* you're interested. It's a minimum of six months, though." Bobby gave him a small, indulgent smile. "Miles is willing to put you up for the six months, if you want."

"Shit." Adam's throat was tight again. "Shit. Miles."

"Yeah," Bobby said. His grin widened. "I thought you might feel that way."

Chapter 28

he winter was hellish. Adam got out of the hospital just in time for Christmas, and managed to stay out of Betty Ford until the middle of January, but that was because he was staying with his mother. She spent a lot of time shuttling him back and forth between L.A. and San Diego, dealing with the fallout from the club poisonings. There were the cops, who grilled him mercilessly about his fight with Neil, and where he'd gotten the drugs that had killed his friends, and whether he'd known how dangerous they were (well, *duh*). He told them what he remembered about Eddie saying it was a friend of Jesse's, but hell, half of L.A. was friends with Jesse, so that wasn't much help. And then there was the inquest, and the funerals.

As soon as his mother decided he was well enough, though, she drove him to the clinic herself. Then it was eight weeks there, not six, and then another week because Evie was having difficulties dealing with some of the restrictions and had gone anorexic, and he wanted to stay and support her through that. Then when they were both out, he had to deal with the record company and the producers and the lawyers, putting Black Varen into the grave beside Eddie and Neil. After that, he dealt with renting out his Santa Monica condo. But finally it was the end of April, and he was on his way . . . home?

The closer the car got to the resort, the tighter his chest felt, until he thought his heart might pound its way clear out of his ribcage. He wished Evie were there so he could hold onto her hand until she bitched at him, and distracted him from the utter terror that had him by the throat. What if Miles really didn't want him there? They hadn't talked more than once a week, and Miles was even less communicative on the phone than he was in person. What if he was feeling something else: pity, guilt, something, anything but what Adam wanted him to feel, which was . . . What? Happiness? Adam had majorly fucked up—what could Miles find in that to be happy about?

He'd gone through some counseling at the clinic, of course, but it mostly left him doubting himself worse than he'd ever done before. He knew his skills, his strengths, and had been pretty sure he knew his weaknesses, but eight weeks at the clinic had made him take a good hard look at himself, and what he saw wasn't reassuring: a thirty-one-year-old adolescent who'd turned his back on the work he really loved for a temporary gig making shit-piles of money. He had never realized that he thought of the band gig as temporary, but in talking to the counselor, he kept saying things like "When I go back to the theater," or "Someday, when I'm back in theater," signs that he really had never taken the band seriously. How ironic was that—the career that practically every teenaged boy dreamed about had fallen into his lap, and he hadn't wanted it.

It wasn't that he didn't *like* the music, or the band—except for when he didn't, which had been pretty often lately, even before the bullshit—or the life. It had been a lot like musical theater, basically doing the same thing night after night, just with more music and a really limited cast. And the touring company he'd been with before had never been pursued by groupies and paparazzi, or had drugs handed out like candy, or had quite so many hangers-on. But performing with the band was still theater. And he loved theater.

But now it was over. The band was gone, the tour canceled, the album in limbo. He figured that Black Varen's staff of producers would take the stuff they'd already recorded, mess around with it a bit, and eventually release it. He supposed they'd write some dedication to Eddie and Neil, and then that would be it. Chuck had already joined up with another rising band who'd lost their bassist, and his name would probably rocket them to at least semi-stardom. Black Varen was going to be a footnote in music history.

He wasn't sure if it was sad that he didn't really care.

Bill, though—Bill had already told him he was sticking around. Despite Adam's decision to go back to theater, and Bill being one of the more notable rock managers in L.A., Bill was sticking. He'd manage Adam's solo career, which Adam wasn't sure about, but Bill was, and act as his agent for the theatrical stuff, which Adam was sure about. That was okay. Bill was good people. Even Eric, who managed Adam's finances and was cynical about everyone, thought so.

But something stupid in Adam kept wondering if Miles would still like him now that he wasn't a rock star anymore. Something *really* stupid, considering that Miles hadn't even known who Adam was when they'd met.

The car pulled into the turnaround where the entrance to the resort was. Adam stared out of the car window.

The chain was gone, replaced with a classy wrought iron gate suspended between two brickwork pillars. On one pillar was a neat, elegant plaque that read, "Indian Lake Resort. Quality Events." On a raised plinth a few feet from the gate was a small transmitter box with a grill and a button. The driver pulled up, rolled down the window, and pressed the button.

"Who is it?"

"Mr. Craig's limo," the driver said. There was a buzzing sound, and the gates swung open.

They'd paved the drive and cut back the overgrowth along the sides, and when the limo pulled into the parking area in front of the resort building, Adam noticed that the place had been painted and landscaped. He got out of the limo and stood there a moment, taking in the changes.

Then the door to the resort slammed open. He looked up, his heart pounding in his throat.

Miles was standing on the porch, a tense, taut expression on his face. His hands fisted once, twice—and then he shot down the steps and across the ten feet of paving stone to Adam, grabbing him and shoving him back against the limo to kiss him thoroughly.

Adam wrapped his arms around Miles and went under, the sheer joy of feeling that strong, steady body against his, of tasting the coffee-scented taste that was Miles, shredding the last of his anxiety into small bits of glitter that blew away on the spring breeze.

When they came up for air, Miles smoothed his thumbs over Adam's cheekbones. "Too skinny," he murmured, and leaned his forehead against Adam's.

"It's been a rough winter. I hated that the doctors limited my phone and internet. What did they think, that I was gonna order takeout? But I'm here now. It's all good."

"Yeah." Miles smiled, then released him. "Come on, get your stuff."

"I got it." The driver popped the trunk and pulled the two suitcases out. Adam reached into the backseat and pulled out his duffel and the Rickenbacker and Fender, each in its own custom case. Miles took the duffel and let him manage the guitars, which was exactly how he wanted it. "Where to?"

"The cottage, if that's okay?" The uncertainty in Miles's voice made Adam smile. So Miles. "The lodge is nicer, but there's a convention this weekend that I don't think you'd like much."

"What? Rabid Reactionary Right-wing Religious Republicans or something?"

"Worse. International Brotherhood of Polka Players and Accordion Enthusiasts."

"Holy fucking shit," Adam said blankly. The driver choked back a laugh. "No, no, the cottage is fine. Is it soundproofed?"

Miles laughed, and led the way.

When they got there, however, he didn't head for his own bedroom, but the junk room Adam had only noticed in passing before. "I cleaned up the spare room for you. I used to use it for storage, but I figured you needed your own space."

Adam set the guitars down on the floor by a futon, and when the driver brought in the suitcases, he paid him off and sent him on his way.

"You don't like it."

Miles's face was unusually expressionless. "No. No, it's fine. I just thought . . . No. It's fine." He smoothed the futon cover where it stretched over the back, and looked out the window. Nice view, anyway.

"You thought you'd be staying with me?"

Miles's voice sounded funny, and Adam turned to see a faint smirk on his lover's face. He grinned back at Miles, relieved. "You dick."

Miles laughed. "I figured you would be, too, but Lisa said you should have your own space for when I drive you crazy."

"Which would be always." Adam crossed the room, back into Miles's arms. "The room is perfect," he murmured. "My guitars already love it. But I don't like sleeping on futons."

"That was my idea," Miles admitted. "I figured you'd hate it and *have* to sleep in my bed."

"I always knew you were a smart man."

"I don't know about that. But at any rate, this room is yours. You can, I don't know, practice or something. Or write. Or whatever you want to do." Miles gave him an awkward grin. "Hide out when you're sick of me."

"I won't get sick of you."

"You haven't lived with me," Miles said darkly. "Not really."

"Not yet." Adam rested his chin on Miles's shoulder. "Thank you for taking me in."

"You make it sound like you're a homeless person or something."

"As of last week, I am. I rented out my condo and put everything in storage. Not that there's a lot. I had the thing you did me—what do you call that, anyway?"

"I call it 'art,'" Miles said.

Adam poked him in the ribs. "Anyway, I had that shipped back here, if you don't mind. I know, it's where it started, but I love that thing and didn't want to put it in storage. I want it with me."

Miles released him and stepped back. "You do?"

"Well, yeah. I mean, it means a lot to me." He blinked. The expression on Miles's face was priceless—completely and utterly stunned. "Miles," he said softly, "it's not only beautiful, but it's something you made me, so it means even more. I love you, Miles. I think you're the first person I ever have."

"But . . ."

"But what?"

"You love my *art*?"

Adam laughed. "Jesus, I tell you I love you and you're more impressed with the fact that I love your fucking art? Yeah, Miles, I love your art. I love your smelly paints and weird concoctions and the way you run your hands through your hair so it stands on end. I love your crazy-ass bird. I love the way you completely lose yourself so deeply in what you're doing that an atom bomb could go off next door and you wouldn't even notice. I love how you look when we've just made love, and I love when you're all pissy and cranky and yelling. I love this cottage and I love this resort and I love this room and I love *your* room. I love you." He took a deep breath and forced himself to meet Miles's eyes. "I love you. Do you . . . can you . . ."

"Moron," Miles said with a grin. "Idiot. Come on." He took Adam's hand and dragged him out of the bedroom and down the hall to Miles's own room. "Look."

"Holy fucking shit!"

There had to be six—no—eight—no, *eleven* portraits of Adam hanging on the walls of Miles's bedroom. Some were pencil drawings, some of them detailed, some of them just loose, wild sketches. Some were oil paintings, of just his face, and some of him onstage with a guitar. He recognized one as coming from one of their promotional shots. But they were all him, and all beautiful, because, he realized, *he* was beautiful in Miles's eyes.

"Do you like them?" Miles asked anxiously.

"These are amazing." Adam turned in place, studying each picture, before turning back to Miles. "Amazing. *You're* amazing. And I'm amazing because you love me."

"I don't want you to go like Elsie," Miles said. He caught Adam's hands in his. "Don't go like Elsie. Don't go at all. Stay."

"If you want me to, I'll stay. Forever if you let me."

"Okay," Miles said.

Chapter 29

ou don't even have to get out of the car," Adam said. "It'll be just like those little drives we take with Harper. You don't freak out on those anymore."

"They last less than an hour." Miles daubed paint on a tiny flower.

"This'll last maybe three, and most of that will be sitting still. In the dark. Watching a movie. Watching *Cabaret*, for God's sake. Come on, Miles!"

"Who the hell runs a drive-in theater anymore, anyway? Those things went out with, with, something, anyway. Roller derby."

"Hey, roller derby is huge nowadays. Anyway, it's some guy just over the Wisconsin border. Bought an old drive-in and is showing classic movies one night a week. It's only about forty minutes away. You can do forty minutes in a car with your eyes closed."

"I do forty minutes in a car *better* with my eyes closed."

"So close your eyes 'til we get there, and then open them. It'll be dark, you won't even see the other people in the cars around us. We'll bring popcorn and Cokes—"

"Coffee."

"Whatever, and we can get in the backseat and neck like teenagers."

"I thought you wanted to see the movie."

"We can watch the movie and neck at the same time."

Miles glanced up at his eager face and raised an eyebrow. "It means that much to you?"

"Dude, when do we *ever* get a chance to see *Cabaret* on the big screen?"

"Me? Pretty much never."

"So it'll be a new experience. Harper says you need to try new things."

"I need to try new things *that aren't too far out of my comfort zone*," Miles said. He narrowed his eyes at the scene in front of him. It needed something else. He picked up one of his tiniest crow-quill pens and dipped it in the red ink. Carefully, he drew a series of evenly spaced red dots around the spray of flowers.

"Miles."

He set the quill aside and turned on the stool to meet Adam's eyes. "Yes."

"Yes, what?"

"Yes, I'll go see *Cabaret* with you. If it matters that much to you. I don't know why—we've seen it three hundred times."

"But not on the big screen. Not in a drive-in. Not like, like a *celebration* or something. An *event*."

Miles took a deep breath. "Okay," he said. "Tomorrow."

"I owe you," Adam said breathlessly. "I owe you big time."

"Yes," Miles said. "You do."

"He okay?" the guy at the ticket booth asked.

Adam glanced over at Miles, who was sitting with his eyes squeezed shut and his hand clamped on the panic bar over the passenger-side window. He was dead white and sweating. "Yeah, he's fine. Hates driving. Prefers a motorcycle."

"Dick," Miles muttered through clenched teeth.

Adam handed the guy cash, and the guy handed him back a slip of paper with a couple of numbers on it. "Dial your radio to that station," the guy instructed, "and you'll pick up the sound. If you have any trouble, call the bottom number and someone will come to your location and help you out."

"Thanks." Adam rolled up the window and turned the air conditioning back on. "Okay," he said to Miles, who opened his eyes and took a deep breath. "Seriously, dude, you *live* outdoors most of the time, but opening a car window freaks you out?"

"Car windows freak me out," Miles said. "*Cars* freak me out, or haven't you realized that?"

"You *own* a car. You drive. And I've seen you drive around the resort with your windows open."

"That's different."

Adam sighed. Of course it was. Over the course of the last five months, since he'd arrived in April, he'd learned that it was impossible to judge what would and wouldn't trigger Miles's reactions, mostly because Miles himself couldn't know. For instance, when they had started driving him off-resort this summer, it turned out he had almost no problems with highway driving, or driving on the little country lanes around the resort, but driving in traffic was terrifying. At least that one Adam could understand, given what Lisa had told him about the accident. But the windows thing was just plain weird.

It was okay, though. Miles had been so patient with Adam, even when Adam was frustrated and impatient with himself. He didn't mind when Adam would go off and sit on the dock by himself for hours, or lock himself in the spare bedroom to write, and he put up with Adam when Adam absolutely had to be with Miles and talking, when he knew Miles would much rather have had quiet and solitude to work. He'd apologized to Miles once, and Miles had only listened quietly, then said, "Well, of course I don't mind. It's you, isn't it?" and that had made Adam feel better than all the protestations and kind words ever could.

So when Miles had gone on his first car trip with Lisa and Harper, Adam sat in the backseat with Miles crushing his chord hand and didn't say anything except, over and over again, "It'll be okay, Miles." And when Adam had gotten so frustrated with the thickheadedness of the other people in the drug program Bobby had recommended, Miles had made jokes about it until Adam had to laugh, and then he wasn't so mad. Miles had held him at night when he'd cried with fear that he'd never be in shape to perform again, that no one would want him, and told him over and over again that *he* always would.

Miles taught Grace to give Adam kisses and to call him "Sexy Thing," the way Adam had taught her to call Miles "Cootchie Papa," and he tried to keep her out of Adam's room so she wouldn't sit on his guitars and scratch them. Adam tried to keep her entertained when Miles was working on one of his oil paintings, because she liked to eat the big brushes he used. Adam backed up Harper when she was pushing Miles, even when he wanted to slap her for it, and Miles backed up Adam when he and Lisa occasionally got into spats over what was best for Miles. Though that wasn't too often; Miles and Lisa fought more than Adam and Lisa did. In the end, they both knew that Miles was the most important thing.

But this was the first time they were actually going somewhere, for a purpose. When Adam had heard about the drive-in theater showing *Cabaret*, he knew that this was *it*. Miles loved the movie, but more importantly, he knew how much Adam loved it. He might not do it for himself, but he'd do it for Adam.

Of course, they had Harper's cell phone number, just in case.

Adam pulled the Jeep into a spot in the very last row, although there were plenty closer up. The theater had been built in the glory days of drive-ins, so the slope was terraced, with each row set slightly higher than the row in front, and each spot had an excellent view of the screen. But he wanted to be close to the entrance, in case Miles just couldn't handle it.

Besides, nobody'd be watching *them*, all the way back here.

He put the car in park, but left the engine running so that they'd have plenty of A/C, since the windows had to stay closed, then looked over at Miles. His eyes were open, but he was staring fixedly ahead at the big screen, which was playing some retro advertisement for popcorn and drinks, and he was still clinging to the panic bar. There was a cooler in the backseat, with bottles of Coke for Adam, and a big thermos of coffee for Miles, but Adam didn't reach for any of that. Instead, he set the radio to the frequency on the paper, then slithered over the gearshift console and into Miles's lap.

Miles jerked in surprise. "What—" he started, but Adam took advantage of his open mouth to kiss him thoroughly. He could feel Miles's tense muscles softening, easing into his embrace. Miles's arms came around him. "See?" Adam murmured. "Necking. In public, sorta. But that's just the start."

"What?" Miles said again.

Adam gave him another kiss, then reached down for the seat lever, pulling it so that the seat slid all the way back. Then he went to his knees on the floor mat. "I think," he said mischievously, "that you need to relax in order to properly appreciate this movie."

"Do I?" Miles sounded like he was choking.

"Oh, definitely." He lifted Miles's long legs so that his feet rested on the dashboard, then squirmed between them before unbuttoning Miles's jeans and undoing his zipper. Miles was already at half-mast, despite his tension of only a minute before. "Definitely," Adam said again, and bent his head to take him into his mouth. Miles groaned and his fingers wove into Adam's hair.

God, Miles tasted good. They'd showered together just before they'd left, and Miles still tasted of coconut and pineapple, like a piña colada. A penis colada, Adam thought, and chuckled, and the vibration made Miles moan again, deeper this time. He ran his tongue up the underside, then around the head, sucking and slurping noisily to make Miles laugh, as he always did, and if the laugh was shaky, that was okay, too.

From the radio's speakers, he heard the beginning strains of the opening of the movie, and redoubled his efforts, so that Miles was whimpering along with the music, and when he started chanting, "Love you, love you, love you," Adam knew he had him right where he wanted him. He let his throat relax and took Miles all the way in, letting the buzz of the lack of oxygen fill his head, and just as his vision started to flicker, Miles cried out and came. Adam swallowed and pulled back a little so he could breathe.

"You make me crazy when you do that," Miles gasped. "You freak me out. One of these days you're gonna pass out and *die*."

"No, I'm not," Adam said with a grin. "I'm crazy, but I ain't *stupid*." He gave Miles's softening cock a last lick, then tucked him back in and fastened him up again. "I've had my snack," he chirped. "Want some popcorn?"

Miles dragged him up into his lap and kissed him thoroughly. "I only ever want you."

Epilogue

espite the Valium, Miles was sweating and bordering on panic by the time the limo pulled up to the Auditorium Theater. He shot Lisa a terrified glance, and she immediately reached out and covered his free hand with both of hers. "Five minutes," she said calmly, "and we'll be in the box. There's a private entrance we can use—Adam showed it to me this morning. You'll be fine."

He took a gulp of water from the bottle held tightly in his fist, choked, and narrowly avoiding spilling it all over his new suit. Doug reached over and took the bottle out of his hand. "Dude, you don't wanna ruin the threads."

"I can't do this," Miles said frantically. "I can't—I need to go home—"

"Home's an hour away, Mikey. The box is five minutes. It'll be just like at the movie, remember? Rob's waiting up there right now—he just texted me that the box is mostly closed on three sides, so you're good. It'll be just like the movies."

Miles took a deep breath and let it out, and did it again, trying to manage the fear the way the therapist had shown him. "That was a dinky little retro drive-in movie theater. I never got out of the car. And Adam was with me."

"Adam'll be there." Lisa squeezed his hand. "He said he'd come up afterward and leave with us. Miles, we're an hour early—there won't be anyone around except us. It'll be good. And just think what this will mean for Adam."

Adam. He had to focus on Adam. Remembering him the way he'd been that morning, wildly excited, nervous, *happy*. All these weeks of rehearsals, not to mention the *months* before that, when Adam was torn between being relieved that he didn't have to fake it anymore, and terrified that he would never get another opportunity to perform again. He'd been scared to death about this, too, even though it was a role he could play in his sleep, because it was about so much more than acting. It was Adam's first public performance as an out actor.

And he'd missed performing, Miles knew. To Miles, being on stage would be the essence of Hell, but Adam thrived on it. *Loved* it. It was part of what he *was*. Being off-stage for over a year while he went through rehab and Miles worked on his own issues—*that* had been Hell for Adam. As terrified as Miles was to come here and sit in a huge theater with thousands of other people around, he knew he owed it to Adam to be here, to be supportive just the way Adam had been, putting off trying to get back to work until he knew that Miles was making progress in his own therapy.

The limo pulled up to the main entrance on Congress, and Doug got out and went into the building. Miles saw the massive stone pillars of the portico and felt a little more secure—the building was solid, strong . . . safe. He swallowed again and gave Lisa a tentative smile.

She bloomed. "Oh, Miles, you are going to *love* the inside of this building. It's so beautiful—the pictures I showed you don't do it justice. It's glorious."

Doug rapped on the limo window, and Miles opened the door. "It's set, come on in. They're waiting for us."

Miles looked at Lisa. She gave him an encouraging nod. He took a deep breath, and for the first time in years, set his foot down on ground that didn't belong to him.

The earth, surprisingly, did not shake. There were no subterranean rumbles. No one ran toward him, screaming, with a bloody butcher knife in hand. No one stared, no one pointed. There weren't even any cars on the street at that moment. It was shockingly dull. He slid out of the limo and stood up. "The air smells funny."

"Bus diesel," Doug said. "Eau de Chicago." He reached down to take Lisa's hand to help her out. She shook out the skirt of her designer dress and tucked her arm in the crook of Miles's elbow.

He took another deep breath and followed Doug into the theater.

Bobby and Evie were waiting for them in the private box on the lower level. A wet bar was set up at the back, with selections of beer and wine. There were hors d'oeuvres on a separate table. "Fancy," Miles said, and took pride in the fact that his voice only shook a little.

Evie, who'd met the other Associated Enablers of Miles Caldwell a few months ago when she'd come out to visit Adam, knew Bobby a little better since they'd met at the hospital. She had a cocktail in one hand, and Bobby's sleeve in the other. If it had been Miles, he would have been nervous, but Bobby only looked amused. "There's gin, thank God, and tonic and limes, if you want something a little stronger," she told Lisa after they'd exchanged air kisses. "Bobby mixes a mean G&T."

Doug gently disengaged her fingers from Bobby's jacket. "He's mine, fag hag."

She snorted and stuck her tongue out at him. "Like it's my fault all the gorgeous ones are gay. With certain exceptions." That last was accompanied by an exaggerated mean squint.

"Don't do that, it'll give you wrinkles." Doug kissed her cheek and said, "How you doin', Skinny?"

"Just super!"

It was difficult, Miles discovered at that moment, to stay nervous when one was happy. Between his friends' byplay and the astoundingly beautiful surroundings—the inside of the theater was even more impressive than the lobby—he was starting to relax, something he'd never imagined was possible outside the resort. Or maybe the Valium was just kicking in. He winked at Lisa. "Can I have a G&T?"

"Not with Valium, you can't. Have a Coke instead."

"You're no fun."

She looked up into his grinning face, and her eyes got wet. She put her arms around his waist and rested her head against his heart. "Oh, Mike," she said, then, "I mean . . ."

"It's okay. You call me what you want, Lise. You've earned it." He hugged her gently, then glanced up to see the rest of them watching, approving looks on their faces. "What are you staring at?"

"Nothin'," Doug said with a grin.

The curtain calls over, the lights came up in the theater, and Miles sat back in his seat, blinking. "Wow," he said. "When the Emcee took off his coat and he was wearing the concentration camp uniform underneath . . . That was powerful. I'd forgotten how dark this play was. And Adam was right—it's different from the movie in details, but it still has that punch."

"It was really different from the movie." That was Eric's wife Melanie. They and Adam's mother had arrived just before the play started, but Miles had talked to them on Skype before, so he knew them. The kids—who he kind of liked, despite them being kids—had been left with Melanie's parents in Sacramento.

"Yeah, the screenplay has a different storyline. I read the script again the other day so I'd have an idea of what was going on—I've seen the movie a billion times, so I wanted to make sure I didn't expect this to be just like that. Of course, I heard bits and pieces when Adam's been rehearsing, but it's not the same thing. The Emcee is the same, and Sally. But the Emcee is such a powerful character. He just drove this play. You could just feel the repressed rage and fear, even when he was singing."

"That's funny," Lisa said. "You said 'the Emcee' instead of 'Adam.'"

"Did I? Huh. I guess that's how good he is—I forgot he was playing him." Miles rubbed his chest, feeling like he was going to burst. It was a good feeling, a proud feeling, like he'd been the one to put Adam up there. "He was really good."

"Better than that, he was really well received," Lisa pointed out. "Three curtain calls and a standing ovation—on his first performance. Where the hell is he going from there?"

"Off-Broadway. He thinks there's a good chance that he'll get tapped for a new revival of it there—he said he's already been contacted by the producers. But he's keeping it hush-hush for now." Miles got up and moved to a seat farther back, away from the crowds of people in the now brightly lit theater who were massing toward the exits. The sight bothered him, but the noise bothered him more, and he put the earplugs his shrink had given him into his ears. But he did it quietly, and while the others might have noticed, they said nothing.

The play had been excellent—all of the actors were good, and Miles had found himself transported the way he was when he watched a movie, caught up in the action and passions before him. He *had* forgotten that the Master of Ceremonies was his own lover, and instead had related to him as the cynical, chilly, repressed caricature he'd portrayed himself as. It was a character so far removed from the way Miles knew Adam really was that he completely failed to see anything of Adam in the Emcee. *That* was acting.

Miles let himself relax—gave himself permission, as his shrink said—and leaned his head back against the velvet of the seat, closing his eyes to relive every moment of the event.

A while later he heard a muffled, "I think he's asleep," and opened his eyes to smile up at Adam. "Not hardly," he said, and took the earplugs out. "Hey."

"Hey." Adam bent and brushed his lips over Miles's. "And other than that, Mrs. Lincoln, how did you enjoy the play?"

Miles laughed. "I coped," he replied, and slid his hand around the back of Adam's neck to pull him into a deeper kiss. He tasted of champagne and smelled of makeup. "You were wonderful," he murmured against Adam's mouth.

Adam sat on his lap. "I know," he said smugly. "Three curtain calls and a standing O. Pretty damn good for a first night."

Doug hooted. "You were *marginally* okay, but that's about it."

Adam gave him a one-fingered salute behind his back, and Doug laughed.

Adam's mother said, "Oh, *Adam.*"

Miles chuckled. "You're in trouble now."

"I am." Adam brushed the hair from Miles's forehead. "I'm deep in trouble, 'cause I'm head over heels for a crabby recluse, and in three months I'm going to be in New York, and far, far away from him."

"It's settled then?" It was good news, but Miles couldn't help feeling disappointed.

"It is. More Off-Off-Broadway than anything, but it's a dream of a lifetime."

Miles frowned. "Dream . . .?" Then he laughed, and laughed. "Sally?"

"*Sammy,*" Adam corrected, his face alight with joy and mischief. "Sammy Bowles, in a gender-switched revival. I couldn't tell you until tonight, when the producers caught me backstage. It's gonna be awesome, baby. And the best part?"

"Is?"

Adam leaned forward, resting his head on Miles's shoulder. Miles curled his arm around him, feeling oddly content, despite the unfamiliar surroundings. "It's so out there, it'll probably fold in three weeks," Adam said with a grin.

Also by Rowan Speedwell

Finding Zach

Kindred Hearts

Bitterwood

Love, Like Water

Hopes & Fears (Dreamspinner Press 2010 Advent Calendar)

Angel Voices

The Florentine Treasure (Dreamspinner Press 2012 Daily Dose:
Time is Eternity)

Flowers for Him (in Promoted by the Billionaire),
with Marie Sexton

About the Author

Born on a mountaintop in Tennessee (or possibly in a hospital in suburban Chicagoland; the data are unreliable), Rowan Speedwell was kidnapped at a young age by time travelers, who dragged her around '20s Paris, '30s Hollywood, ancient Egypt, the twenty-third-century Federation, and Imperial Spain before dropping her into the latter half of the twentieth century, from which she has miraculously escaped into the first half of the twenty-first. She still misses the Federation, though. And she wonders why, after all her vast experience with time, she has so little of it.

What time she does have, she spends writing, reading, sewing, reading, doing calligraphy and illumination, reading, making jewelry, reading, researching obscure topics, reading, shooting arrows (badly), and petting her cat. And reading.

For more information about Rowan, please visit her website: www.rowanspeedwell.com, or check out her Twitter feed @rowanspeedwell.

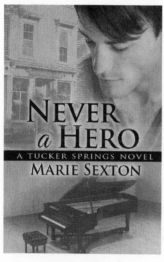

22869810R00158

Made in the USA
Charleston, SC
05 October 2013